Unforgettable, My Love Has Come Along

Ann Marie Bryan

To order additional copies of this book, contact:

Victorious By Design, LLC
www.victoriousbydesign.com
orders@victoriousbydesign.com

ISBN-10: 0-9851-4680-X
EAN-13: 9780985146801

DEDICATION

I dedicated this book to Orville, my wonderful husband, best friend and partner. I love you. Thank you for your prayers, unconditional love, affection, inspiration and unwavering support.

CONTENTS

ACKNOWLEDGEMENTS

First and foremost, I am exceedingly grateful to my Lord and Savior Jesus Christ who is the author and finisher of my faith. Thank you Lord. My life is a ministry for you.

I am indebted to my circle of love who helped to make this book a reality.

Orville, my husband. You are the one my heart loves. Thank you Honey for your patience while I write. Your love, prayers and remarkable ideas helped to fuel my desire to write to the honor and glory of our Lord and Savior, Jesus Christ.

My wonderful mom and siblings, especially my six gorgeous sisters for their unfailing love, joyous laughter and invaluable advice. I love and appreciate you more than you will ever know.

Bishop John E. Baker, my dynamic pastor, and First Lady Ann-Marie Baker, his beautiful, spirit-filled wife, for imparting timely and relevant messages from God's word to strengthen my relationship with the Lord.

My amazing spiritual sisters and brothers, whose steadfast love and support keep me grounded in the word. Your prayers have been a source of strength and comfort, pulling me through the many seasons in my life.

Angie Singleton, author of *Diamond's Fate*, for her motivation and encouragement to write and share my personal experiences about God's love, grace, mercy and goodness to draw others to Him.

Extra special thanks to all the wonderful individuals whose great outpouring of love and tremendous support helped to foster the perfect plan of God so that "Orane" and "Annalisa" could have an unforgettable season.

No book comes together without a talented team. For their countless hours of editing, leadership, spirituality and giftedness, my sincere thanks to Millicent Battick, Shaun Battick, Ayana Matthews and Julianne Veira. Your friendship blesses me beyond measure and I am deeply grateful to you.

PROLOGUE

THE ONE

Not again!

A surge of trepidation caused me to bolt upright on the off-white overstuffed sofa in my living room. I stared at the cordless phone as if it had just burst into flames.

This was like a bad recurring dream.

"Sister Harri," I said in a measured tone, "I already told you that I'm not interested." As a mark of respect, the younger members of my family added "Sister" before the names of our three eldest sisters, Maydine, Bella and Harriett, whenever we addressed them.

"Annalisa don't you think..." Harriett was not in the least bit put off by my lack of interest.

"Why do we keep having this conversation?" I asked impatiently, while I silently plotted a respectable exit strategy.

"No pressure, but you should reconsider," Harriett insisted.

"No thanks Sis. I'm good," I replied grumpily. Her persistence was becoming annoying.

"Annalisa please!" she pleaded gently. "Why don't you talk with Mr. Conway then make a decision?"

Did she not hear me? I forced myself past the screaming wall in my head and spoke quietly. "Sister Harri, let's talk later."

"Okay. Call me later," Harriett said, stifling her frustration. "Remember to check your email for our flight itineraries."

"Okay!" I murmured, staring unconsciously at the phone before dropping it on the sofa.

A deep sigh escaped my lips as I leaned back on the sofa, totally perplexed. *Why was Harriett so persistent?* This kind of behavior was very uncharacteristic of her. Two years later and she still kept inserting Mr. Conway's name in our conversation.

Harriett met Mr. Conway while he was conducting business at MayPo Middle school in Jamaica where she was the principal. She admired his character and business-like manner and was totally convinced that he could be THE ONE...for me. "Mr. Conway is a Christian," she stated proudly during a prior conversation. She knew that I would never entertain a relationship unless the man professed the Christian faith.

Still, Mr. Conway was not up for consideration.

To have a successful relationship, both persons need to at least live in the same vicinity. I could not fathom how a long distance relationship would work. Above all, I had no desire to disturb my uncomplicated life.

Truthfully...

I would definitely disturb my simple, well-ordered, uncomplicated life if the object of my affection was in close proximity. That would be a less challenging relationship to maintain. Well, at least in my mind. Long distance relationships seemed way too complicated.

If only I could get this across to Harriett, the third born in my family of six sisters and four brothers.

As the last female born in my family and divinely assigned the eighth spot, I acquired four guardians for my life - Mama and my three eldest sisters. Quite often they exercised their motherly rights.

"Annalisa, are you dating anyone?"

"When are you going to get married?"

"Do you plan to have children?"

Then to add fire—"Your biological clock is ticking. You may be too picky, no one is perfect."

In their defense and without a doubt, I know that they care about me. Nevertheless, I must admit that the constant questioning was aggravating at times.

I wanted to fall in love. I desired the joys of being in love; the rush, the tingle, the breathlessness, the friendship and the anticipation of genuine affection and adoration. But finding love was challenging, even daunting at times. I've had crushes but love, love eluded me. I had been in love or so I thought; lost love and was still hoping to find love. I had days of fasting and praying for a husband. But then, I also had days of crying and feeling sorry for myself. I tried not to bond with those who believed that there were no good men left in the world. How could I? My husband was out there.

So, I waited with bated breath to know the delights of having that special someone in my life. Secretly, I asked God to send me someone special. So, I waited and waited...

While I waited, I was determined to live life to the fullest. This was NOT the suffering period before meeting someone. I simply went about the business of living my life in Godly purpose. In the deep recesses of my heart, I was convinced that God would come through in this area of my life. And come through beyond my wildest imagination.

THE STORY OF US

"This was the Lord's doing; It is marvelous in our eyes." (Psalm 118:23)

CHAPTER 1: THE SURPRISE

"Welcome back!" I smiled, hugging my sisters, Maydine and Harriett in the arrival area of Tallahassee Regional Airport.

Harriett joyfully clapped her hands. "It's good to be back!"

"Good to see you Anna!" Maydine said smiling. Her light brown eyes sparkled with excitement. "Let me look at you!"

I giggled foolishly as Maydine twirled me, while belting out squeals of excitement. I was nine years old again. I grew up with Maydine, the first born in our family. She hugged me tightly and then lightly cupped my face with both hands. "Let me see what has changed."

I grinned at her. "Nothing has changed."

"Right," Maydine said, with raised eyebrows.

"I am going to cancel your mothering rights," I playfully warned her.

Maydine chuckled, admiring my slender, 5' 7" frame. "No more fun at your expense. You look great."

"Yes, you do," Harriett said, joining the conversation.

"Awww! Thanks!" I beamed. "I feel like doing a group hug."

"Just don't start crying out here," Harriett said, and we all giggled.

A few minutes later, we loaded the suitcases and carry-ons in the trunk of my burgundy Toyota Camry and drove away.

"What's on our itinerary?" Harriett asked, snuggling comfortably in the passenger seat.

"I hope you're ready to roll," I responded smiling.

She groaned loudly. "We only have two weeks!"

"A lot can happen in two weeks," I told her comfortingly.

"Yes Harriett, Anna will make sure of that!" Maydine chimed in.

"Definitely," I said confidently. "As usual, I have a great line up of activities including a picnic on the beach."

"A beach trip?" Harriett exclaimed while Maydine broke out in hysterical laugher.

"We must go to the beach," I insisted dramatically. "It's calling!"

Harriett chuckled. "It's calling you! You know, we cannot swim."

"Be brave my sisters," I begged in a perfect British accent, "throw caution to the wind."

"Since you put it like that, I'm ready," Harriett declared unreservedly.

"So am I," Maydine quipped softly.

"Alrighty!" I piped up. "So, how is it going in my sunny homeland?"

"Jamaica is great!" Maydine responded spontaneously.

"Yes," Harriett agreed. "We are experiencing heavy rain island-wide but we needed it."

I smiled at Harriett. "Perfect!" *Beautiful Jamaica! Sometimes I miss the island life, the people, hmm definitely the food.* "Did you bring any Jamaican food?"

"Food?" Harriett exclaimed with knitted brows. "Ohhh no! All that complaining about gaining weight when we are around."

I snickered and Maydine chuckled softly. My sisters were not only great company but talented cooks. Usually, I do all the eating and the evidence of their superb cooking stayed with me long after they were gone.

"No complaining this time round!" I reassured her giggling. "I'll wait until you leave."

"Shameful!" Harriett playfully scolded me while Maydine laughed loudly. "But, thanks for the heads up!"

"I promise to be good!" I said innocently.

"I am sure you will be," Harriett said, rolling her eyes. "Tallahassee I miss you!"

"I can tell Tallahassee misses you too," I teased.

"Yes," Maydine said playfully.

Harriett pressed her lips together and her eyes narrowed. "O... kay, so it's going to be like that, both of you joining forces against me."

"No!" Maydine and I responded in unison, way too quickly.

"Right!" Harriet retorted in a dry voice, still taking in the scenery.

"We all love Tallahassee," Maydine said, tapping Harriett on her shoulder.

"Yes," I acquiesced quietly.

Tallahassee, Florida. Hmmm?

Four years later, who would have thought I would be here? My plan was to complete my studies then relocate to a faster growing metropolitan area. But, through the years, the city grew on me. I enjoyed living in Tallahassee, with its serene settings and peaceful environment.

As we journeyed home, the Wednesday afternoon heat finally gave way to showers of rain. I heaved a sigh of relief and flicked on the windshield wiper hoping to see through the white rain. It was a perfect respite from the heat on this hot summer day.

"Anna, drive slowly." Maydine sounded breathless. She was perched at the edge of the back seat with a strangled hold on my head rest.

"Yes Sister Maydine," I replied reassuringly.

"Tallahassee and the white rain," Harriett murmured. "Can you see the yellow line?"

"Yes Sis and I have my hazard lights on."

"Good, good," Harriett said softly.

Shortly thereafter, the rain subsided into a drizzle and we made it safely to my beautiful three-bedroom townhome.

✳ ✳ ✳

A week later...

Home sweet home! Time to feast!

These were the thoughts that invaded my mind as I drove home from work. As I anticipated, my sisters certainly did not disappoint me. The wonderful aroma of their cooking greeted me the moment I closed the door. Within minutes, we sat down to a sumptuous meal of authentic Jamaican brown stewed chicken, steamed rice and peas, fried plantains, tossed vegetable salad and carrot juice. The food was truly satisfying to my body; albeit, my clothes were getting a little bit snug.

"I know that look!" Harriett's voice permeated my wondering thoughts.

I grinned at her as she eyeballed me at the round four-seater mahogany dining table. "What look?" I asked, stalling for time.

Maydine chuckled softly as she watched the drama unfold.

Harriett refused to back down. "If I hear anything about gaining weight, I will..."

"Sis, take it easy." I smiled, patting her shoulder. "Thanks to you both, I just had a great meal. I promise, no talking about gaining weight."

"At least not today," Maydine declared grinning.

"Stop it!" I pushed my chair away from the table and feigned a look of shock and hurt. "Is that a good thing to say?'

Maydine burst into a fit of laughter. "If only you could see your face," she said, managing to get her laughter under control.

"Don't let me cancel your mothering rights," I warned her as Harriett pursed her lips and sighed.

I touched Harriett's hand and flashed a smile that was supposed to ease the hurt. "Pay no attention to what Sister Maydine just said. You know that I enjoy your cooking."

"Way too much," Maydine interjected chuckling.

"Mother! Behave yourself." My eyes were filled with laughter as I eyeballed at her.

"Fine!" Maydine jerked upright and her eyes lit up as she stretched lazily. "Let's watch a movie."

"Sign me up. Relaxation! I am in," I responded, rising to clear the table.

Harriett loudly cleared her throat to get attention. "I know you are not saying that!" she exclaimed, looking at me quizzically.

"What?" I inquired, totally puzzled.

"I asked you to go walking with me after dinner, and you said no."

"It's too hot!"

Harriett grinned. "You are getting a little round in the middle."

"Huh?" I gaped at her and they burst into laughter at my expression. I recovered rapidly. "I am going to pray for both of you."

A few minutes later, we stacked the dirty dishes in the dishwasher and moved to the living room.

"Let's watch NCIS (Naval Criminal Investigative Service)," Harriett requested. She was hooked on NCIS, a TV series involving a team of fictional agents who investigates crimes involving the U.S. Navy and Marine Corps.

"I don't mind if we can't find anything else," I responded, leaning back in the sofa.

"Not again!" Maydine winced, nestling comfortably in the sofa across from me. "Anna, please see if you can find something else for us to watch."

"Fine, you two!" Harriett murmured. She was seated in the small sofa next to me, sighing as she savored a cup of green tea.

I propped my feet up on the coffee table and scrolled through the channels. After an unsuccessful search for something of interest, we settled on NCIS.

By the second commercial break during NCIS, Maydine was soundly sleeping. *Typical Maydine.* I smiled knowingly.

"Don't forget to give me the photos," Harriett broke into my thoughts. "You haven't given me any recent photos of yourself."

"Yes, I remembered." I quickly walked to the entertainment stand and opened a drawer.

"You don't have to do it now," she exclaimed.

"That's okay. I already created your little pile." I pulled out stacks of photos and located hers. "Here you go." I handed her the pictures and placed the rest in the drawer.

"Thank you!" Harriett beamed and promptly began looking through the stack.

"I will add more before you leave," I said, burrowing in the sofa to find a comfortable spot.

"Okay," Harriett replied. "Nice shot!" She held up a picture of me sporting a full-length red satin evening gown. "You look fabulous."

"Thanks Sis! You know I try." I grinned at her before turning my attention to NCIS.

Suddenly, Harriett's mumbling caught my attention. *Am I getting paranoid? Did she say Mr. Conway?* "What did you say," I asked tentatively.

"I was just saying that I would show Mr. Conway these photos."

"What?" I gasped loudly, sitting up. "Please don't show my pictures to Mr. Conway."

"Annalisa please!" Harriett pleaded, clearly frustrated.

"What's…going on?" Maydine was fully awake. "Mr. Conway. Who is Mr. Conway?"

Without sparing any details, Harriett filled in the blanks while I stared at her in frustration. Suddenly, Maydine knitted her brows then she leaned back in the sofa and crossed her arms.

"Mr. Conway! Conway …" Maydine's voice trailed off, then a bright smile lit her face.

I stared at her, surprised at her burst of emotion.

"I know Mr. Conway," she said, looking totally amused.

A loud gasp escaped Harriett's lips as she wrestled with the turn of events.

"You know him?" I inquired, with arched eyebrows.

"Yes, Annalisa Jones!" Maydine smiled. "He is a nice gentleman. I haven't spent any quality time with him because every time he comes to my office, I'm usually on my way to a meeting or attending to something." Maydine was the principal of Creek Cross Elementary and Middle School in Jamaica.

The room grew quiet and they stared intently at me.

"What?" I gave a hollow laugh and flopped backward on the sofa. "I am still not interested."

"He seems very nice, very business-like," Maydine encouraged.

"I told her," Harriett jumped in.

Maydine looked me straight in the eye, and said, "I can tell you this. He's always very encouraging and inspiring."

I looked away as my heart raced. I did not respond. Actually, nothing came to mind.

"Does he know that you are busy finding him a mate?" Maydine joked, reclining in the sofa.

"No, but I know he is seeking a wife," Harriett responded, making her case.

"He seems very confident. I am sure he has many choices," Maydine stated.

"He is not looking for just any woman," Harriett remarked sharply. "He is seeking a special lady, a Christian lady."

"Well, I hope he finds that special someone," I blurted out.

"I am sure he will," Maydine said wholeheartedly.

"Oh yes," Harriett agreed. "There must be ladies vying for his attention and affection."

Maydine smiled knowingly. "If my memory serves me right, he is a very classy dresser, quite dapper."

"What's his first name?" I interjected half-heartedly.

Harriett gave an awkward laugh. "I don't…remember his first name."

"O…kay then, so much for knowing your Mr. Conway," I said, barely concealing my annoyance. I was taken aback by her lack of knowledge in this regard.

9

"Annalisa, let me give him your number," Harriett begged.

I shook my head in frustration and rolled over on the sofa. "Let's get back to NCIS."

The room grew quiet and I turned to look at my sisters. They were both staring at me in disbelief. I laid there hoping that something would pop into my head and give me the magic answer. No convincing excuse came to mind. "Don't give him my number, give him my email address."

I had no intention of responding to any email from Mr. Conway.

CHAPTER 2: LOVE CALLS

Summer ended and I was glad for the change in the climate. Cooler temperatures prevailed reminding me that winter was on the way. Tallahassee's subtropical climate was characterized by hot, humid summers and cool winters. Last summer was particularly hot and occasionally temperatures were above 100 degrees Fahrenheit.

I was home comfortably snuggled under sheets in bed, when the phone rang. Ouch! My right hand hurt as I reach for the phone.

"Hello!" I answered cheerfully.

"Hello! How are you?" a deep, strong masculine voice asked.

"I am great! Thank you," I replied, trying to identify the voice.

"That's great to hear," he chuckled softly. He knew I could not place his voice.

"Jamie? Aldane, I know it's you," I said, stretching my hand to release the knots in my limb. My nephews are a treat, using what I call their Bond (007) voices.

"No, this is not Jamie or Aldane."

Feeling slightly embarrassed, I glanced at the caller ID. The call was coming from Jamaica but I did not recognize the number. "I'm sorry, who is this? You have the wrong number."

"I have the right number. I am blessed to have your number," he declared in a self-assured voice.

Strangely, an unexpected tingle of nerves hit me. "Who is this?"

"Is this Annalisa?"

"Yes, this is Annalisa."

"I am Conway, Orane Conway."

Orane Conway! Orane Conway! Why does his name sound so familiar? My eyes widened involuntarily and my bottom lip quivered from

nervous tension. I had totally forgotten about Mr. Conway. "Who?"
I asked, trying to regain my composure.

"Orane Conway. Your sister, Dr. Harriett Selby gave me your
number," he stated calmly.

"Oh. Oh." Words failed me.

"I am sorry to call so late, but I was thinking about the right
time to call and finally felt the go ahead."

Did he actually say that he was thinking about the right time to call?
I chuckled softly and quietly rolled on my side to turn on the bedside
lamp. "Well, if you feel the need to call, who am I to send you away?"

"Yes," he replied. "You do not want to send away the messenger
before he gives the message."

Laughter bubbled up within me. *A sense of humor! Great! Stay
on neutral subjects, I cautioned myself.* "So, how are you? I asked.

"Like you, I am doing great. God is good."

"Are you a Christian?" *That is not a neutral subject!*

"Yes!"

"That's great to hear! How is your walk going?"

"I take it one day at a time. I have fallen off the wagon a few
times but God is good," he stated quietly. "How has your walk been?"

"It has been very exhilarating. God is always up to something.
Which church do you attend?"

"Riverdale Pentecostal church. I have been there for a few
years."

"Sounds good," I remarked.

"My pastor is a great role model," he continued. "I have learned
valuable lessons from hearing him preach the word."

"That's great."

"What about you?" he asked.

"I attend Hope Apostolic Church. This is my first involvement
in an apostolic ministry. My pastor is an extremely dynamic preacher
and teacher of the word. I am growing."

"So it has been a good experience. Great! I spent most of my life attending Pentecostal churches. I love being in the house of the Lord."

"Me too!' I responded enthusiastically. "I love praise and worship."

"Same here and I cannot get enough of the word."

"The word of God is truly powerful," I said quietly. "I want to walk in His ways."

"That's just beautiful!" Orane said in a deep dramatic voice.

Spontaneous laughter erupted from me. "You're funny!"

"Yes. I have jokes," he chuckled. "It was nice talking to you. I just wanted to say hello. You have work in the morning, so I won't keep you. "

Ouch! That's my line!

Secretly, I wished that we could talk more but I did not want to appear eager. "You are right. It was nice talking with you too. Thanks for calling."

"May I call you during lunch tomorrow?"

I paused. *Did Harriett give him all my numbers?*

"Yes," I responded, then hesitantly asked, "Do you have my cell number?"

Orane chuckled sensing my apprehension. "No. You are going to give it to me now."

I laughed too, knowing that he knew where I was coming from.

"I love to hear you laugh," he remarked with a hint of a smile. "You seem like a wonderful person."

"You've been hearing things about me," I said in a leisurely tone.

"All good," he chuckled softly.

Orane and I exchanged numbers then said goodnight. A slow smile crept up the corners of my mouth as I placed the cordless phone back on its base. *A refreshing and interesting man!*

I lay back on my bed and closed my eyes, giggling softly. Neutral subjects were clearly not my thing! I hoped my questions were not too direct for a first conversation. I did not want to come across as uptight or overly professional.

I grabbed the sheets, pulling them closer to me. There was a strange feeling in my stomach, nervous excitement. I totally surprised myself; I gave my heart permission to speak freely with him. Sleep came much later after I replayed our entire conversation in my mind.

* * *

The following day, I woke up smiling then screaming when I saw the time. I must have slept through the alarm. Usually, I have devotion before sliding out of bed but that morning, I could only say a prayer. I threw my legs over the side of the bed and ran to the bathroom. A few minutes later, instead of my habitual spread for breakfast, I ate a cheese sandwich and drank tea.

Thankfully, I had taken out my work attire the night before. I quickly pulled on a dusty pink shirt, black skirt suit and accessories, then applied light makeup and a touch of perfume. As I struggled to put on my shoes, I caught sight of my reflection in the mirror and started to grin. "I am going out with joy," I declared boldly. I grabbed my purse and was on my way.

That day, my cell phone was closer than a brother. I took it everywhere I went, a very strange occurrence for me.

Hours later, during lunch, the anticipated call came.

"Hello," I answered, moving to exit the building.

"Hi Annalisa! This is Orane. We spoke last night."

"Hi! How are you?" I asked cheerfully.

"Great!" he responded. "It sounds like you are having a wonderful day."

"Yes, I am. I just finished lunch," I replied, taking a seat in a nearby gazebo.

"What did you eat?"

"Ah, a little something that I threw together, brown stewed chicken and steamed white rice. It was tasty though."

"Are you a good cook?"

"I can help myself in the kitchen but I would rather just eat. Can you cook?"

"You are being modest," he laughed. "Yes, I can cook, but like you, I rather just eat."

"Shameful!" I teased him mercilessly. "This is not good."

"Guilty. I embrace it," he chuckled. "Your sister told me that you live in Florida."

"Yes. Tallahassee, North Florida. I work at my alma mater, Colgana University as a senior personnel officer."

"HR. I can tell that you love your job."

"I do," I grinned.

"Not sure if your sister mentioned that I operate a small business that offers information technology services."

"Yes, Mr. Entre...pre...neur!"

Orane chuckled. "I always wanted to own a business."

"What did you do before you started the business?"

"I started out as an accountant. Later, I joined the sales team at an Information Technology company and a few years after that, I started my own business."

"Nice going!"

"Thanks!" I could hear the smile in his voice. "I know that you have to get back to work. May I call you at home later?"

"That's fine. I will listen out for your call."

"Great talking with you again. Talk with you later."

"Bye."

I gazed at my cell phone. *Way to go Annalisa Jones! I will listen out for your call. Not even suggesting a time to call.* I burst into senseless giggles as I walked back to my office. Unsurprisingly, my mind slanted toward optimism. *I am showing my interest, I told myself.* I giggled even more.

Ann Marie Bryan

Naturally joyous, I daydreamed on and off as I worked, laughing softly as my thoughts were hijacked by buoyant pieces of my conversation with Orane. I looked forward to talking with him again and...perhaps again.

※ ※ ※

A chill of nervous excitement began in my stomach when my home phone rang around nine o'clock that evening.

"Good evening!" I answered pleasantly, curling my long legs beneath my body and leaning back on the green cushions on the off white love seat in my bedroom.

"Hi Annalisa."

"Hey Orane! How are you?" I felt spontaneous knowing mixed with excitement as I greeted him.

"I'm good! Are you doing good?"

"Yes, I'm good. I was just catching up on politics."

"You're interested in politics?"

"Yes. Actually, I wasn't so totally involved until Barack Obama decided to run for President."

"America could have its first African-American President."

"Imagine that, in one of the greatest countries on earth," I exclaimed.

"Senator Obama is a natural orator. His delivery is excellent."

"Yes," I agreed wholeheartedly. "So classy, natural and conversational."

"The whole world is watching," Orane said thoughtfully.

"So true. I am now officially a political pundit," I declared.

"It's like that."

"Yes."

"At one stage I thought I would get involved in politics," Orane confessed. "I worked at the community level."

"Why didn't you?"

16

"Life happened back in the day," he sighed heavily. "I still have aspirations but I am waiting on the Lord for the right timing."

"Alright, Senator Conway!"

Orane chuckled. "So apart from politics, tell me something interesting about Annalisa Jones."

"Okay, let me see...I cry at the drop of a hat."

"Seriously?"

"Yes, it's a family tradition. I would hate to be the one to break it."

Orane laughed softly. "So you cry whether you're happy or sad?"

"Yes. My tear ducts are always full," I winced. "I cry at the movies, weddings and funerals. I cry because of God's love for humanity, you name it, I will cry. I am a crier."

"I will walk with a handkerchief."

"Best to do that." I grinned. "I take it, you don't cry easily?"

"No. I don't cry easily."

"I can teach you. Let's practice. Boo-oo, booh! Boo-oo, booh!"

Orane burst out laughing. "You are something Annalisa."

"I told you, I have a lot of experience in that area."

"I would rather you teach me how to laugh."

"Okay. Ready. First you..."

"You are unbelievable," he chuckled with satisfaction.

I giggled, feeling an increased level of comfortableness with him. "So tell me something interesting about yourself."

"I'll prefer if you discover that," he responded in a leisurely tone.

"Ohhh, smooth operator!"

"I'm just saying."

I pressed him gently. "Get me started. Tell me one thing."

"I like hot cocoa and bread."

"Cocoa and bread! Seriously?"

"Yes, and for the records, I do cry before the Lord sometimes when I pray."

"Awww! That's just beautiful."

Ann Marie Bryan

Orane inhaled then exhaled. "So there! All my business out in the open."

"Just a little," I grinned. "I gathered that you live in MayPo."

"Yes. I have been living in MayPo for over ten years. I am originally from Ocho Rios."

"Ocho Rios! Great place to live. Back in the day, some friends and I would drive from Kingston to Ocho Rios just to hit the beautiful beaches."

"I understand. The beaches are phenomenal. Do you miss them?"

"Definitely," I exclaimed. "Jamaica has mighty fine beaches."

"How long have you been away?"

"Seems like forever. But really, only four years. Before I left, I worked in human resources at Enterprise Bank in Kingston."

"HR again. You like dealing with people."

"Yes. It's my calling, my destiny. People and cultures fascinate me."

"I take it that you like traveling."

"Absolutely! I would put traveling on my list of fun things to do."

"I enjoy cultures too," Orane mentioned. "Isn't it amazing that we are all created in God's image?"

"That's what fascinates me," I said in hushed tones.

Orane laughed out. "I can tell."

"Guilty!" I responded, chuckling with delight.

"Hope I didn't call too late. I would have called earlier but I stopped at church for bible study."

"Not a problem. Are you actively involved in church?" My lips curled in a smile and I pulled the green cotton throw around my shoulders. *This will be an all-nighter...a wonderful all-nighter.*

"Yes. I participate in men's fellowship and help with the youth ministry."

"That's great! Dancing is my ministry."

18

"Dancing!" Orane sounded pleasantly surprised. "I am not exposed to dancing as a ministry."

"Ohhhh, it's wonderfully liberating to dance under the anointing of the Holy Spirit."

"How long have you been dancing?"

"Forever!" I said dramatically. "I breathe and sleep dance. It is an effortless activity for me."

"Really?"

"Yes. I began dancing from my childhood days during family events. I danced through high school but it was during college that I was exposed to dancing as a ministry. There began my love affair with the ministry of dance. I am overseeing the dance ministry at my church."

"What age groups do you teach?"

"We have three groups. The pre-juniors—those are the little ones, the juniors are teenagers and the seniors are adults."

"I cannot wait to see you in action." I could hear the admiration in his voice.

I smiled. "I'll see what I can do to make it happen."

Our conversation continued into the wee hours of the morning. No topics or questions were off limit. We were on the same level mentally and interested in some of the same things. We discovered our mutual fascination with empowering lives. I was particularly impressed with his sentiments and testimonies about the goodness of God.

Sleep did not come quickly as thoughts of Orane began to inhabit my mind. His voice kept reverberating in my head as I replayed our entire conversation. I found him to be extremely knowledgeable and disarmingly candid. I smiled briefly as I considered my future romantic probabilities. Orane was opening my eyes and perhaps, my heart.

CHAPTER 3: PICTURES PLEASE

Classified.

My friendship with Orane was hush-hush for almost two weeks before I finally confessed to Maydine and Harriett. They were elated and promised to keep it top-secret. They called nightly for a status report. "Look at you both, enjoying my private life," I often teased them amidst their girlish giggles. Soon, Orane began relating to them on a more personal level.

I filed my experience so far under, *Totally Happy* in the classified section of my heart! There was a new bounce in my steps as my friendship with Orane continued to blossom. Never have I seen or experienced any such thing. There was no explanation for the sustained kick in my energy level. I found myself smiling as pieces of our conversation floated through my mind. This was a new level of happiness.

My interest in Orane spurred my curiosity.

What is it about him that makes him different from any other man?

My situation with him is different but still common sense and common rules apply. In the beginning, it was great daydreaming about him but reality could present a whole different picture. Certainly, I may be setting myself up for disappointment.

In light of this, I doubled up on my prayers, seeking God about my new found joy and the subject of my attention. I prayed that I would not create a distorted perception of Orane. I asked the Lord to show me how to keep my heart with all diligence. I did not want to run ahead of myself or worst, ahead of God. As I sent up fervent prayers to heaven, my spirit was refreshed and peace flooded my soul, beyond my own comprehension.

Orane took our friendship in stride. He planted subtle seeds of love but no pressure came from him. He kept up what he began earlier, reserving lunch hours for brief conversations and nights for longer conversations.

While Orane's words were capturing my attention, I had no idea what he looked like.

Was I living on the edge?

No! Definitely NOT!

I was waiting, sometimes impatiently and even a little apprehensively. Orane had promised to email me pictures which seemed to be taking forever. In the meantime, I tried not to weave a web of thoughts and paint an ideal image of him.

"Where are the photos?" I asked Orane during one of our nightly conversations.

"I haven't forgotten," he responded. "I will be taking the new shots soon."

"What happen to the old shots?"

"Trust me, you would prefer the new shots."

I sighed, flopping backwards on my bed. "Okay Orane, send them before I turn a hundred years old."

He chuckled softly. "You are rough."

"A diamond in the rough." I giggled. "Be patient."

Maydine and Harriett's description of Orane did not put me at ease. "He looks nice," they reported.

What exactly does that mean?

Plain and simple, I would absolutely love to see the man behind the voice. The suspense was too much.

Finally, weeks of anticipation inched closer to fulfillment.

During a lunch hour conversation, Orane informed me that he had emailed the new pictures. I was ecstatic; I wanted to climb on a soap box and announce it to the world. My heart soared with excitement until…it suddenly hit me.

Am I ready to see this man?

I sat in my office gazing at my cell phone in self-imposed mental anguish. *Should I view the pictures now? Could I handle it?* I was tempted, surely tempted but I dare not look at my email. Privacy was required.

All sorts of emotions ran through my brain as I watched the workday creep to an end. I could hardly wait to get out of the building. A part of me desperately wanted to see what Orane looked like but another part did not want to be disappointed. Five o'clock sharp, with an extra pep in my steps, I burst through the exit door of my office, for the privacy of my home.

Half an hour later, I climbed the stairs at home and entered the study. My laptop purred to life and I logged into my email account. The screen registered Orane's message. I could hardly wait to see the man who was steadfastly holding my interest. After several deep breaths, I double clicked with eagerness then scrolled down the page to see two thumbnails of him.

I gasped and my mouth fell open.

My breathing became shallow and I quickly signed out.

What on earth is wrong with me?

Why didn't I enlarge the pictures?

I looked cautiously at my laptop as if it had grown two horns. Questions rushed through my mind as my palpitating heart subsided. The effect was still very unsettling. My breathing slowed somewhat and I reopened the email. I enlarged the two pictures briefly.

Orane wrote: *"I hope that you are sitting down."*

I smiled and responded, *"No need, you are quite handsome. Thanks for sending them."*

✳ ✳ ✳

Two hours later, a smile was already on my lips as I answered the phone. "Good evening, Orane! How is it going in your neck of the woods?"

"Woods? What woods? I don't live in the woods." he joked.

"Okay my good man, at your dwelling," I grinned, stretching out on my bed.

"It's going great, my lady!"

"Sounds wonderful."

Orane paused. "I wasn't going to call tonight."

"Uh huh! I understand, those pictures were pretty ghastly," I said jokingly.

He gasped dramatically. "I thought you said it was not about the physical."

I chuckled softly. "It's not, but looking fine sure helps."

He winced. "My bad for disappointing you, my friend."

"Luckily for you, no disappointment," I responded playfully. "The pics look good."

"Those are pictures of my cousin."

"Your cousin! Which cousin?" I harassed him lightheartedly.

"Even if I told you his name, you would not know him Annalisa." Orane laughed out, delighted at his mini victory.

"Right! You didn't tell me you're short," I badgered him.

"There you go again, talking about the physical."

"Uh. You're funny!"

"What's wrong with being short?" he asked, looking for a "fight".

"I am not taking you on today," I uttered confidently.

"Come on, make my day!" he begged, laughing softly.

"No Clint Eastwood, no fighting today."

"Do you have an issue with short people?"

"Sir, you are badgering me," I stated calmly. "Nothing is wrong with being short."

Orane chuckled heartily. He was in a great mood. "Now, we are on the same page."

"You are something Orane Conway!"

"You are a sweetheart Anna," he said playfully. "Can I call you Anna?"

"Knock yourself out!"

"So Anna, what's new?"

"I just spoke to my friend, Ari. She is coming for a short visit next weekend."

"Who's Ari?"

"Arianna and I met while we were studying at Colgana University. She lives in Georgia."

"Good for you ladies."

"I'm looking forward to seeing her. I haven't seen her in over a year so I was glad she decided to stop by."

"Great. Next weekend, my church is having a convention."

"Sounds like a plan. You're helping out."

"Yes, doing my part," he responded. "I am going to call you back. I have to…"

"Noooo!"

"I want to talk with you but I have to do bank reconciliations."

"I forgive you then. Handle your business."

"Before I go," Orane said in a deep husky voice, "be honest with me. Do you have a problem with short people?"

I could not help but laugh at his foolishness. "Orane Conway, stop!"

"You didn't answer the question, Anna."

"Do you see where this conversation is going?"

"Yes, Anna."

"Me too! It's going nowhere."

Orane laughed softly. "You are way too smart, lady."

"Aren't I just," I giggled, "totally smart!"

"Totally!"

"For the records, you are not short."

"I know that Anna." Orane chuckled confidently. "I am nearly six feet tall."

"Forgive me, Mr. Tall," I teased.

"You are forgiven," he drawled dramatically.

I giggled softly. "Bye!"

"Talk with you later," he chuckled.

I burrowed further into the pillows. *I like this guy!* I smiled, basking in the stimulating conversation we created. Soon, we would have to make the difficult decision that would shape the nature of our relationship. Our conversations have undoubtedly created a bond between us, making possible a deeper connection. I thoughtfully watched as the yellow sheer curtains swayed lazily in the mild breeze. Whether I liked it or not, I was becoming hooked.

CHAPTER 4: CONNECTED

God is first place in our lives.

That was our agreement going forward as Orane and I continued to communicate. It had been just over a month but the bond between us grew stronger with each passing day. I admired Orane's relationship with God and I loved the thoughts of his heart. He kept me informed about biblical and world events and we started nightly devotion.

Our friendship was made to order, with just the right amount of everything. We delighted in each other's "company", learning about each other, praying together, exchanging jokes and talking about life. An effortless rapport existed between us. It was becoming easier to cue into each other's feelings. We were inexplicably connected.

We enjoyed challenging each other's mind. I discovered Orane's engaging personality. He was extremely alert, astute and intellectually stimulating. During our many heated "debates", he would often start with what I called the regular perspective before dropping the "bomb", a new, fresh, bold perspective, "stirring the pot a little".

Totally exhilarating!

I marveled at the strength of his mind.

Orane revealed his playful side and I frequently felt the brunt of his pranks. Many times when I answered the phone I would say a few "hellos" before he chimed in with *"don't shout"* then burst into a fit of laughter.

Annoyed! Yes I was.

Nevertheless, I looked forward to talking with him every day. We enjoyed every millisecond that we were in touch. Our spirits were quickly becoming intertwined as we found favor with each other. It felt like we had known each other for years…maybe forever. We had not confessed our feelings to each other but I believed that we both knew. We were just letting our friendship happen.

And speaking of feelings...

I had become enamored with Orane. It hit me like a ton of bricks one day while I was in the kitchen at home baking banana bread. The realization sent me in a state of panic then shock. My heart beat took off in a sprint without notifying the rest of its counterparts. I paused and gripped the cupboard for support to get my breathing under control. I had been trying very hard to suppress it, thinking it was impossible. But, it was a little too late. I may not be completely in love with him, but I could feel myself falling...

❊ ❊ ❊

In the wee hours one Saturday, I perched on several pillows on my bed, talking with Orane. My ear was hot and tender from the telephone cradled between my neck and shoulder.

"Have a wonderful night or should I say morning," I said, stifling a slight yawn.

Orane chuckled softly. "Is this your final attempt to end our conversation?"

I grinned. "You just like talking with me. Admit it!"

"At least, I can admit it," he hinted quietly.

"Have a good morning, Mr. Conway!"

"Annalisa..."

Something in his voice drew my attention. "Yes. I'm still here."

"I feel so connected to you," he said softly.

Unexpectedly, my mouth went dry and my heart pounded so hard that I could feel the throbbing in my ears. "I know what you mean," I replied. "I'm just totally amazed at our friendship."

"Yes. We are good with each other," he said thoughtfully. "I believe that we could join each other on the journey to the next level."

"I feel that way too," I confessed, trying to get my breathing under control. "I have never been so free with anyone."

"I feel special," he said tenderly. "You are such a wonderful person."

I was all choked up. "Thank you!"

Orane paused. "Why aren't you married?" he asked quietly.

"The right person has not proposed."

"Have you received proposals?"

"Yes, a few. I actually thought I would get married the last time."

"What happened?"

"We both had very different reasons for wanting to be married. I needed emotional support and I was not getting it. Also, I did not like the thoughts that flowed from his heart."

"Sounds like you know the qualities that you desire in a partner."

"Yes!" I paused, blatantly waiting for him to ask the obvious.

He chuckled knowingly. "Would you like to share them?"

A giggle I could not hold back escaped my lips. "Okay, since you're insisting! I desire a man of God, a praying man. My husband and I must bear fruits for God. Of course, friendship is important. I also look for potential and the fruits that flow from his life. For me, it's not how you start but how you finish or desire to finish."

"Yes. God likes finishers," he interjected.

"Oh yes. Of utmost importance is how my husband processes then articulates his thoughts."

Orane inhaled then exhaled. "I am glad that you can enunciate what you desire in a mate."

"Thanks. I do so prayerfully. Do you wish to be married?"

"Yes. I desire to be married and have a family. It is something that I have always wanted. I am asking the Lord to choose for me. God must be at the center of my relationship and marriage because I know that's the only way it will stand the test of time and last a life time."

"Yes," I agreed softly.

After Orane and I said goodnight, I laid in bed thinking about him, over and over again. Without a doubt, I would be fortunate to have him in my life. But, is he the 'real McCoy'?

Can I truly be in love with someone I have never met?

Is this an illusion?

Wishful thinking.

A fantasy.

I had no intention of losing my most valuable resource, my heart. Yet, I had to be true to myself. I was getting attached to Orane and the feeling was being reciprocated. He did not want to let me go and I...I didn't want him to. Again, I committed our friendship to the Lord and asked for His continued guidance.

CHAPTER 5: SISTERLY ADVICE

I smiled at Arianna across the dining table as she swallowed the last bite of her fried egg. "This is an absolutely beautiful Sunday morning."

"Yes," she agreed. "I love days like this, sunny blue skies and cool temperatures to put everyone in a great mood."

"I am so glad that you decided to visit." I eyed her while sipping my green tea.

A bright smile lit her face. "Me too. Yesterday was fun."

"Yes, it was," I responded, automatically returning her smile.

It was good to have Arianna in town for the weekend. Saturday morning passed in a blur of joy as we roamed the city, basking in the warmth of the sun's rays. We spent the afternoon shopping and later enjoyed a movie at the theater in Tallahassee Mall.

"I have finally decided to leave my relationship," Arianna blurted out.

My eyes widened with compassion. "Oh Ari!"

"You know that we have been dating forever, and still no marriage proposal. Ray has all kinds of excuses." She sighed in frustration.

"I know it's not easy to leave a relationship," I said comfortingly, "especially one that you have invested in."

"Tell me about it," Arianna said sarcastically. "Seven years later and no ring. I kept hoping that Ray would change."

"Ari, I know it's hard but…"

"The white picket fence collapsed before my face." She sighed and her gaze dropped to the wooden floor.

I nudged her. "You know you deserve the best and don't you forget it."

"I know Anna." She exhaled deeply. "I have been building back my relationship with the Lord. But I still feel that I need to have my head examined for staying in the relationship so long."

"Don't beat up yourself. In fact, don't even think it; that's the plan of the enemy to keep you in bondage."

She smiled slightly, resting her elbows on the table. "You've always been so encouraging."

I tapped her shoulder. "You know that you deserve someone to treat you like the queen you are."

Arianna nodded and her slender frame drooped as she looked sadly into the distance. "I am so afraid to start over," she said quietly.

"Ari, any man would be extremely blessed to have you. Don't short change yourself."

Her large blue-grey eyes brightened. "Thanks my friend! I forgot that I am a child of God."

"Girl, God loves you so much."

"I know. I have been crying out to Him. I need someone to treat me right but I need to start believing that I should be treated right."

"We learn as we go along," I consoled her. "I know you've been reviewing the scriptures on love."

"Yes, still going through. I need to get me back!"

"There you go my friend. I have been praying for you!"

"Yes, I know. Thank you for being there...for your prayers... and your love."

"Don't even mention it, that's what sisters do. When one door closes, you better prepare yourself because in the right season, God will open double doors for you."

"High five!" Arianna yelled, grinning as our hands met. "Yes Lord, double doors, please!"

"You should begin to think about the qualities that you desire in a husband," I suggested.

"I'll do that. Do you know the qualities that you desire in a mate?"

"Of course! He must definitely be a Christ…"

"Girl, I know he must be a Christian. What else?"

I giggled at her mock sternness. "He must be a praying man with a heart after the Lord."

Arianna rolled her eyes then grinned. "Yeah, yeah, all of the above."

"Good to see you smiling Ari."

Arianna sighed deeply. "Sometimes you meet someone you like but he doesn't like you. Then another time, someone will like you and you don't feel the same way. I believe one day, one day all that will be synchronized for me. In the meantime, I'm gonna live it up." Arianna began to sing and dance her rendition of *"Single Ladies (Put a ring on it)"*, Beyonce Knowles' popular song.

I laughed loudly and cheered as she danced from the dining room to the living room and ended with a dramatic pose. "Go on girl, take back the power. You are a survivor."

She grasped the edge of the sofa for support. "Ohhhh, that was my stress reliever!"

I giggled even more as she sprawled out on the sofa.

"So, what about you?" Arianna asked breathlessly. "I saw you blushing on those calls. Yes girlfriend, I saw you. Let me have it."

"Okay," I said sheepishly, flopping down on the sofa across from her. "FYI *(for your information)*, I am developing a friendship and hopefully a relationship."

"Yippee! Yippee!" Arianna screamed dancing around.

"Shush!"

Her smile broadened and her eyes widened. "Who is the lucky man?"

"His name is Orane. We have not yet met. We've been communicating by phone. I will be spending Christmas in Jamaica so we will meet then."

"Ooooh!" Arianna threw her hands in the air. "This is good news."

I gave her the short version of how Orane and I began. By the time I was finished, she visualized Orane and I walking off into the sunset.

"Here comes the bride," she sang, pretending to walk up the aisle.

"Sit down and stop being a mess," I playfully scolded her.

She giggled and with squeals of delight, collapsed on the sofa. "Have you chosen a color for your wedding?"

I looked at her in utter disbelief. "Stop it."

"I think you should start preparing yourself," she continued cheerfully. "By the looks of things, it will be quick."

"I am not the type to start wedding plans before I get a proposal," I said with disdain. "I am not even in a relationship."

"Don't be a spoil sport, let's visit wedding sites and save them to Favorites."

"Seriously Arianna Simpson, you are 'off the chain'!"

"Come on," she said, grabbing her laptop from the coffee table.

"I cannot be involved in this foolishness," I said, hurrying towards my bedroom. "I have to prepare for church."

"Annalisa come on, you know we have time."

I threw myself across my bed. *Thank God, I escaped.* I was barely acclimatized to having a special friend in my life.

"Anna, come here a minute please!" Arianna shouted.

I slid off my bed and stood in the doorway. "Yeessss!"

Arianna was still on the sofa in the living room, gazing intently at the screen of her laptop. "Are you coming to look at the wedding sites? I will email you other links when I get home."

"Nope!"

"Spoil sport!" she pouted.

"I don't want to be involved in all that."

"I think burgundy is an awesome color. Please don't go with pastel shades." Her eyes were filled with excitement. "Do you have any color in mind?"

I looked at her as if she had lost her mind. "Let me see...Nope."

"Okay, if that's the way you're gonna be."

"I am going to get ready for church." I lifted my hands in the air and danced. "I have to get my praise on."

"Fine! At least show me his picture."

I stared blindly at her. *Ouch! Brain freeze!*

"What is wrong with you? I only asked to see his picture."

"Let me get to my email."

My hands felt sweaty as I logged into my email account on her laptop. "There he is," I said breathlessly.

"What are you all nervous about? He is a nice looking man."

"He is?" I swallowed hard. "He is."

"Yes, he is," Arianna said, with one eyebrow raised. "Let me enlarge it…let see 150%…there, very nice."

"O…Okay, can I close out now?"

"Yes ma'am! Keep that nice man locked away. I'm definitely preparing for your wedding."

I looked at her baffled. "Did I mention that I am not in a relationship?"

"But you are. You just won't admit it," Arianna said pointedly.

I glared at her and she burst into hysterical laughter.

"You should see your face," she said, heading upstairs to the guest room.

"Oh stop it!" I yelled, and with that I bolted for my bedroom.

After church, I waved goodbye to a giggling Arianna. Her jet black curly hair bounced up and down with her movements as she joyfully gestured to me before pulling away. She was still in full blown preparation for my wedding day.

CHAPTER 6: COVERT ACTIONS

"Father, let your will be done on earth in our lives as it is established in heaven," Orane earnestly prayed.

That night, I sat on the carpet in my bedroom as Orane and I bombarded heaven with prayers. As Orane prayed, the atmosphere was charged with the presence of God. I wept before the Lord, thanking him for His goodness and mercy throughout my life.

"Annalisa, are you okay?" he asked calmly at the end of the prayer.

"Yes. I'm just in awe of God's love for us."

"God is awesome."

"Totally," I agreed quietly. "I have always felt that the Lord watches over me."

"He does. He will never leave you nor forsake you."

"Yes," I acquiesced softly, adjusting my position so that my back rested against the wall.

"Are you baptized?" Orane asked.

"Yes. I was baptized the summer before I left for college in Jamaica."

"I was baptized twice," he remarked, "the first time was in my early teens and the second, when I recommitted my life several years ago."

"Praise the Lord," I cheered.

"Annalisa," Orane paused.

"Yes." Unconsciously I held my breath; something in his voice requested my undivided attention.

"I know that we have not met but there is a settling in my spirit about us. I would like to get to know you more and if all goes well, I would like to marry you, if you would have me. You already have my heart."

Ann Marie Bryan

Someone please check my pulse!

My eyes widened and my heart pumped with excitement as I spoke. "Orane, I have never felt so connected to anyone. Yes. I will marry you if all goes well with us."

"Great!" he shouted with exuberance. "I have found the one my heart loves."

My mind raced and butterflies danced around in my stomach as his words pierced my heart.

Then the "bomb" drop occurred.

"I know that you'll be in Jamaica in another two months but I would like to visit you in Tallahassee," Orane said quietly.

I was shocked into silence as several emotions swirled through my mind.

Visit me!

Say something! "I...I..."

"You can think about it," he said. His words sounded light but I could hear disappointment in his voice.

"No!" I exclaimed, trying to steady my heart rate. "I mean, I would really like that." I buried my head in the pillow to muffle my screams of delight.

"Great! I'm thinking of visiting you in three weeks' time."

My heart palpitated so hard that I could hardly hear myself think. "Three weeks' time is good," I responded breathlessly.

Orane exhaled deeply. "Now I can say, see you soon!"

I giggled softly. "You sure can!"

After Orane and I said goodnight, I laid in bed praying and thinking. Orane's heart was fully committed to our friendship and potential relationship. However, I was not ready to articulate my feelings for him. I needed to conduct checks and balances, because of all that was at stake. I was too close to the situation to properly assess it.

I needed more eyes.

Godly trained eyes.

It was time to call in reinforcement.

Two days later, I asked Kay, one of my closest friends to meet me for lunch. To know Kay is to love her. She was a wonderful, kind-hearted and gracious woman of God. I met Kay through Maydine and Harriett, five years ago during my summer vacation in Tallahassee. A year later, during my period of study, I worked as Kay's teaching assistant at Colgana Elementary School.

I knew that Kay would be honest with me as I solicited her help with navigating my newfound friendship.

"You are glowing," Kay remarked, when she joined me for lunch at Zali Italian Restaurant.

"No, look at you! You're looking great." I smiled at her. Kay was still rocking a new blunt cut hair style. "How are the boys and hubby doing?"

"They are doing well. So what's...?" Kay asked breathlessly, only to be interrupted by Jovan, the waiter.

We quickly ordered soups.

Kay eyeballed me. "You had me on pins and needles coming here. What's up?"

"I met someone," I blurted out, grinning from ear to ear.

Kay clapped her hands with glee. "Yes," she exclaimed, throwing her hands in the air.

"Ah, let me rephrase."

My conversation with Kay was punctuated with ohhhs, ahhhs and loud outbursts of laughter as I brought her up to speed on my friendship with Orane.

"You and Orane are incredibly attached to each other," she commented as Jovan placed our soups on the table and left.

"Yes but I don't believe in long distance relationships. They can be challenging and difficult at their worst."

Kay swallowed a few spoons of her soup then looked intently at me before speaking. "I hear you say challenging and difficult, but not impossible."

I smiled knowingly. "Right. I will miss the face-to-face inter-action, the frequency of seeing him whenever I desired, not to mention maximum trust is required. We already spoke about the trust factor."

"I am not down-playing any of that," Kay reassured me. "I know that you are praying and so will I. Since you have not yet met him, take it in stages."

"Yes, that's true. Let me not run ahead of myself. We did say that we would get to know each other more."

"That's great. Keep doing what you are doing, clarifying each other's values, beliefs and commitment."

"Yes," I replied thoughtfully.

I swallowed a spoon full of soup then looked up to find Kay grinning at me.

"Have you spoken about finances, sex and all?" she asked.

I blushed. "Of...of!"

Kay laughed then suddenly stopped with raised eyebrows. "Yes, you did! Knowing you, all topics and subtopics were covered."

I grinned at her. "You know I covered every topic in the book and out of the book"

"Your name would not be Annalisa Jones if you didn't," Kay beamed, stirring her soup. "Does Orane know what he is getting into?"

"Oh stop it! He knows Proverbs 18:22." I smiled sheepishly, feeling an unexpected tingle of nerves.

Kay laughed and repeated the scripture verse. "He who finds a wife finds a good thing, And obtains favor from the Lord."

"Amen!" I declared.

Kay gently smiled at me, her spoon full of soup poised in front of her mouth. "He must be a special man. I have never seen you so energized and alive."

"Yes. He is special," I beamed.

"Great! So continue to keep each other informed about family life, friendships and daily events to keep your relationship alive."

"Yes. If we commit to a relationship, we also need to set the limit on how long we will be apart."

Kay nodded. "Remember, God is good. Commit everything to Him and trust Him."

"Thanks Kay! I appreciate you," I said softly.

"You'll be alright. Just take it in stages."

"I will."

Half an hour later, I journeyed back to work feeling more enlightened and in touched with my feelings about a long distance relationship with Orane. Orane and I needed to be extremely secured and satisfied with each other for our long distance relationship to work successfully.

❋ ❋ ❋

The next day, I placed a call to Melissa, my seventh 'adopted sister'. Melissa and I met during our college years in Jamaica and we have been close friends ever since. An intercessor and prayer warrior, Melissa was a remarkable woman and a wonderful human being with an amazing personality.

Melissa was elated when I informed her of my friendship with Orane. Her shouts of joy echoed through the telephone and she openly thanked God for His faithfulness.

Since Melissa operated as the Branch Manager for a full service bank, I knew that she was sharp at garnering information from her clients so I told her to utilize her skills on Orane. I had arranged for Orane to pick up a small package from her before his trip to Tallahassee.

"I'll see what I can find out," Melissa modestly promised.

Melissa had strict instructions to observe him, in conversation and body language.

"You should be ready to answer any question I ask you concerning Orane," I warned her.

In her usual manner, Melissa laughed. "I will do my best. Take everything in stride. The Holy Spirit will guide you."

"Thanks Mel, I appreciate you!"

The next day, I emailed Melissa:

"...Last night, Orane told me that his heart is fragile so I am not to destroy it. He feels that we are not totally on the same page emotionally. I told him that it takes me a while to make up my mind. I feel pretty good about him. Actually, I can't wait to see him. All I do is pray. I do not want to have a broken heart myself. My head space can't take it so I am cautious...with one foot out."

❋ ❋ ❋

Almost two weeks later, Melissa informed me that Orane would be picking up the package that day. I was on pins and needles awaiting word from her. Finally, during lunch, the long awaited call came.

"How was he?" I asked excitedly. I had camped out at my usual spot, the gazebo near my office.

"Oh, he is good to go," she said calmly.

"Mel, this is no time to hold back," I threatened playfully. "Tell me!"

Melissa chuckled. She clearly anticipated my reaction. "He's deep in terms of his walk with God and his purpose in life. He spoke about his love for the Lord and indicated that he desired a wife who loves the Lord. In fact, that's what he desires most in a wife."

"Nice!"

Excitement filled Melissa's voice. "He believes that you fit the bill even though he has not met you."

"What else?" I whispered breathlessly.

"He is well groomed and well spoken. I know you would like that."

I giggled knowingly. "Mel, you are too much."

"He seems like a very serious man," she pointed out.

"Oh yes. He is quite something. Describe him."

"He is medium height say 5'9", slim, dark, lean, nice looking man."

"What's his shoes size?"

"Nine, ten, eleven, who knows," Melissa said laughing.

"My, you're good," I said playfully. "I will definitely use you for my next investigation."

Melissa giggled. "I also did some digging."

"That's what I am talking about!" I beamed. "You are officially Private Investigator M. What did you find out?"

"Good reports so far. This lady's reaction was immediate and spontaneous. She said that Orane is always sharing about the goodness of God."

"Alrighty!"

Melissa went into hushed tones. "Another lady told me that he is very particular about his reputation. She also said that he takes care of his physical appearance."

"Mel, you are a gem. I cannot thank you enough."

"No problem! Glad to be of service. Remember to look your very best when you pick him up at the airport. You know first impression really does last."

"Absolutely!"

"If you are still in love when you meet him, then I see no reason why you shouldn't get married shortly."

I gasped even though I was delirious with excitement. "Sure Mel!" I responded sarcastically.

"How's December?" Melissa asked enthusiastically.

"Girl stop!"

"Ok, January then."

I broke out in a hollow nervous laughter. "Your lunch time is passing and you are having way too much fun at my expense."

Melissa paused. "Annalisa, I know that you will make the right decision. The Lord knows everything about Orane. I will continue to pray for you both."

Ann Marie Bryan

"Thanks Mel, I appreciate you. Say hello to Simon and the kids for me."

"I will! Enjoy the rest of your day as I know you will. By the way, should I put Reverend Fuller on standby?"

"Yes, do that." I threatened. "Bye!"

A few days later, I emailed Melissa:

"I am not sure why I feel so calm about this. I am so looking forward to seeing this man. I really like his spirit and he makes me laugh so hard. We have a very unpretentious relationship. Seriously, we talk foolishness sometimes too. He has a real relationship with God and I know it. Harriett and Maydine just love him to life. They speak very well of him.

He said that I should not worry about our friendship but all I have been doing is praying. He said that God has fulfilled the desires of his heart. He has never had this kind of naked and unashamed relationship with anyone. Actually, neither have I. He said that it does not matter what I look like, he has found his wife. Okay, let me stop here. Blessings!"

CHAPTER 7: FACE TO FACE

My shock and awe campaign…

Definitely NOT my recommendation to anyone, for any occasion, time or season.

For his short weekend visit, Orane requested the room rate of the hotel nearest to my home. I checked the rates at RBC Hotel, which was a ten-minute drive from my home. Much later, after careful consideration, I told him that he could be my guest.

"Are you sure?" he asked, surprised by my offer.

"Don't worry," I told him. "I plan to put you in chains upstairs."

Orane was not the only one astonished by my offer. I believed that Maydine, Harriett, Melissa and Kay thought that I had lost my mind.

"Annalisa, this is so unlike you!"

"Are you sure you want to do that?"

"That is not a wise decision!"

"Have you thought this thing through?"

Simon was extremely distraught and spoke to Melissa about the situation. "Babes, ask Annalisa if she is sure about this. This is unlike her."

Actually, very uncharacteristic of me!

Quite frankly, I would never recommend such an action.

I acted on emotions rather than principles and that is NEVER EVER a great idea. While I was not totally comfortable with my decision, Orane and I needed to spend quality time together. I must confess that I had asked Arianna to spend the weekend with us. But, as Orane's visit drew closer, I released her from the commitment because Orane and I had built up an element of trust.

Finally, the day arrived. Happy Thursday!

I slept in a little, only to be awakened by the blaring sound of my cell phone alarm. I half-opened my eyes and smiled widely as excitement filled my body. But, that was short-lived.

A big sigh escaped my lips, like a deflating tire.

Sometimes, the highly anticipated pleasures of a special day automatically create joy and great contentment; perhaps, even a deep all-pervading excitement. Today is not, one of those days.

Joy. Yes.

Contentment. No.

Shivers of trepidation attacked me and a tiny war raged within.

Will Orane and I still have our special connection when we are face to face?

Will I like him physically?

Will he like me physically?

Halfway through the morning, my cheerleaders - Melissa, Kay, Arianna, Maydine and Harriett called to boost my seemingly faltering courage.

The day went by quickly and before I knew, it was time to make my airport run. Dinner was already prepared and I made sure that my home was looking superb. I added red accents to the kitchen and living and dining rooms which were mainly decorated in off-white and forest green. So glad that I did! The vibrant red created a warm and engaging atmosphere.

In my attempt to achieve the right look, I changed outfits several times then ended up wearing what I had initially planned, my navy jeans pants and jacket, gold tank top and navy sandals. My black hair was brushed sleek beyond my shoulder.

Before leaving home, I powered up my laptop and checked Orane's flight status. His flight was arriving ten minutes earlier than scheduled. I would be late.

So much for first impression!

It was a beautiful evening. The evening sun shone brightly as I headed to Tallahassee Regional Airport. I voiced my faith instead of nursing and rehearsing my fears. I could feel my temperate slowly rising as I drove into the arrival area.

Orane saw me first. He moved confidently towards the car, with an easy smile. I drew in a shaky breath, opened the trunk and got out of the car.

"Annalisa!" he exclaimed smiling, with wide open arms.

Hesitantly, I wrapped my hands around his waist. "Orane, great to…" My greeting was muffled by our embrace.

"Let me look at you." Orane held me at arm's length. He looked calm and at ease.

"Sorry, I'm late," I said, blushing under his intense scrutiny. "Welcome to Tallahassee!"

"Thank you. I feel at home already," he said gallantly. He placed his carry-on in the trunk and closed it. "Ready when you are."

His smile was lethal! He was handsome, with amazing dark brown eyes and gorgeous kissable lips. *Resist! Resist girl! Now is not the time to be led by your raging hormones.*

I returned the smiled. "Let's go!"

"Would you like me to drive?" Orane asked as we pulled away.

Pure mischief was in his eyes, eyes that just pulled me in and played on my heartstrings. "Hmm! Let me see, tomorrow perhaps! I am giving you a break since you had a long flight. How was your flight?"

"It was good. Thank God, I arrived safely. It's really good to see you."

"You too." My senses were a mess. I felt nervous and excited in the same breath. *Breathe, I cautioned myself.* "We'll be home…in twenty minutes," I mumbled.

"Are you okay?" Orane asked.

"Yes, just processing." I sighed then held on to his left hand. "I am having an out of body experience."

"It's me," he said reassuringly. "The same one you talk to every day and night."

"I know." I smiled at him. "It will be a bit cold while you are here."

"I realized so I came equipped."

"You don't look like your photo at all. You should fire your photographer," I joked.

Orane laughed. "Are we still talking about the physical, Anna?

I giggled. *Caught again!*

"Hope you are not disappointed," he said.

"Of course not, look at you."

Orane had one eyebrow raised and amusement was in his eyes. "That's your favorite expression."

"Ouch!"

He nudged me playfully. "Yes. You always say that."

We burst into laughter at my poor attempt at shock and disbelief.

"Yes," I concurred. "I do use that phrase a lot."

"If I may borrow your phrase, look at you! You're almost back."

Orane squeezed my hand and part of my defense melted away under his gaze. A few minutes later, I drove into my garage.

"Welcome home," I exclaimed as we exited the car.

He smiled charmingly. "Thank you. I was feeling a tad bit unwanted."

"Never!" I murmured ushering him through the door. "This is my humble abode."

Orane dropped his carry-on near the door. "Come here!" He held my hands. The gentleness in his eyes stilled me. "If you are not comfortable, I can stay at a hotel."

"No. I am good. I promise!" I placed my head on his shoulder and he held me and prayed.

"Thank you." I smiled at him. "I just felt overwhelmed. I am good now."

"That's alright, as long as you're okay."

"I'm good."

He winced. "Now, where is the bathroom?"

My eyes widened and a loud gasp escaped my lips. "Right there!" I pointed to the half bathroom nearby.

"Thanks," he said, moving with lightning speed towards the bathroom.

As soon as the bathroom door was closed behind him, I muffled a scream of delight. I could not believe that he was here. I could barely contain my excitement as I entered the dining room.

The dining table was already set for two with gold placemats, burgundy and gold napkins, gold chargers, white dinner plates, silverware, wine glasses and serving utensils. A transparent vase containing fresh yellow and white roses stood in the center of the table evoking a feeling of warmth and happiness.

Across from the dining room, I entered the kitchen, washed my hands and started warming dinner in the microwave. I had prepared brown stewed chicken, steamed rice and peas, corn casserole, steamed cabbage and tossed salad.

"Look at you," Orane teased. I turned and saw him sitting on one of the bar stools around the counter that separated the kitchen from the dining room.

"No, look at you Mr. Conway."

"Are you good?" I could hear the concern in his voice.

"Yes, I'm good, really good."

"Great! What can I help you with?"

"Are you sure you want to?" His eyebrow lift sent me into fits of giggles. "Okay, please pour the drinks. The glasses are in the top cupboard to my right and drinks are in the refrigerator."

"What will you have to drink?" he asked.

"Orange juice, please. I'll take a small glass. I intend to have tea. Would you like tea too?"

"Yes. Great idea! Should I put the vegetable platter on the table? Nice arrangement!"

"Thank you! You are too kind." I smiled at him. "Please take out the Italian Vinaigrette dressing for me. You can select the dressing you like."

"Sure will."

As I moved around the kitchen and dining room, I observed Orane scrutinizing and making mental notes of my physique.

"Like what you see." I posed briefly for sudden impact.

"Yeah, very much so," he responded with exuberance. "Now, I am convinced that you are back."

"Ahhh let's eat, that's if you are not too full."

He reached for me and I grinned and slipped out of his reach.

"Allow me." Orane pulled my chair out.

"Thank you, kind sir."

"My pleasure!"

Orane took his seat and blessed the meal. "What is this?" he asked.

"It's corn casserole. It's great, not too sweet. A friend taught me how to make it."

"I like it," Orane said, chewing on the corn casserole. "You're right. It's not too sweet. I don't like a lot of sweet stuff."

"Me either, give me fruits all day," I said, sipping my cup of green tea.

"I love fruits too. This food is delicious." He eyed me. "As I suspected, you are a great cook."

"Thanks. Just one of my, ah let's say, many skills." I snickered at my own melodrama.

Orane laughed. "Annalisa Jones, you are something."

"Yes, I am!" I smiled mischievously. "Ah pictures. How could I forget?"

I had recently purchased a digital camera and simply loved being a photographer. I retrieved my camera from the end table nearby.

Orane grimaced. "I don't like taking pictures. I always look like I'm from the wilds."

"It's not your fault. It's the photographer," I teased as I clicked away.

"I'm going to hold you to that," he winced.

"Don't look self-conscious; relax, just be yourself."

"That might not be a good idea."

I giggled. "It's not a good idea, it's a great idea."

"Right! Aren't you finished?" he begged after several shots.

"Just one more! I'll take more tomorrow," I said smiling. "Did you just roll your eyes?"

"No. I was just lifting my eyes to the sky."

I shook my head. "Naughty man!"

He chuckled. "Would you like me to take pictures of you?"

"No. Thanks," I said, taking my seat at the table. "You can do so tomorrow."

"Okay! You are...what are you staring at?"

I blushed. "Nothing!" I did not realize I was staring.

Orane looked cross-eyed. "Thanks! You are really helping my self-esteem."

I grinned and touch his shoulder playfully. "You know what I mean."

"You are not eating."

"I am not hungry, late lunch. Plus, there are other interesting things to look at."

"Go right ahead. Don't let me stop you. There is nothing much to see."

Are you kidding me? I smiled and gently looked at him. "There is a lot to see." His photos did not do justice to his classic good looks. His strong, well-kept body and winning smile made him look as if he ought to be on the cover of a magazine. He was wearing navy jeans, white shirt and black shoes. His navy vest rested on the bar stool.

Twenty minutes later, Orane wiped his mouth with the napkin then asked, "Should I pour the wine?"

"Yes, please."

The phone rang as Orane headed towards the refrigerator and he reached for it on the counter and handed it to me.

"Thank you." I smiled at him before answering. "Hello my sister." It was Harriett and I knew Maydine was nearby.

"Hi dear, just checking if you're okay. Did Orane arrive?"

Ann Marie Bryan

"I'm great. Yes, he arrived."

Immediately, Harriett went into hushed tones. "Just say yes or no to these questions—Are you comfortable? Is he what you expected? Is he nearby?"

I clenched my teeth to stop myself from laughing out. "Yes, yes and yes to all of the above. I will definitely talk with you tomorrow. Please let Sister Maydine know that all is well."

"Okay dear! Talk with you soon!"

"Bye." I just knew my circle of love would not be falling asleep any time soon.

"That was Sister Harri, aka Dr. Selby, calling to find out if you arrived safely."

"That's very thoughtful of her. Is she doing alright?"

"Yes!"

"Great!" Orane said, opening the refrigerator. "Which wine is it?"

"It's the Diviera."

"Found it!"

"I hope we'll like it. Two friends recommended it."

Orane peered at the label. "I thought you didn't drink alcohol."

"I prefer non-alcoholic wines. Alcoholic beverages taste so bitter, not to mention bad for my body."

He chuckled softly. "Babes, this wine has more alcohol than beer."

"Really?" I moved closer to inspect the wine bottle.

"Yes. I will let your sisters know that you gave me alcohol so you can take advantage of me. Unbelievable."

"Right, to all of that." I smiled at him as I accepted my glass of wine.

"I have very high expectations of you," he cautioned playfully as we moved back to the table.

"In that case, I am going to restrain myself."

"Please don't!" Orane chuckled. "Let's toast—to long life, great health, Godly wisdom to make decisions and an even closer walk with God."

"Amen to all of the above!"

"Annalisa, this has a lot of alcohol."

"Eeeeh yes! It's fruity though."

"Babes, I don't think we should drink this."

"I agree," I said, putting my wine glass on the table.

Orane placed the wine in the refrigerator. "Let's move to the living room, if you don't mind."

"Not at all," I replied, leading the way.

Orane exhaled, reclining in the center of the largest sofa and I curled up at one end. We observed each other perceptively then burst into laughter. We both knew what was going on.

"Look at you! I thought you were a little short lady."

"Uh-huh!" I poked him. "Who is talking about the physical now?"

He smiled lazily at me. "Birds of a feather flock together."

I wagged my head. "Right. Poor excuse!"

"You planted that seed in my head," he teased, poking my side.

I giggled and moved out of his reach. "I can be a little short lady, if that tickles your fancy."

He chuckled, totally amused. "You know, I'm no fun when I am hungry. Now that I am full, I..."

I eyeballed him grinning. "You will be fasting from now on."

He gasped playfully. "You are a mean lady; a beautiful mean lady."

"Beautiful is good." I smiled at him. "I may give you a little food."

"Thank you. You are gorgeous."

I shrunk back, my voice teasing. "Flattery will get you no-where."

"Seriously," he said quietly, "you are beautiful. When I decided to visit you, I wondered..."

Here began our story time. There was much laugher as we openly shared our thoughts about meeting face to face.

A few hours later...

I woke up feeling slightly disoriented. I lifted my head from Orane's shoulder. He was still asleep.

"Orane wake up!" I shook his shoulder gently.

"Huh?" He rubbed his eyes and groaned. "Tired."

"It's late."

He stretched murmuring, "Yes, it's late."

"Let me show you to your room."

As we passed the kitchen, the microwave clock indicated after midnight. Orane grabbed his vest from the bar stool then picked up his carry-on and climbed the stairs behind me.

"Make yourself at home," I said, entering the guest room. I pointed to the blanket on the bed. "You will need the blanket, nights and mornings tend to be a little cool. The bathroom is on your right. You can use the stack of towels on the shelf."

Orane's eyes pierced mine. "Thanks Babes."

"Anytime. Have a wonderful night."

"Good night," he whispered as we hugged. "I will see you in the morning."

I could feel his breath on the side of my face, breaking my body out in chills so I quickly disengaged from our embrace and headed for the door. "Yes, tomorrow," I murmured.

"What about my chains? I don't know if I can stay here by myself. I may have nightmares."

"No chains or nightmares." I chuckled softly. "Sleep tight."

"Have a wonderful night too. Thanks again for everything."

"You are welcome." I beat a hasty retreat.

Downstairs, I quickly stacked the dishwasher and turned off the lights. I could hardly wait to get to my bedroom. Once there, I jumped on my bed and buried my head in my pillows to stifle my screams of joy. *Thank you Lord.* I finally met the man behind the voice. I have always wondered what it would be like to set eyes on him. Now that I have, I was not disappointed. His personality was even more attractive than I had imagined.

Surprisingly, I felt a little off in the beginning. My mental adjustment to the new parameters of our friendship did not go according to plan. The visual cues were overwhelming. I found it slightly difficult to communicate with him in the flesh. Nevertheless, we had successfully passed the first hurdle. Going forward, my plan was to read his non-verbal cues and discover his true personality. I prayed that I was not harboring any unrealistic perceptions of him.

I communed with the Lord in hushed tones, praying for wisdom. Sleep came much later as the evening's events replayed over and over again in my head.

CHAPTER 8: RAGING HORMONES

I jumped, startled out of my slumber by the buzzing of my cell phone on the nightstand. I rolled over in my bed, reached for my cell phone, and squinted at it before turning off the alarm. It was 7:00 AM. Without warning, a swell of excitement swept through me and my heart skipped. I bolted upright with a wide grin across my face. I could hardly wait to lay eyes on Orane again. There was no denying it.

I showered and slipped into a pair of gray cropped pants piped with pink and the matching sleeveless blouse. There was no sign of him when I entered the living room. I tiptoed up the stairs and pressed my ears against the guest room door. He was steadily breathing.

I sighed happily. *Sleeper! I have a sleeper on my hands.*

I ate breakfast—egg omelet with cheese, tea, toast and orange juice. Half an hour later, I propped myself up on two pillows on my bed, communed with the Lord then began to read one of the many books that I had started.

I must have dozed off, because the next thing I heard was Orane calling my name. I awoke with a start then struggled to full consciousness and saw him standing outside my bedroom door.

"I fell asleep," I murmured self-consciously.

"That's okay," he said, averting his eyes and moving from the door. "I'll be in the living room."

"Okay," I responded, rolling out of bed. I checked myself in the bathroom mirror then entered the living room. Orane was seated on the sofa. "Happy Friday!" I greeted him. "Did you sleep well?"

His dimples deepened as he smiled at me. "Happy Friday to you too! I slept well. Did you?" His athletic frame was dressed in forest green cargo shorts, white t-shirt and black Nike sandals.

"Yes, I did," I replied pleasantly, trying not to look self-conscious as I joined him on the sofa.

Smiling, he held my hand lightly, his thumb stroking the back of my hand. "It did get a little cold last night," he said. "Thanks for the blanket."

Having him touch me that way, made me feel just a little too excited for my own comfort. "You're welcome!" I said coyly as he released my hand. "How about breakfast? I can do egg omelet with cheese, tea, toast and orange juice."

"That sounds great but no orange juice please."

"Got ya."

"This is for you." He handed me a pink and green gift bag that was sitting on the end table.

"Thank you. Should I look now?"

"Please do."

I pulled out an emerald green and yellow cotton and spandex workout t-shirt with cap sleeves and matching knee length pants.

"Thank you. I like it." I smiled and hugged him.

"You are welcome."

I eyed him playfully. "How did you know my size?"

"I have skills and connections," he said mysteriously.

"Good job!" I was very impressed with his gift because during a prior conversation, I told him that I had purchased a set of DVDs for a 6-week home-based aerobic and resistance exercise program. I placed the items back into the gift bag and rested it on the barstool. Orane took up position on the next bar stool. I flipped on the kitchen pipe, squirted a little of the dishwashing liquid and washed my hands. "I know that you like eggs," I remarked as I dried my hands.

"I love eggs. Can I have two egg omelets please, with franks?"

"You sure can."

"I'll make my cocoa."

"I'll reheat the water. Check the cupboard to my left for a packet of cocoa. The cups are one cupboard down."

"Did you eat? he asked, reaching for a cup.

"Yes. As you know, I am an early riser. I tried to wait on you though."

"Is that right? he teased, tickling my side.

"Oh stop!" I giggled, escaping his hands. "I did."

"Jet lag. I will be down early tomorrow," he said, stirring his hot cocoa.

"No problem! Any time you rise is good."

"Thank you kind lady." He hugged my shoulder.

Ohhh! He smelled so good! "Anytime," I replied coyly, mesmerized by his closeness.

A few minutes later while eating, Orane asked, "What would you like to do today?"

My hand flew to my chest and I eyed him. "Don't you have that backwards?"

He did not hesitate. "I can find my way around."

A soft giggle escaped me. "I know what that is, you got too much sleep!"

He poked me in my side. "You've got jokes!"

"Yes, I do! Let's hang out here for a short while then I will give you a tour of the city."

"Sounds great!"

I turned on the camera that was resting on the table. "Time for your photo shoot."

"Not again," he said, avoiding the camera.

"Just relax; it will be over in a moment!" I took several shots. "Very good! More animal, bring out the animal in you! You're a dangerous beast."

Orane laughed softly. "I don't know what I'm going to do with you."

I smiled at him. "You are enjoying this. I know you are." I had stopped taking pictures to adjust the zoom setting when I glanced at

Orane. For a moment, I saw something in his expression. He was uncomfortable with my picture taking frenzy. "Okay, let me stop harassing you."

"Let me take some of you," he said smiling.

"Sure!"

He took several shots. "You are enjoying this."

"Very much so!" I giggled.

He shook his head then handed me the camera. "You are something!"

"The camera loves me."

"Will I see these pictures before I leave?"

"If you are nice all weekend."

He smiled at me. "You know I'll be!"

The midday sun was slowly waning and the temperature was falling when we left home for our city tour. Ever the consummate guide, I narrated the tour of some of Tallahassee's landmarks and attractions such as the New Capitol Building, Florida Agricultural and Mechanical University, Florida State University and Mary Brogan Museum of Art and Science, recounting historical details which were committed to memory.

Orane was quite the gentleman, opening the car door and holding my hand as we toured. We ended up window shopping at the Tallahassee Mall. Soon, we rested our aching feet at the food court in the Mall and ate Chinese food. Our heartfelt laughter rang out as we ate and shared about funny occurrences during our school days.

Orane held my hand as we exited the mall. "Look at you!" He smiled at me with raised eyebrows. "You are having a great time."

"Absolutely," I responded happily. His prolonged eye contacts did not go unnoticed during our meal at the food court.

It was early evening when we returned home.

Orane peered at me after he closed the door leading to the garage. "You look beat."

"I'm a bit tired."

Reaching out, he pushed a strand of hair behind my ear. "Let's rest and pick up later."

I sighed. "Yes. I hear my bed calling me."

"Are you going to need a wakeup call?" he asked.

"Maybe," I teased.

"You know you love to sleep. No shame in that."

I eyeballed him. "Didn't you wake up at 10 o'clock this morning?"

He winced. "Hey, jet lag remember."

"Jet lag it is." I grinned at him. "I will set my alarm."

"Come here," he drawled with a slight smile playing on his lips.

I just stood there, shifting my feet and toying with my hair. He closed the gap between us and kissed my cheek. "Thanks for everything," he whispered as his grip tightened on my waist

I froze. My stomach did a small flip and chill bumps raced down my spine. *My word! Help! Raging hormones! Absolutely, must gain the upper hand!* "You're welcome," I said, bashfully disengaging from our embrace.

"See you in a bit," he said softly.

"Okay," I murmured, hoping that my wobbly knees would take me to my bedroom. *Phew!* I closed the door behind me and leaned on it. I inhaled then exhaled slowly before bursting into soft giggles. *Raging hormones!*

Within minutes, I showered, put on a robe and slipped under the comforter. This was just what the doctor ordered.

Later, I awoke to soft knocking on my bedroom door. "Annalisa!" Orane called out.

"I'll...I'll be out in a minute Orane." I was still half asleep when I checked the time on my cell phone. *Mercy!* It was after eight. I checked the alarm button and a soft chuckle escaped me.

Within minutes, I entered the living room. "You look beautiful," Orane said smiling. I was decked out in a red full-length fitted bodice dress with flowing skirt and halter neckline.

"Thank you," I said, joining him on the sofa. His muscular legs were on display. "You're looking great too." I admired his navy cotton twill shorts with cargo pockets and matching navy and white Polo shirt.

"Thanks, even though you are a sleeper." He harassed me gently.

"Sleeper!" I grinned at him. "My alarm button was set at the off position."

"I see that's how it going to be."

"Oh stop," I said, punching him lightly on the shoulder.

He laughed. "I have to take you with the good and the bad, right?"

"Whatever!" I threw my hands in the air in mock disbelief.

"Come on over here woman and let's get the show on the road." I grinned at him. "Before we get too settled, are you hungry?"

"Not very, I could eat something though, nothing too heavy."

"Ham sandwich?"

"No, remember I don't digest pork well."

"Ah, I forgot."

"Let's order pizza."

"I am not much of a pizza fan but I'll eat a slice."

"Let's eat something else," he suggested.

"We can order pizza. The truth is I don't usually eat this late."

"I can tell." He chuckled, using his hands to outline my slender figure in the air. "Please order. I will pay for the pizza and all the good treatment you're giving me."

I gleefully clapped my hands. "It's about time I get paid for all I do around here."

He smiled at my antics. "You will be paid and amply too."

"I like the sound of that!"

"How far is the pizza place?" he inquired.

"Very near, less than ten minutes."

"Let's pick up. What toppings do you like?"

"Pineapple and pepperoni," I responded.

"I don't like pineapple."

"No problem, we can have another topping."

"No go with pineapple and thin crust."

"Thin crust it is."

I sat on the barstool and located the phone number for Zixla Pizza Place in the telephone directory that was sitting on the counter.

"What size?" I asked.

"12-inch please."

I placed the order for the pizza.

"Ready to roll!" Orane said, turning off the TV.

"Let me get my purse and jacket. You should put on pants. It's a bit chilly."

"Okay. Give me a moment."

A few minutes later, I parked and we held hands and walked towards Zixla Pizza Place. The cool evening breeze whipped around us and I smelled his cologne as it floated in the air. *Um! Very nice.* He smelled as inviting as he looked.

"Let's sit while we wait on the pizza," Orane said, pulling me towards two empty chairs. "I have a joke to tell you."

I perked up. "A joke?"

"Yes. Pastor John Hagee recounted it in one of his sermons. It goes something like this—A man called 911 to report that his wife was in labor. Of course, he was frantic, very frantic because he did not know what to do. The 911 operator asked him—Is this her first child? The man bellowed—No, no, this is her husband."

I exploded with laughter. "That's funny," I told him breathlessly, tears streamed down my face at the absurdity of it all.

Later at home, we cleared the coffee table for the pizza and drinks.

"Politics!" Orane exhaled as we listened to history in the making on CNN. "What a phenomenon? President-Elect Barack Obama."

"Change has come to America," I said dramatically, drawn in by the tide of history.

"He has energized the whole country," Orane remarked, biting into his pizza.

"Yes. I am energized. He is a world changer, shattering more than 200 years of history."

"Are you going to the inauguration?"

I swallowed a bite of the pizza. "I would love to. I might jump on the bandwagon with those at work."

"Washington D.C. will be very cold at that time."

I grinned, watching as President-Elect Barack Obama's voice rang out on CNN. "Hey, I would take frost bites to be a part of history."

Orane chuckled. "I know you will be taking lots of pictures."

"Oh yes." I smiled at him. "I remember your political aspirations."

"Yes. I believe that I have something to offer."

"You should do it. It's on your heart." I took another bite of my pizza. *With his charisma and heart for humanity, he would go far.*

His eyes seared into mine. "I will. My father was involved in politics in Jamaica."

"I'll put that on my prayer list," I encouraged.

He gazed at me tenderly. "A praying woman. I love it."

I smiled in acknowledgement as his dark brown eyes penetrated my being. *Help! Diversion Needed! Raging hormones!*

"Let's watch a movie," I grinned coyly.

We channel surfed and found an action packed movie. Orane reclined in the center of the sofa and I nestled comfortably in his arms as we watched.

Well, that was the plan.

A few hours later, I woke up. I was curled up at his side and he was snoring softly. *Oh Lord, this feels good.* I relished the steady beating of his heart and the warmth of his flesh. A heavy sigh escaped my lips and his arms automatically tightened around me. Involuntarily, I leaned closer. *Oh no, not good! I cautioned myself.*

"Orane, Orane." I shook his shoulders gently.

He groaned instantly and pulled me closer, burying his head in my neck.

"Orane, Orane," I called out desperately.

Abruptly, he moved out of our embrace and stared at me. "I fell asleep," he murmured, stretching then pulling himself to full height.

"It's bed time!" I said gently.

He opened his arms and I fell in them. "I'll see you tomorrow," he whispered, squeezing me tightly.

"Have a good night," I murmured, hoping that someone would yank me out of our warm embrace.

Orane gently released me from his arms. "Have a wonderful night."

"Thank you!" I choked out before we parted from each other.

Holding it together was difficult after he left. My natural instinct was to chase upstairs, two steps at a time and sleep in his arms.

Thankfully, sanity prevailed! Great thought but wrong season!

CHAPTER 9: STAYING STRONG

"Stop taking my picture," Orane begged, looking like a caged animal. We had just finished breakfast at home.

"I'm the paparazzi." I giggled at him as I packed up my camera. *A very small price to pay for love, I thought.*

He gazed at me as I sat at the dining table. "You were quiet at breakfast."

"Really, I didn't realize."

"I understand."

"Okay." I knitted my brows.

"I live alone too," he said chuckling.

"What am I missing?"

"You are not accustomed to seeing anyone in the morning."

"Is that so?" I laughed coyly. "What say you, no morning faces?"

"No morning faces, please," he said, tickling my side.

"Oh stop that," I giggled. "I'm afraid of my side."

"Let me help you get rid of it then." He reached for me and I pushed my chair away from the table.

"You know what I mean." I grinned at him.

Shortly thereafter, we headed to Governor's Square Mall nearby and shopped at Macy's and JCPenny. We discovered Zinne's Pretzels, a pastry shop and indulged ourselves with cinnamon sugar pretzels. Zinne's Pretzels was a sweet little spot, for what I hoped was a temporary sweet tooth.

Later at home after dinner, we relaxed on the sofa, very aware that our time together was getting shorter.

"Any regrets that you came?" I asked nonchalantly.

"None! All good! I love you more, now that I have met you."

I smiled and gently punched his shoulder. "Look at you. I like you too."

Orane gave hollow laugh. "You are so good for my ego."

"It will get better. I promise!" I looked at him coyly, then looked away. I looked back and he was gazing at me. "Stop it!" I playfully nudged him.

He closed his eyes then opened them. "I forgive you," he drawled. "How's your mother?"

"Mama is doing great. I spoke with her this morning."

Mama was an exceptional woman and the heartbeat of our family. God had blessed her bountifully. Eleven children later, she was in great shape. Mama was also an amazing prayer warrior. From childhood days, she would rise early to seek God. She prayed for each member of the family, lifting us up before the Lord.

"I admire the closeness in your family," Orane remarked. "Your sisters are great."

"Thanks. We have always been a close bunch, a band of brothers and sisters."

"Your father would be proud of you all."

"Yes. I believe he would be."

The death of my beloved father over twenty years ago brought much grief and sadness to the family but we trusted God. "It's going to be alright," Mama told us. "God is good." Mama, along with my three eldest sisters, worked hard to raise the younger members of the family. We received great support, encouragement and comfort from relatives, friends, acquaintances and those who sorrowed with us.

"It will take me a while to remember the names of your family members," Orane remarked.

"Don't worry, it took me a while too!"

He eyed me with undisguised amusement. "Right!"

Laughing softly, I nudged him. "It sure did! Anyway... did I tell you about my little tirade with Natasha during my childhood days?" I giggled just thinking about it.

"Natasha?"

"Natasha, my sister, the fifth born in my family. Come on now, you must keep up!" I teased him.

He grimaced and poked my side.

"I was about five years old or so at the time. Natasha taught me how to spell my name, Annalisa Jones and that was fine. Then, she insisted on teaching me how to spell my middle name, Abigail. I got so upset, ranting and raving. I told her in no uncertain terms that I did not wish to spell Abigail because they gave me too many names. Oh, you should have seen me; I put on quite a show."

Orane laughed out, doubling over.

"Okay, carry on. Have fun at my expense."

"That is funny."

I grinned. "That's a lot of work for a five-year old. How are your mom and dad doing?"

"Very well. God has been good to them. Their later days are definitely greater than their former." Orane shared deeply about his childhood, his past and vision for the future. I listened keenly, weeping at times and asking appropriate questions at the right moments. He concluded with Philippians 3:13-14, *"Brethren, I do not count myself to have apprehended; but one thing I do, forgetting those things which are behind and reaching forward to those things which are ahead, I press toward the goal for the prize of the upward call of God in Christ Jesus."*

"Indeed! Amen!" I responded quietly.

"God is good," he said enthusiastically. "He continues to do great things in my life."

"Yes. God is awesome."

Orane touched my shoulder and his warm eyes seared into mine. "Do you realize that we have not spent any time in the word since I have been here?"

You could hear a pin drop as I flipped a strand of hair from my eye and regarded him shrewdly. "You mean together. I have devotion early morning and most times before I go to bed."

"I know." He leaned back on the sofa with his hands clasped at the base of his neck. "I just want us to be careful."

Suddenly, I felt so annoyed.

I took a deep breath, centering myself as I prepared to be honest with him. "So, why didn't you ask me about devotion or prayer before this?"

Orane looked puzzled. "Are you upset?"

I got up from the sofa then squatted down again. "A little... peeved."

He reached over and touched my hand. "Don't be."

I pursed my lips before responding. "I just sensed that you are laying it all on me."

"No. I am not Babes."

"I don't know!"

"Babes, I'm in no way blaming you. Never."

I thrust out my chin. "You know that I love spending time in the word and prayer."

"Of course, I know that. I just miss us spending time in the word as we usually do in the nights. I don't want us to lose that."

I inhaled then exhaled and my annoyance slowly evaporated.

Orane held my hand. "Babes, there is no reason to be annoyed."

"Okay. Let me not take on that wrong spirit," I said quietly.

He gave me a quick smile and squeezed my hand. "Where is your bible?"

I took my bible from my bedroom and gave it to him. He read Genesis Chapters 1 and 2 and zeroed in on Genesis 2:2, *"And on the seventh day God ended His work which He had done, and He rested on the seventh day from all His work which He had done."*

"Does God need rest?" Orane questioned.

"I know for sure that God was not tired," I replied grinning. "Our God was not tired from creating. It simply means, He ceased to perform all His creative work."

Suddenly, the room grew quiet as we considered our all-powerful, all knowing God.

"God sent you in my life at the right time," Orane revealed quietly.

"That's a nice thing to say," I said softly.

He looked thoughtful. "I asked the Lord for a relationship that would lead to marriage."

"Me too. You're in my life at the right time too."

He chuckled. "Babes, you need to get your own lyrics. You cannot just borrow my lines."

"Why reinvent the wheel?" I poked him in his side, grinning as his eyebrows rose.

"Tell me what qualities you desire in a husband."

"Again?" I rolled my eyes dramatically.

He chuckled. "Do I need to put you in the naughty corner?"

"Noooo!" I flashed him a smile. "I need a prayer partner, a God lover, a friend and someone who will give me emotional support. The way I see it, if my husband truly loves the Lord there will be evidence of the fruit of the Spirit in his life."

In a deep drawl, he asked, "What about physical love?"

I swallowed then laughed nervously. "Oh, that's a given. Physical love is a definite must have."

"We have great chemistry," he stated, gazing into my eyes, deep into my soul with love and acceptance. .

My breathing became shallow and there was a shift in my body as my temperature climbed rapidly. "Yes, we do," I murmured looking away.

He chuckled softly. "Don't worry, I understand. Let me get some water. Would you like some?"

"Ah, no." I stared at my bible as Orane moved to the kitchen.
Lord, help us!
I could break my decision right now.
Ah! Perish the thought!

We had already made a firm decision to remain celibate until marriage.

"Penny for your thoughts!"

I did not realize that Orane had re-entered the living room so I made a valiant attempted to keep my voice nonchalant, unwilling to betray any emotion of sort. "Oh, it's nothing."

"Nothing! Sex is something," he said quietly, gazing at me. "Can we hold each other accountable for our sexual purity?"

At first, I nodded, fearing I might say no. Then, I said boldly, "Yes we can."

Never mind the struggle that I just had.

"Thank God for you. You are a wonderful person."

I fought the frog in my throat. "Thank you."

He touched my arm. "God has done a great job with you."

I smiled at him. "He's been working and I have been squealing. As soon as I overcome one hurdle, here comes another."

"Sounds like life! You said that you wanted your mate to be your prayer partner. I have always wanted that. I also desire someone to support me and help me make decisions."

"Thanks for saying that because some men have issues with women in that regard."

"I am not one of those men," he said confidently. "Let us commune with the Lord."

We sang *"I worship you almighty God"*, kneeled before the sofa and earnestly sought the face of the Lord. I prayed first, followed by Orane.

A few minutes later, we hugged and said goodnight, still relishing the absolutely divine effects from a beautiful, spirit-filled time spent in the presence of God.

CHAPTER 10: OVERWHELMED

How can it be?

Orane and I burst out laughing when we spotted each other in the living room. We were in matching colors for church. I was dressed in a purple skirt suit, stockings, black shoes and gold accessories. He sported a black suit, purple shirt, purple and black striped tie and black dress shoes.

"Great minds think alike," Orane concluded, still chuckling.

A tingle of excitement hit me as I pulled into the parking lot of the church, some fifteen minutes later. *What will it be like to worship with Orane?* I tried to maintain my usual confident demeanor as Orane held the door for me to enter the sanctuary. He looked at ease as we greeted several members of the congregation before taking our seats in the center pews.

I attended a vibrant church that focused on quality worship, prayer, studying the word of God, fellowship and community outreach. Bishop Jonathan Barker, a remarkable man of God, held the office of Lead Pastor. After the opening prayers, we experienced an awesome time of praise and worship to kick off the service. The tambourines, guitars and drums were in one accord and everyone clapped and sang wholeheartedly. Our hearts were prepared and ready for the unadulterated word of God and we listened attentively as Bishop Barker explained God's love for humanity. As anticipated, Orane was cheerfully acknowledged during the welcome segment. We left church feeling uplifted and thankful.

Later that day, my joy was even more evident.

I giggled foolishly as Orane attempted to feed me with lobster pizza at A & O Seafood Restaurant. We were absolutely stuffed by the end of our main course—grilled lobster tail, steamed snow crab legs, garlic shrimp scampi, baked potatoes and steamed broccoli.

Orane persuaded me to have dessert, strawberry sorbet and I was so glad he did.

I moaned as I savored the delightful taste of the fruity sorbet. It had just the right amount of tartness. "Gym here I...Orane are you okay?" He was deep in thought and his countenance had completely changed.

"Yes, I'm..." His voice trailed off.

"What is it?" I asked, reaching across the table to touch his hand.

He looked off in the distance. "I'm good."

I eyed him with great concern. "What's going on?"

"I know that we are good together but..." His voice trailed off again as he tried to find the right words. "I don't think a relationship between us is going to work."

My eyes widened and my heart quivered. Thankfully, I was sitting down for this mind-numbing bit of news. "You think so?" I offered a weak, shaky smile.

He did not respond.

I played with my sorbet, trying to hide how seriously traumatized I was. My mind began to swirl and I glanced at him, desperately trying to read his expression.

I could not!

What is this?

Did I open my heart too quickly?

Could he have hidden his emotions that well?

"We'll be alright," he said calmly. "Let's give it more time."

A number of comebacks came to my mind but I chose silence. My stomach felt sick. *Was I blinded by my desire, hoping for something that apparently never existed in the first place?*

I gazed blindly at the salt and pepper shakers as Orane started another conversation. I did not respond. I continue to pick at my sorbet hoping not to fall to the floor. For a moment, he assumed that something was caught in my eyes. I was blinking back tears. *He doesn't believe in 'us' and probably never did.*

70

"Annalisa…" he said, reaching for my hand.

To avoid his hand, I reached for my water glass. "It's okay," I managed to squeeze out without choking.

Get it together, I cautioned myself.

"We'll talk when we get home," he said comfortingly as he paid the bill.

We'll talk when we get home. I knitted my eyebrows and had to restrain myself. I wanted to glare at him. *Talk about what?* "Back in a moment," I mumbled, escaping to the restroom.

Tears welled up in my eyes as our many conversations ran around in my head. I locked myself in one of the bathroom cubicles and spoke encouraging words to my spirit. Within minutes, I emerged from the restroom hoping that I would have a game plan by the time we made it home.

The ride home passed in a blur. Conversation between us was difficult for me. I was busy ordering my heart to change course. The car hit a few rough patches in the road, which consistently forced me back to the present. I attempted to push away unwelcome thoughts but reality kept intruding.

Later at home, while Orane packed, I entered the study and downloaded the pictures from the camera then burned them to a CD for him. I tried to think about what had occurred in a positive light but all kinds of negative emotions ran through my mind. My head was spinning and my confidence started to ebb.

Someone had just pulled the rug from under my feet.

How could I have I convinced myself that a relationship between us would work?

Months of fooling myself!

The realization was excruciating and a strangled sob escaped my lips as I knelt before the Lord in my bedroom. No words could express how I felt and I groaned under the weight of my burden. As I travailed before the Lord, I felt the comfort of the Holy Spirit. I knew that my inarticulate groans did not escape my omniscient God. I rose up and encouraged myself in the Lord.

Ann Marie Bryan

Breathe! I told myself. I pressed my hands against the sides of my head, willing the ache in my heart to go away. I needed to talk with someone about the situation.

But who?

Which one of my cheerleaders could handle this...not so good news? Perhaps all!

I was sitting on the sofa in the living room, listening to Maydine's words of wisdom, when Orane came downstairs and sat beside me. "Sister Maydine, I will talk with you later...Bye."

I felt extremely self-conscious as I briefly gazed at him. *How do I move away from him?* I wanted to say something but my nerves were too raw.

"Annalisa." His choked voice caused me to pause from my mental deliberations.

Not trusting myself to speak, I nodded without meeting his eyes.

"Please forgive me," he said softly.

I laughed nervously. "There, there is..."

"I can't believe you gave up on our relationship so easily."

"I, I..." I was hit again.

"I, I nothing. You tried to save yourself instead of our relationship. All your walls went up and you locked yourself in."

"You shocked me." I made a valiant attempt to regain my composure. "I did not see it coming."

"You could have said...of course a relationship between us would work. In fact, it would be downright wonderful!"

'I..."

"Babes having a successful relationship takes guts and marriage takes laying down your life."

"You took me off guard. You came out of left field."

"Oh yeah? I bet you never saw this coming either." He held my hands in his for a few moments. "I am deeply in love with you— body, mind, soul and spirit." It came from deep within him; everything fell away.

72

He gathered me close and I gasped softly as his right hand caressed my cheeks. "You are beautiful. Even before I laid eyes on you, I knew that I wanted you in my life forever. Now, I cannot imagine having to spend my life without you. I love you. Babes, will you consider marrying me?"

Marry you!

My heart pounded and my mind screamed unintelligibly. I wrapped my arms around his waist and buried my face in his neck. "I love, I love you too. I will definitely consider marrying you."

He cupped my face with his hands and looked at me tenderly. My heart fluttered as he leaned in and gently kissed my lips. "You are my baby," he murmured, wrapping me in his arms again.

"Yes, I am," I murmured softly, purring with delight at the sheer pleasure of it all.

"I would like you to meet my family when you are in Jamaica," he said as we disengaged from our embrace.

I smiled at him. "I look forward to that!"

"I would also like you to see me in my environment before you make your decision."

"That would be great."

I hugged his shoulder with one hand and he rested his head on my shoulder. We had disarmed each other and now enjoyed the bliss of emotional intimacy.

Within minutes, I was brought back to reality by the overwhelming thought of Orane leaving. A quiet battle ensued within me. Tears welled up in my eyes and before long they rolled down my cheeks and I began to sob uncontrollably.

"Babes, why are you crying? Orane pulled me in his arms, comforting me with easy stokes over my back. "Stop, you're breaking my heart."

I wept even more.

"Babes..."

"I'm going to miss you." I lifted teary eyes to his.

"I knew this would be hard. I love you," he said, kissing my forehead.

"I love you too," I said softly as our eyes met. His eyes were like hot liquid chocolate and they smothered with blazing desire as his lips moved towards mine. My body felt weightless as our lips found each other naturally. His fingers moved affectionately to the nape of my neck, and my arms wrapped comfortably around his shoulders. I wanted to stay enveloped in his arms forever.

Forever!

Protest! Tell him to stop. I am going to...any moment now.

Without warning, Orane pulled away, mumbling apologetically. "Sorry, I...I didn't mean to do that but you looked so, so beautiful."

"Don't apologize," I whispered, resting my head on his shoulder.

He wrapped his arms around me. "I had to call on the Lord for help." He spoke softly above my head. "I wanted to forget my commitment."

"Yes, yes," I agreed quietly.

It was a difficult moment as we struggled to bring our desires under the subjection of the word of God.

Good sense prevailed and we honored the Lord.

I curled up in Orane's arms until way after midnight. No words were necessary. We just held each other. Now, we were exposed and vulnerable, completely open with each other. It was one of those moments that I imagined; only, it was even more wonderful.

❋ ❋ ❋

Early the next day, Orane and I experienced the agony of parting as we journeyed to the airport. We kept our conversation light and frivolous, hoping to soften the difficult situation. I had tried to mentally prepare for our parting but I knew that it would be hard.

I dropped Orane at the departure area and left to find parking. When I rejoined him, he was checking in. I waited patiently, hoping not to mentally freak out. As Orane watched my expression, he smiled knowingly.

A few minutes later, we sat on a dark brown leatherette sofa in the waiting area near the security checkpoint.

"Will you be on time for work?" Orane asked.

"Yes. I'm only fifteen minutes away."

"I will call you as soon as I hit land," he said reassuringly.

"Yes, that would be nice. It was really good having you here."

Emotions welled up in his throat. "It was great to be here. Thanks for everything."

I managed a smile. "You are more than welcome."

"It's that time. Will you walk with me to the checkpoint?"

"Yes and I'll wait until you go through."

"Let's go," he said, holding my hand.

Near the security checkpoint, Orane cupped my face in his hands and I swallowed and held my breath. His lips curved in a grin and he kissed my forehead after mentally deciding that a simple lip contact might not be enough.

"I love you!" he said, gazing into my eyes.

"I love you!" I whispered as we embraced.

He kissed my cheek. "I will call you soon."

"Okay!" I gave him a tiny smile.

With that, he grabbed his carry-on case and moved towards the checkpoint. It took everything in me to stay grounded. *Oh Lord, I cannot watch him leave.* I walked slowly towards the exit doors as he went through the scanning device. I glanced around and he was collecting his items. I had no desire to wave goodbye so I exited through the sliding doors, fearing I might start weeping.

Too late!

The dam broke and tears spilled to the floor. Dabbing my eyes, I rushed to my car. *Happy thoughts! Happy thoughts, I told myself.* No words could comfort me as I drove to work, tears just rolled down my cheeks.

CHAPTER 11: THE DECISION

"How is life without THE ONE today?" Melissa emailed me.

"Oh girl, I am still having withdrawal symptoms!" I responded.

Withdrawal symptoms!

That's exactly what I went through after Orane left. I went through all kinds of strange and unfamiliar emotions. Thoughts of him constantly invaded my mind, triggering subconscious meanderings about our future.

With a heavy sigh, I covered my eyes with my hands and flopped backward on my bed. Truth be told, I missed him terribly, yet I was still uncertain about our future together. I was grateful that he had proposed and did not expect an answer right away. This gave me time to think and continue seeking God for direction in this regard.

I had always felt that I would be married. As I waited, God pruned me so that I would know what mattered most. Over the years, the qualities that I desired in a husband changed from a long list to two must haves—a praying man and a friend. I desired a husband who would live a God centered life and seek God first in all situations.

While I felt strongly that I wanted to share my life with Orane, I did not want to be *"caught up in love"* but face the reality of my situation. We lived "worlds" apart. If we decided to get married, immigration proceedings would take some time. Aside from all of that, the thought of being married was rather unnerving.

Was it time to give up my single life?

Was I ready to give 100% of me, my most prized possession?

Was marriage something that I still desired?

Was I prepared to love God's way?

Was I ready to say "we"?

I had more questions than answers so I continued to pray for wisdom to make the right decision.

A week after Orane left, I had lunch at TCD Golf Club with Marisa, a co-worker and friend. With her vivacious personality, Marisa was the life of every party. Married for over ten years, she had always encouraged me to follow in her footsteps.

"You're dating," Marisa said perceptively as we ate.

"Ah, yes!" I grinned at her. "Shocking! I know."

"I knew it," she beamed. "There is something different about you." Her expression begged for more.

"I am still trying to figure it out. He lives in Jamaica."

"Do you love him?" she asked excitedly.

"I really do."

"Oooh nice! High five!" She laughed enthusiastically as our hands met.

"He's wonderful. His name is Orane."

"Oooorane," Marisa squealed with delight.

"Oh stop," I grinned foolishly.

"So, what's the hold up? You have issues with him."

"No, not really, just wrestling with a few matters that he mentioned." *Matters that I felt were not appropriate for me to share.*

"Annalisa, you know persons beyond age thirty have a lot of clutter."

I nodded vigorously.

Marisa's eyes stretched to their limit as she concluded. "Or have situations! You know—people drama, not to mention bad credit score, unfiled tax returns, financial troubles, set behavior patterns and the list goes on."

I chuckled at her melodrama. "I do realize that people go through all kinds of stuff that leave marks on their lives."

"Yes, all kinds of stuffs," Marisa said knowingly. "Pray and fast about the matters. Allow the Lord guide you."

"Yes. I'm doing that."

Marisa looked pensive. "If he has learned from these situations and moving forward, that is great."

"I believe he has."

"I like his honesty," she said, gently nodding her head.

"I do too. He did that right out of the starting blocks. I'm very glad he did."

"Well, learn all…," Marisa paused as the waiter placed our bills on the table and left. "Learn all you can about his past but I say focus on the future."

"Yes. I will," I responded smilingly.

"Something tells me, he has proposed."

Marisa eagerly awaited my response as I slowly placed cash on the table to pay for my lunch. I grinned coyly. "Yes. I'm thinking about it."

"Yippee! Another high five please!" Marisa yelled, giggling as our hands met.

"I'm excited but I need to think about it," I warned her.

Marisa touched my hand and her eyes widened. "Do you know how difficult it is for a man to propose? The courage, not to mention the nerves he has to muster up. You better hurry up and decide your mind. Good men are hard to find."

"Yes," I agreed solemnly. "Soon. Very soon."

Ouch! I did not think about that!

I was so focused on myself that I had not fully realized that Orane had really placed his heart in my hands. While I had not taken his proposal lightly, I did not consider how much courage it took for him to propose.

"Is Orane pressuring you to make the decision?" Marisa asked as she paid her bill.

"No. Not at all!" I responded thoughtfully.

"Then, there is no excuse for your lackluster expression."

I grinned widely. "No excuse! I am good."

Marisa smiled. "You'll be alright. Let's get back to work."

I nodded in agreement and we collected our purses. "Thanks, for your words of wisdom."

"I have more," she teased.

"I bet you do!" I grinned as we exited the restaurant.

Later that day, I was sitting cross-legged on the floor in the study at home, selecting music for dance ministry rehearsal, when I became deeply aware of my own clutter. Life certainly brings baggage and the longer we live, the more baggage we tend to carry. But, I have learned to do what Jesus encouraged in St. Matthew 11:28-29, *"Come to Me, all you who labor and are heavy laden, and I will give you rest. Take My yoke upon you and learn from Me, for I am gentle and lowly in heart, and you will find rest for your souls."*

I knew that I could not change Orane's past situations so I placed them on the altar before God and focused on our present and future. I smiled softly as I thought of us as a couple, Orane and Annalisa. Orane was certainly not dragging his feet. He was in a marriage mind-set. I definitely needed to take decisive action. The last thing I wanted was a repeat of how I handled Nedrick's proposal some six years ago.

Ned and I dated for about six months. We were having a conversation on the phone when he proposed.

"Did...did you ask me to marry you?" I asked tentatively.

"Yes, I did," he replied in a dry voice.

I was speechless.

Lord help me! "Thanks Ned. But remember we have certain issues to resolve in our relationship before we go in that direction."

Ned exhaled. "Annalisa, I cannot believe that I proposed and you are saying we have issues."

"I'm sorry Ned. I am not discounting your proposal but before we consider marriage, we need to deal with our issues, especially our communication problem."

With all of his wonderfulness, the more I prayed about marrying Ned, the more restless I became. Thoughts of marrying him were not sitting well in my spirit. Moreover, in my "girlish thoughts", a marriage proposal should take place in a certain setting.

Ned politely ended our conversation.

A month later, Ned and I were seated on the sofa at my home, watching TV.

"Will you marry me?" He asked so quietly that I almost missed it.

Ugh, not again!

Help me Jesus; I want to answer him correctly! We still have unresolved issues.

"Why do you want to marry me?" I questioned calmly, stalling for time.

Ned's arched eyebrows and wounded eyes told me that he did not anticipate such a response. "What kind of question is that? What do you mean, why do I want to marry you?" He made a valiant effort to control his rising temperature. "Who gives an answer like that to a proposal?" Ned moved speedily towards the front door.

Scrambling to my feet, I chased after him. "Ned, I ..." I touched his back and he flinched then slowly turned to face me. His dark grey eyes were tinged with pain, his demeanor detached and distant. I gave him an encouraging smile. "I appreciate your proposal but I wanted to know your reasons for desiring to marry me so that we can be on the same page." I needed to hear something from him. I was not even sure what that something was.

Ned was livid. He would have none of it. "Do you know how many ladies would love to hear those words out of my mouth? If they could see me now, I would be a laughing stock."

"Ned, please sit down. Don't make it sound like that. You are upsetting yourself unnecessarily."

He glared at me. "I had to speak with a friend after I proposed to you the first time." My arched eyebrows did not impress him. "Yes. I felt that I needed help. My friend suggested that I do it face to face. Do you know how difficult it is for a man to propose?"

"Please sit down. I will think about it."

Ned paused. His internal struggle was obvious. "May I borrow your phone?"

"Sure!" I responded. "Who are you calling?"

"Melissa. She can probably explain why you are refusing to marry me."

So, Ned made the call, only Melissa was out, instead he spoke with Simon. He briefly explained the situation and after listening intently for a few minutes, he hastily concluded the conversation.

"What happened?" I asked curiously from the sofa.

"Simon said maybe you just don't feel the same way I do." Ned grabbed his car keys from the coffee table and again headed for the front door. "Bye!"

"Ned, please don't leave like this."

"I'm off."

Summoning the last ounce of strength left in him, Ned closed the door behind him. With screeching tires, he left the apartment complex.

Two weeks later, proposal number three marked the beginning of the end of our relationship. The ringing of my home phone woke me from a deep sleep. Semiconscious, my eyes fluttered from the faint light streaming through the curtains from the streetlights. I squinted and struggled to reach the phone in the darkness.

"Hello." I rolled on my side and flipped on the bedside lamp.

"Annalisa, are you asleep?"

I could hardly recognize his voice, "Ned?"

"Yes, sorry to call so early."

"It's okay. What time...it's after one," I said after glancing at my cell phone. "Are you okay?"

"Yes! Will you marry me?"

Suddenly, I was wide-awake.

Lord, please help me...no, help him.

Not down this road again. I do not wish to hurt this man.

"Ned, remember that we decided that we wouldn't. I appreciate your love but I don't think that we should get married."

Ned never proposed again and as expected our relationship eventually ended. We were on two different paths.

I concluded that I was not honest with myself or with Ned. I ignored early telltale signs that indicated trouble in our relationship. Excuses ruled—*No one is perfect! It will get better.* In retrospect, I could have saved us both from the unwelcomed heartaches that resulted from a relationship that was going nowhere.

Having learned several invaluable lessons from that relationship, I pressed on. In so doing, I asked the Lord to keep my heart and to teach me how to love.

When I was younger, I associated love with an adrenalin rush, butterflies in my stomach, a fluttering heart and senseless giggles. I may have even used the phrase *"fall in love"*. But as I grew older, I discovered a significant aspect of love - Love is a decision, a commitment to each other with an emotional component. It is my pledge to prefer or put someone ahead of me and to operate in the best interest of that person.

Marriage demands such a love and this is well-defined in 1 Corinthians 13:4-7,

> *"Love suffers long and is kind; love does not envy; love does not parade itself, is not puffed up; does not behave rudely, does not seek its own, is not provoked, thinks no evil; does not rejoice in iniquity, but rejoices in the truth; bears all things, believes all things, hopes all things, endures all things."*

Yet, considering a sacred lifetime institution as marriage was no easy task. In my mind, marriage and work seemed synonymous. It was clearly a labor of love and a unique commitment. I wondered if I would submit to my husband. Submit sounded so outdated. Yet, the Lord requires submission out of love in a marital relationship. I felt that my submission to the Lord would definitely help me to be a submissive wife. I was encouraged by Ephesians 5:28-29, where husbands are commanded to love their wives even as their own bodies.

The scripture concluded that a man would not hate his own body but instead would nurture and treasure it.

As I searched the scriptures, I concluded that marriage was not for the faint hearted or the selfish. The relationship between a husband and wife must be a reflection of God and the church. Jesus Christ gave His life for the church so marriage requires dying to self to bring forth oneness. I admired this oneness; it seemed deep and beautiful. There is nothing more powerful than the fervent prayer of two united by marriage under the influence of the Holy Spirit.

Even as I contemplated marriage, my thoughts flowed to honor! Usually, I can tell a lot about a person's character by looking at who they choose to honor. Thankfully, Orane honors God. *"...; for those who honor Me I will honor, and those who despise Me shall be lightly esteemed." (1Samuel 2:30)*

Knowing that there is nothing new under the sun, I took comfort that many have gone ahead of me in the journey of marriage— Mama, Maydine, Harriett, Bella, Melissa and Kay, just to name a few. These ladies kept me grounded. They offered wise counsel and some fasted and prayed with me as I attempted to navigate my new terrain.

Nevertheless, I knew that ultimately I would be responsible for my decision regarding Orane's proposal. In the depths of my heart, I was ready to intentionally love him.

CHAPTER 12: HOME BOUND

Oh happy day!

In a matter of minutes, I would see my love and my sunny homeland.

Harriett visited me for a few days and we traveled to Jamaica during the week of Christmas. As I looked out the window of the aircraft, my mind drifted to Orane. It was surreal how instinctively we understood each other. We delighted in each other's company and our spirits were in love. We were relaxed, utterly at ease with each other and brimming with affection.

The breeze was barely blowing in the warm evening air as Harriett and I exited the arrival area at the Norman Manley International Airport in Kingston, Jamaica.

Home sweet home!

Orane spotted me and we hastily move towards each other.

"Welcome home. You look wonderful." He looked at me fondly after locking me in a warm embrace.

I was dressed in white jean pants and jacket, gold ruffled tank blouse and gold sandals. My curly hair style and light make up added to my wow factor.

"Thank you. Great to see you," I said, laughing softly. "It's good to be home."

Orane heartily hugged Harriett. "Dr. Selby, welcome back."

Harriett flashed a radiant smile, overjoyed to see Orane. "Good to see you Orane, all the very best for the Christmas season." It was two days before Christmas day.

"Same to you Doc, to you and your family."

While Orane greeted Everton, Harriett's husband, Harriett eyed me crazily. "You look great together," she mouthed, giggling softly as she secretly gave me two thumbs up.

I grinned right back at her, nodding foolishly.

Within minutes, we left the airport in Orane's black BMW M6 Coupe for MayPo, a town approximately forty five minutes away.

"Look at you," Orane said, squeezing my shoulder.

"No. Look at you!"

"Are you happy to see me?" he asked.

"Totally," I said dramatically and then burst into a fit of girlish giggles at his raised eyebrows.

"I'm happy to see you too," he chuckled.

"I cannot believe that I kept myself away from this country for over four years. It was so hard to leave."

"It's called out of sight, out of mind," he teased.

"Of course.... not. I was laying and anchoring my foundation in my new country."

He smiled at me. "Now you have good reasons to be back."

"Oh yes," I grinned.

"Come now, let me hear you speak patois. Say, 'I am going over there' in patois."

"What?" I asked in dismay.

Orane laughed as he waited to hear my Jamaican Creole. "Let me help you, Mi a go dung deh so."

As I attempted to repeat the phrase, he really got a kick out of it. "Are you finished?" I asked, pursing my lips.

"Yes, I am. No, say it again." He laughed loudly.

"Go on, take advantage of me."

"Never, ever my love."

I touched his shoulder. "Sounds good to me."

"I mapped out our itinerary, but let me know if you would like to add anything else."

"No. Nothing else. What we discussed is good."

"Look in the cup holder. I have a cell phone for you."

"Honey, that is so thoughtful. Thank you," I said, picking up the cell phone.

"You're welcome. Roaming may be too costly for you to use your own cell phone. The charger is there too."

"Thank you."

"Anything for you, my girl."

"Anything? I will make a list."

"I give you an inch and you take a mile," he said smiling. "I plan to stop by my home before taking you to Mrs. Mohan."

"To my sister? I thought I was staying with you," I teased.

"Right! As old as you are, Mr. and Mrs. Mohan would be so disappointed in you...cohabiting."

"Yes. I can hear that conversation now. Anyway, it's not even about them. It's about our relationship with God."

"That's my girl."

"If you like, you can refer to her as Sister Maydine instead of Mrs. Mohan."

"Nooo. I prefer to use Mrs. Mohan...right now."

"Okay."

"I have dinner for you."

"That's what I am talking about, taking care of your girl."

"Yes. I am trying to impress you. I hope I succeeded."

I smiled at him. "Yes. You can check that off your list. After dinner, I will give you a honey-do list so you can impress me further."

A few minutes later, Orane looked much at ease as he showed me around his home, a beautiful three-bedroom single family house.

"I have something for you," I beamed across the square four-seater glass dining table after dinner.

"Okay."

I pulled the gift from my bag. "Guess, what's in it?"

"I'm not playing that game today," he said, trying not to appear eager.

"Fine, spoil sport!" I handed him the gift and he tore the wrapping away.

"Annalisa!" He jumped from his seat and hugged me. "Great minds think alike," he said smiling as he looked at the eight by ten framed photo of me.

I smiled at him. "Yes. I saw the same picture in your bedroom."

"But I like this larger frame. You look great."

"Thank you."

"I took this picture of you in Tallahassee. I like it," Orane said, staring at the photo. "Nice shot."

"Thought you would like it."

"I will keep this one in the living room."

With that, he placed the photo on the entertainment stand then stood back to admire it. "Okay, let's get out of here," he announced.

✻ ✻ ✻

The following day, Orane picked me up at mid-morning and gave me a tour of his business place. He intended to close down operations until the New Year. His work life was extremely hectic and I could see why he was in such great shape. I met a few of his employees, mostly sales personnel and his administrative assistant. They were very courteous, but I could see curiosity in their gaze.

At midday, we picked up Merck, Orane's cousin, in the town and transported him home. Merck was already smiling when I met him. He was anticipating our meeting. A tall man perhaps a little over six feet, Merck's broad shoulders rested well on his lean frame.

"Hello Annalisa," he greeted me as he entered the car. "How you doing?"

"I'm great! Nice to meet you Merck!" I extended my hand and he shook it heartily.

"Likewise Annalisa, likewise."

Orane greeted Merck. "Ready to roll."

"Yes sir," he responded.

"Annalisa welcome home," Merck said as we drove off.

Ann Marie Bryan

"Thank Merck! I feel as if I never left."

"Yes. There is no place like home. Now you have good reasons to be back."

Orane chuckled. "She sure does!"

"Yes, I do!" I confirmed.

"You have a good man on your hands," Merck offered. "He will take care of you."

"Thanks Merck! I realize that!"

Laughter filled Orane's eyes as he glanced at me. "Merck and I grew up together."

"Yes. Wild adventures!" Merck laughed. "I had to rescue him several times."

"Annalisa, do not believe him. It's the reverse. I had to rescue him from girls, his siblings and his parents. He was just a bad kid."

Merck chuckled. "Cousin, let's put it down to youth. Unforgettable times! I know you enjoyed the adventures."

Orane laughed knowingly. "Yes, yes."

"It was like that huh?" I teased.

"Yes," Orane responded. "Merck got me in trouble with my parents several times because of his antics."

"He was a bookworm. I was trying to break him out a little," Merck said as Orane stopped at a white single family house.

Merck exited the car. "Annalisa, please come and meet my wife and kids!"

I looked at Orane who nodded approvingly.

"Audra!" Merck called out as we approached the house.

No response came so he opened the front door. "Audra," he yelled, looking towards what I assumed to be the kitchen. Sounds of the washing of dishes were coming from there. "Audra, we have guests. Orane and..."

"On my way dear!" Audra entered the living room, wiping her hands with a small white towel. "Hello, nice to meet you Annalisa!" she said, after Merck's introduction. Audra was bright eyed and her voice had a cheery ring to it. She was brimming with energy.

88

"Nice to meet you too Audra." I smiled as we hugged.

"May I call you Anna?" she asked.

"Anna is fine. Where are the children?"

The three children seemed to appear from nowhere. They must have been waiting in the wings.

"Nice to meet you Miss Annalisa," they greeted me shyly as their mother introduced each by a wave of her hand, Cathy, Simone and Joseph.

"So nice to meet you," I said as I smiled and shook each hand.

Audra and Orane greeted and shortly thereafter, we left.

"Ready to eat?" Orane inquired.

"Definitely," I responded.

We ate lunch at Catirean, an open air seafood restaurant and entertainment center. Within minutes, the restaurant was crowded with locals, all of whom seemed to know each other. They kept the waitresses busy with their orders.

I enjoyed a splendid meal of steamed red snapper, steamed white rice and steamed vegetables while Orane ate jerked conch served with sweet papaya sauce, steamed rice and peas and tossed salad.

Orane touched my arm and smiled at me across the square wooden table. "You are really enjoying your meal."

"Ah, yes! It is deeelicious. Thank you!"

"Glad you're enjoying it."

"I'm gonna need a bed after this," I teased.

He winked and beckoned for me to come closer and I leaned forward. "Don't worry, I'll roll you out of here," he whispered, chuckling softly.

"Roll? I can't believe it. What about carrying me?"

His expression softened as if explaining to a child. "I'm trying to do the safest thing."

I eyeballed him. "I forgive you."

He laughed softly and squeezed my hand.

After lunch, Orane took me to his home.

"Don't move," he said, as we walked into the living room.

I sat my purse down on the coffee table and perched on the edge of the large, dark brown leather sofa facing the TV, as I waited with bated breath. Orane returned with an electronic portable keyboard.

"I'm a bit rusty so I'm not sure what is the driving force behind this," he said.

I clapped my hands enthusiastically. "You didn't tell me that you can play. You know that I absolutely love music. "

"I'm rusty," he smiled sheepishly. "I played way back in the day for my former church."

I flashed him an encouraging smile. "What can you play?"

"Let's do a worship song, *You are Alpha and Omega.*"

"Ohhh, I don't know that song."

"It's easy. You can learn it."

Orane taught me what turned out to be his favorite worship song. He was a little rusty on the keyboard but what did I care; it was music to my ears.

CHAPTER 13: PERFECT TIMING

A beautiful time for all the senses!

All of nature was clothed to perfection and out in splendor to celebrate the birth of Jesus Christ. It was a beautiful day for a celebration. Perfect weather! The sun peeked through the clouds blessing MayPo with a clear mild sunny day. The birds chirped celestial songs from trees that swayed in the cool breeze.

Maydine decorated her home to ring in the season and blared Christmas carols all day. Several of my siblings and their families and friends came to the celebration. We rearranged the dining room to accommodate more tables and chairs then placed additional chairs and tables on the lawn.

Orane and I ate until our hearts were content. I could not get over the deliciousness of the baked chicken and the pleasing aroma of the beautifully decorated roasted beef pulled me in at the buffet station. Not surprising, Maydine prepared macaroni and cheese, potato salad, steamed rice and peas and baked ham. I was so full that I did not get a chance to sample the array of desserts but I did have a piece of the amazing freshly baked Christmas cake.

More family members got a chance to meet and chat with Orane and I kept a close eye on him, just in case he needed to be rescued from any uncomfortable situation. Thankfully, there was no need for that! For someone who grew up in a small family, Orane handled himself brilliantly. *Check, check!*

❋ ❋ ❋

The day after Christmas, Orane and I journeyed to Ocho Rios, a town on Jamaica's north coast, to meet and stay with some of his family members. I was nervous yet somewhat excited, because I

Ann Marie Bryan

would be meeting his mother for the first time. Orane's appreciative glances did not go unnoticed when he arrived to pick me up. Maydine and I selected my outfit—navy jeans and jacket, a slate gray sweetheart neckline blouse and silver sandals. Orane looked suave in khaki shorts and a peach polo shirt. The shape of his dark-tinted sunglasses placed him squarely in the movie *"The Matrix."*

Orane prayed and we were on our way, singing and rocking to the rhythms of Michael W. Smith's *"Worship"* album. In between switching worship CDs, the radio played *"Tell Him"* a duet by Celine Dion and Barbara Streisand. We bellowed out the song in all kinds of strange keys. Orane laughed loudly as I raised my voice to a silly falsetto. After what seemed like an hour later, we stopped at a restaurant for mouthwatering jerked chicken and coconut water.

It was early evening when we arrived in Mahtel, a little town on the outskirt of Ocho Rios and entered the Zuger subdivision. Orane pointed out his old church and the community center where he and his friends played soccer and attended many community events. Oftentimes, he called out to neighbors, some of whom were surprised to see him.

Orane smiled at me as he stopped the car at the gate of an off white single family house. "Are you ready?" he asked

"No, but once the door is opened I will be."

"That's my girl," he said, squeezing my hand before exiting the car.

He opened the gate and held my hand as we walked in lock step towards the house. I could see three figures awaiting us on the front porch.

"Aunt Joy!" Orane greeted a petite smiling woman. Her delight was obvious. I politely said hello to the smiling man and woman who were curiously looking at me.

"Aunt Joy, meet Annalisa," Orane said smiling. "Annalisa, this is my mother." Orane had already informed me that sometimes he referred to his mother as Aunt Joy. This was a family tradition.

"Pleasure to meet you!" Aunt Joy embraced me warmly.

"Nice to meet you Aunt Joy," I said smiling.

Orane continued with the introductions. "And this is Uncle Ernest and Aunt Bee."

"Nice to meet you," I said, politely extending my hand to Uncle Ernest.

"Pleasure dear," he responded with a firm hand shake.

"Nice to meet you too." I extended my hand to Aunt Bee who gently pushed it aside to hug me heartily. "Welcome," she squealed.

Uncle Ernest took our suitcases to our rooms and we sat on the front porch. Aunt Bee served lemonade and plain cake while the trio quizzed Orane about happenings on his side of the island.

Aunt Joy was soft-spoken. She obviously loved and admired her son. Their respect for each other was mutual.

"Anna, are you happy to be back?" Aunt Bee's warm voice drew me in the conversation.

"Yes, very glad. Now, I am wondering how I left all of this."

Aunt Bee touched my shoulder. "Well, I'm sure you will have good reasons to be back soon."

Everyone laughed knowingly.

"What time will you be ready for dinner?" Aunt Bee asked.

"I'm sorry Aunt Bee, I should have told you," Orane said remorsefully. "We already have dinner reservations. We won't be here for long so I wanted to show Annalisa a little of the town."

"O...kay," Aunt Bee said with mock disapproval.

"Please forgive me," Orane said hugging her. "The food will not go to waste."

I tossed Aunt Bee an apologetic look.

"I forgive you both," Aunt Bee said, looking directly at me.

I grinned. "Aunt Bee, I promise you, I had nothing to do with this. It was all Orane."

"Throw me under the bus Annalisa, please."

"Oh come on, Orane," I responded playfully.

Orane pretended to be shocked. "You just took the T out of team."

Ann Marie Bryan

Everyone laughed.

"Let me take Annalisa to her room," Orane said. "I know she's tired."

"Thank you for accommodating me," I said, moving towards Orane.

"You are more than welcome," Aunt Bee responded and the others murmured their agreement.

"Can you be ready by 6:30?" Orane asked as I followed him.

"Two hours. I can do that."

"Come here," he smiled with wide open arms and I fell in them. "Hmmm! This feels so good."

"Totally!" I exhaled softly and slowly extracted myself from our warm embrace. "Thank you Honey. See you in a bit." I giggled softly as he winked then moonwalked down the passageway.

Instead of lying on the bed, I opted to rest on the small sofa. Sleep did not come easy as my eyes flitted all over the room which was nicely decorated in baby pink and white. I felt the crisp fresh evening air as the curtains blew in the wind. I pulled the sofa closer to the window making sure that I did not scratch the wooden floor.

Almost an hour later, I woke up when my cell phone alarm went off. I showered and dressed in an elegant white one-shoulder knee length chiffon evening dress with starburst side pleats. I topped it off with bronze accessories and evening sandals. My hair was brushed straight and sleek. While most of the tresses rested on my back, a few escaped and nestled on my shoulder.

Orane was conversing with his mom when I entered the living room. "Anna, you look wonderful!" Aunt Joy beamed.

"Thank you Aunt Joy!"

Orane looked totally moved as I walked toward them. "Babes, you look beautiful."

"Thank you," I responded, smiling at him.

"Are you ready?" he asked. He looked cool and confident in a black suit with a white shirt opened at the neck and black dress shoes.

"Yes, I am."

"Aunt Joy, we will see you a little later," Orane said, holding my hand.

"Have a good time," Aunt Joy said smiling.

"We will," I responded and Orane closed the door behind us.

The cool evening breeze greeted us as we stepped off the front porch. Orane took a light hold of my arm just above my elbow. He opened the car door and made certain that my hem was tucked in before closing it. As I settled comfortably in the passenger seat, I could not help but think that I was on a beautiful journey.

"Are you okay?" Orane asked gently as we pulled away from the gate. "You seemed far away."

"I'm wonderful. Thanks so much for taking me to dinner."

"You are welcome. I wanted us to spend quality time together."

"I am just happy to be with you."

He chuckled softly. "Do I sense a stirring of love?"

"Yes sir, that's the sound of love."

He gazed into my eyes, seeming to forget the road completely for a moment. Whatever he saw there must have encouraged him. "Great!" he said heartily.

Half an hour later, we exited the car in the parking lot of Celebrate Now Restaurant and Lounge.

"You will like it here. They offer the best Jamaican dishes," Orane mentioned.

"I'm doing all Jamaican food right now."

"I know," he chuckled, offering his arm as we walked to the entrance. Music was playing softly in the background as we entered the reception area.

"Good evening! Welcome to Celebrate Now Restaurant and Lounge," said a smiling female receptionist. "Do you have a reservation?"

"Thank you! Yes, under the name Conway, Orane Conway."

"Yes sir! One moment please." The receptionist motioned for the waitress to escort us to our table.

Ann Marie Bryan

We passed other guests, some already seated with their meals and others nursing cocktails. I could see why Orane thought that I would like this restaurant. It had a rustic, Victorian look with a lush garden. We were escorted to an air-conditioned room with private booths that had full view of a magnificent waterfall surrounded by an exotic array of orchids. Dimly lit chandeliers hung from the wood beam ceiling to create an intimate setting.

Orane seated me before sitting.

"I am Becky," the waitress said. "I will be back in a moment to take your orders."

"Thank you Becky," Orane responded cordially.

"Honey, I love the ambience and decor. Great choice!"

"Thanks Babes!" He smiled at me. "Hope you will like the food."

"You know I will." I returned his smile before glancing over the menu. "I already know what I am having."

"You are good. What are you having?"

"Cream of broccoli soup followed by stewed beef, herbed rice and steamed cabbage. I will have fruit punch and let me see...perhaps bread pudding for dessert."

Orane chuckled. "I will have to roll you out of here also."

"Do what you have to." I laughed softly. "I am a very healthy eater."

A smiling Becky returned. "Are you ready to order?"

"Yes. Babes please go ahead."

Becky took my order. "And what will you have sir?"

"Cream of pumpkin soup, jerked chicken, herbed rice and steamed cabbage and carrots. I will have sweet potato pudding for dessert."

"Great!" said Becky. "Will you be having anything to drink?"

"Babes, what did you select for your drink?"

"Fruit punch," I replied.

"Yes, make that two please."

"If that's all, I will be back in a moment with your soups."

96

"Thanks, Becky," I responded and she nodded and left.

I flashed Orane a smile before asking, "Can we take pictures near the waterfall after dinner?" Suddenly, he lost his hearing. "Orane Conway, I know you heard me."

He winced. "Not again."

"Pretty please." I pouted playfully. "I need pictures."

He let out a defeated sigh. "Okay, we can."

"Thank you Honey, you put the L in love."

He winced playfully. "Did you say that I put the hell in love?"

"Ah, let me think...never." I laughed, squeezing his hand before placing the large yellow napkin on my lap.

I stared at the beautiful cascading waterfall thinking how far we've come. *This is a sweet home coming.* "I imagine this place is even more beautiful in the day light when its natural beauty can be observed," I remarked.

"Yes it is. It's quite a hot spot for lunch and dinner," Orane said as Becky placed our soups on the table.

I smiled at her. "Thank you, Becky."

"You are welcome," she responded before leaving.

Orane blessed our meal.

"This looks good," I remarked, stirring my soup.

"Mine's good."

"Oh yes, this is good too." I savored the delicious taste of the soup.

"Glad you like it. Are you having a great time?" he asked, gazing at me.

I smiled at him. "Honey, I could not ask for more."

"I could," he said, looking at me mischievously.

"I bet you could." I giggled softly, buttering my roll then taking a bite.

"I love you," he said quietly.

I reached for his hand across the table and gazed into his eyes. "I love you too."

He chuckled softly as I hastily released his hand and began to eat my soup.

"Annalisa!" His tone caused me to look at him. "Don't be afraid of our chemistry. It's a great thing." He smiled and looked deep into my eyes.

A bout of shyness overtook me. "I'm working on it," I responded softly.

"So am I," he said reassuringly. "I am glad you chose me."

"Chose!" I laughed softly. "I fell in love!"

"Right!" He was not convinced. "You know love is a decision."

A slight smile parted my lips as I looked at him. "Yes, it is. An act of the mind before it becomes an act of the heart."

He swallowed spoons of soup then gazed intently at me. "Haven't you forgotten something?"

I blushed. "Oh yes, there is the eee-motional component."

"Glad you remembered that!"

We both laughed recalling my last reaction.

"Here comes our main course," I said enthusiastically. "I know you don't mind me having extra meat on my bones."

"Do your thing!" he drawled.

"Thanks Becky," I said as she placed our dinner on the table.

"Would you like wine?" Orane asked, signaling for Becky to wait.

"No thanks. I am barely going to make it to dessert."

"Thank you Becky," Orane said, and she promptly left. "I thought you would have a non-alcoholic chardonnay or your old favorite. What's the name of the wine you gave me when I visited?"

"You are unforgiving." I grinned at him. "I had a moment there. Bringing up my past is so not cool." I lifted a fork full of food to my mouth. "Would you like me with more weight on?"

He looked puzzled and his eyes asked what had brought this on. I refused to back down and waited for a response.

"I don't think you can gain a lot of weight. Your bone structure will not allow it," he said thoughtfully. He chuckled as I pouted. "But that's not the question. Yes, I will love you, no matter your size."

"Ahhhh, that is so nice." I winked at him before sipping some of my fruit punch.

"Babes," he said quietly. "My loving you is not about your physical appearance, fine as you are. I am in love with your spirit."

A bright smile lit my face. "Thank you. I feel loved."

"You are loved." He looked at me tenderly. "I am so glad that you are here."

My heart skipped a beat as I smiled at him. "Me too!"

Warmth radiated from his eyes. "You are my reminder that I cannot ask God for too much. How about spending the rest of your life with me?" He reached across the table and held my hand. "Will you marry me?"

Adrenalin surged through my body and my heart fluttered continuously. "Yes," I replied without hesitation.

Orane jumped to his feet and hugged me tightly. His lips were warm on my cheek. I hugged him back, twice as tight, elated and giddy at the same time. *I have found the one my heart loves.*

We ate dessert basking in a state of euphoria and enjoyed our finest dining experience ever. After Orane paid the bill, we took pictures by the waterfall, laughing and making faces as the water sprinkled us. My hair was ruffled by the cool December breeze and Orane reached out and moved the strands behind my ears. He wrapped his arm around my shoulder as we made our way to the parking lot.

"Do I hear music?" I smiled, emotionally stirred by Diana Ross and Lionel Richie's beautiful romantic ballad *"My Endless Love"* as it filled the airwaves.

"You're good," Orane teased.

"Yes, totally gifted," I giggled.

"Let's dance," he said, taking me in his arms. He seemed to have come alive with the vision of our marriage in sight. I rested my head on his shoulder and wrapped my hands around his waist. We moved slowly to the rhythm.

"I love you," he whispered above my head.

"I love you too," I said, burrowing into his neck.

The song ended but he tightened his hold. I could feel his heart beating; it was as rapid as my own. Tenderly, I pulled slightly out of his arms and touched the side of his face, my thumb stoked his cheek. A smile tugged at the corners of his lips and a hidden fire blazed in his dark brown eyes.

"You are beautiful," he whispered huskily, smoothing my hair as a cool breeze whipped around us.

My lips curved in a smile and I sighed happily, gazing at the healthy glow of his dark brown complexion under the moonlight. "Thank you," I responded breathlessly. "You are an amazing person."

"Thanks, Babes." His smile widened and he gently ran one of his hands down my arm, sending delicious shivers up my spine. Longing coursed through my veins and my heart hammered within my chest. I shuddered, wanting him to kiss me passionately ... and take me to new heights.

"Are you cold?" he asked.

"No," I murmured as he pulled me closer and kissed my cheek.

"Hmmm!" He groaned softly. "I am going to take us home before we get ourselves in trouble."

"Okay," I whispered, "if we must." I wanted to stay cradled in his arms forever.

Orane draped his arm around my shoulder as we walked to the car. Happy emotions enveloped me as I considered our lifetime of togetherness. His love touched me to the core of my heart.

I fastened my seatbelt and pushed the seat back, thinking about our whirlwind relationship.

"Are you okay?" Orane asked as we pulled away.

I nodded, still giddy with love.

"Yes, you are," he chuckled softly.

"Thank you Honey. I had a great time."

"Glad you did. So did I."

He looked so happy.

I am in love with a great guy!

Back at the house, we hugged and said goodnight, delirious from an evening that will be cherished forever. As I prepared for bed, I thought about the events that had unfolded earlier. *Will you marry me?* His words replayed in my mind, over and over again. The look on his face when he said it was etched in my memory forever. I clapped my hands and danced around before throwing myself on the bed, giggling as I rolled from side to side then stared at the ceiling.

I'm getting married.

Our wedding day...A mild and sunny Saturday in spring!

Or perhaps summer!

Happiness filled my soul.

Sleep came much later after I placed a quick call to Maydine. In the end, I was not the only one screaming, she was 'off the chain'.

CHAPTER 14: PRECIOUS MOMENTS

The sun was just starting to rise and its rays cast a golden hue on trees by my window. A few sunbeams made interesting patterns on the wall, providing incandescent light across my bedroom. In a flash, the realization of what had occurred the night before hit me, and I broke into a wide grin followed by an avalanche of giggles. I felt so happy, undeniably happy.

I dedicated the day to the Lord, showered, curled my hair then dressed in dark blue jeans, a leopard print wrap blouse and dark brown sandals. I applied light make up and made my way to breakfast. I could hear an inaudible conversation amidst laughter as I entered the living room where Aunt Joy, Aunt Bee and Uncle Ernest were having a vibrant discussion.

"Good morning!" I greeted them with a smile.

"Good morning!" they responded joyfully.

"Did you sleep well?" Aunt Joy asked.

"Yes, I did. Thank you!" I looked around for Orane.

"Orane is not up," Aunt Bee said. "Would you like to eat now?"

"I will have tea until he's up."

"I am up. Good morning all," Orane said pleasantly as he entered the room.

"Good Morning, Orane!" we responded.

"Everybody doing okay?" Orane asked.

Murmurs of yes and okay rang out.

Orane smiled unashamedly at me and I blushed as he hugged my waist. "I have good news," he announced exuberantly and everyone turned to face him. "Last night, I proposed and Annalisa accepted."

Spontaneous applause and cheers of joy rang out as everyone hugged and congratulated us.

"We will keep you posted on our wedding date," Orane informed them in the joyful atmosphere.

Deep and abiding love welled up in my heart as I watched Orane. He smiled lovingly at me before stating in a deep dramatic voice, "On behalf of my wife and..."

Laughter broke out before he could finish and I grinned from ear to ear.

"I am practicing for our big day," he said smiling.

"Nephew, you are a piece of work," Uncle Ernest said, slapping Orane's back.

"That's my son," Aunt Joy said, still laughing.

"I have entertained you enough for one day," Orane said, amidst laughter. "Time for breakfast."

With that, he took my hand and led me to the breakfast nook, with Aunt Bee in tow, still snickering.

"Thank you for breakfast, Aunt Bee," Orane said smiling. "This looks like your handy work."

"What gave me away?" Aunt Bee asked lightheartedly.

"Let me see!" Orane smiled at her. "Is it this wonderful spread of boiled ackee with salt fish and roasted breadfruit? Breakfast is looking good!"

"Thank you!" Aunt Bee responded happily.

"I bet it tastes good too," I remarked.

"I hope you will enjoy it," Aunt Bee said proudly. "Do you need anything else?"

"I'm good. Thank you," I responded.

"Thanks Aunt Bee. I'm good too," Orane said. "We appreciate you!"

Aunt Bee smiled. "You are welcome. I will be on the front porch if you need anything."

"Okay!" Orane said, and we sat down and ate heartily.

After breakfast, Orane took me on a short tour of the neighborhood and I met a few of his relatives and friends who welcomed me with opened arms. Everyone cheered excitedly when Orane introduced me as his future wife. They shouted congratulatory words and some of the men slapped his back, saying, "You're the man."

I smiled bravely as I listened to their words of encouragement.

When we returned home, Orane chatted with Uncle Ernest on the front porch while the ladies showed me the lush garden at the front of the house.

"Who has the green thumb?" I asked.

"Guilty!" Aunt Bee said, throwing her hands in the air.

"Aunt Bee is really good at gardening," Aunt Joy confirmed.

"The garden is beautiful," I remarked, glancing at the variety of roses.

"I love gardening," Aunt Bee said. "It puts me in a great mood."

"Let me confess right now, I don't have a green thumb," I said bashfully. "Not at all!"

"You cannot be good at everything Annalisa," Aunt Joy teased.

"Ahhh!" I grinned at them. "Nevertheless, I love flowers, especially roses."

"So romantic," Aunt Joy said, playfully touching my shoulder.

"Aunt Joy!" I eyed her, giggling softly, "You're a naughty lady."

She giggled right back, grabbing on to Aunt Bee for support.

"Can I get pictures of you ladies?" I asked.

"Noooo!" they hollered in unison.

"Please!" I gave them my pretty please look.

It worked! I took my camera out of my purse. "Let the model in you emerge," I encouraged them.

The ladies giggled like teenagers as I asked them to strike various poses in the garden.

Half an hour later, Aunt Joy and I sat on a bench in the garden looking at the pictures on the camera.

"Anna, I am so glad that we met! God bless you."

I smiled at her. "It is nice to finally meet you too Aunt Joy."

"I don't have a daughter so you are a wonderful addition to the family."

"Thanks Aunt Joy. That's a beautiful thing to say." I gently hugged her shoulders. "I appreciate you."

She smiled reassuringly. "Orane will make you a wonderful husband."

"Thanks for saying that. I love him. He is very caring and giving."

"Very! He takes care of all my needs, medications and all. He's on time and joyful about it."

"He considers it a joy to provide for you."

Aunt Joy smiled contentedly. "I thank God for him."

I reached out and touched her hand. "Me too."

As we digested this, Orane's voice rang out nearby. "Annalisa."

"Excuse me Aunt Joy," I said, moving towards the sound of his voice. "Yes Orane!"

He was still sitting on the front porch with Uncle Ernest.

"Are you ready?" he asked. "We have to go."

"Yes. Ready when you are!"

"Let me get my car keys."

"Aunt Joy," I called out, "we will talk later. I am hitting the streets with Orane."

"Okay dear," Aunt Joy responded, waving her hand.

Half an hour later, Orane and I toured the unique and very beautiful attractions in Ocho Rios. We visited the Craft Park and I purchased souvenirs for some of my co-workers. After several fittings in a department store and much to Orane's relief, I finally purchased a pair of navy jeans that beckoned, *"I am yours."* Orane purchased a black shirt for himself and two blouses for me. We made Burger King our lunch spot before heading home.

Two hours later, I was in full-blown preparation to attend the wedding of Devon, Orane's friend and Mona, his wife to be. I quickly showered to spend time on my curly updo with wavy tendrils then applied foundation, bronze lipstick and earth tone eye shadow to complement my elegant outfit. Taking a last look in the mirror, I made my way to the living room.

"Gor...geous!" Orane sounded breathless. "You look quite picturesque." He admired my black full length, slightly flare chiffon skirt and fitted bronze toned beaded sleeveless top, completed with striking black earrings and bronze evening sandals and purse.

"Thank you, Mr. Conway. You look the same."

"I look picturesque?" He smiled and waited patiently as I formulated my comeback.

"My bad, poor choice of words; let me rephrase that. You look very distinguished." I showed appreciation for his dapper attire, a cutting-edge classic two-button charcoal suit, burgundy shirt, burgundy and black striped silk tie and black dress shoes.

"You both look very nice." We turned and saw Aunt Joy smiling at us.

"Thank you!" we responded.

"Aunt Joy, we are about to leave," Orane said purposefully. "We will see you later."

"Bye Aunt Joy," I said, moving towards the door.

"Have a good time," Aunt Joy replied as she followed us to the door and closed it behind us.

We drove to the wedding site, Abacoya Gardens and encountered the splendor of nature displayed by well-cultivated flowering plants and trees. Orane parked and we looked around the beautiful botanical garden, adjoining the spectacular cascading falls.

"The architecture is exquisite," I commented, looking at the elegance of the great house, reminiscent of Jamaica's colonial past.

"Yes. It is Spanish architecture," Orane informed me.

"Alrighty!"

He smiled at me. "Don't forget I grew up in this town. I believe they also have a museum displaying a bit of Jamaica's history."

"Really?"

"Yes. The museum is focused primarily on the Taino Arawak Indians, Jamaica's first inhabitants."

I patted his shoulder. "History buff!"

He placed his arm around my shoulder and we stood for a moment, enjoying the scenery before entering a well-maintained lawn in the midst of the garden. We were greeted by an usher who seated us. *Oh no, rain!* A water drop landed on my hand.

"Rain! Run!" someone screamed and we all took off.

"We have to run back to the car," Orane said as everyone ran in different directions. We made it just in time. "Showers of blessings!" he declared wiping his face. "Running in the rain with the one I love."

"Very poetic. Right back at you!" I grinned at him. My grin turned into grimace. "No outdoor wedding for us."

"I agree. It can be beautiful but the weather is unpredictable."

"This place is absolutely beautiful." I touched his shoulder. "This is your kind of setting."

"Call me Mr. Nature," he said playfully.

"So, it will be."

Orane smiled fondly at me. "When do you want us to get married?"

I returned his smile. "Next Summer or Fall."

He poked a finger in my side. "You could have said tomorrow."

"Tomorrow then." I giggled trying to avoid his fingers.

Thankfully, it was a brief downpour. By the time we walked back to the lawn, the bridal party had arrived but the bride and groom were nowhere in sight.

"The seats are all taken," Orane said, offering his arm. "Let's find a comfortable standing spot."

We took up position under a tree on the outskirt of the lawn to have a clear vision of the wedding ceremony. While we waited, Orane greeted and chatted with Rayton, a childhood friend and brother of the groom.

"The bride and groom just arrived," I said enthusiastically, interrupting Rayton and Orane's conversation.

Ann Marie Bryan

"I have to go," Rayton said. "Annalisa, it was nice meeting you."

"Likewise Rayton."

A few minutes later, the bridal party took their places at the altar and Mona made a grand entrance, wearing a white cap sleeved satin A-line gown, pearl necklace and matching earrings and white high heel evening sandals. A bouquet of pink orchids completed her graceful appearance.

I carefully watched the entire wedding ceremony, hoping to glean helpful tips. *Will I be nervous on our big day?* A soft smile spread slowly across my face. *No nervousness! I will release all my nervous energy, way before that day. The whole day must be surreal...wonderfully enchanting.*

Orane's gentle nudge and charming smile brought me back to the present as he gently took hold of my hand and escorted me to the reception area, a pavilion elegantly decorated in burgundy, gold and white.

An hour later, the Master of Ceremonies announced that dinner was buffet style so we picked up our food and returned to our table. Rayton and Jenna, his sister, joined us at the table.

"I would love to get married, if only I could find the right lady," Rayton announced before sipping his water.

"Of all the ladies you know, don't tell me none is suitable," Orane questioned.

"None, my brother! None!"

Orane shifted in his seat and wrapped an arm around my shoulder. "As you know, I found my special lady," he said, looking at me fondly.

My cheeks felt warm and tingly as all eyes focused on me.

"Congrats again, my brother!" Rayton exclaimed. He stood up and bowed deeply towards me.

I smiled and mouthed, "Thank you."

"Thanks Ray!" Orane said. "We will keep you posted on our wedding date."

Half an hour later, Orane toasted the groom. The guests laughed as he spoke about Devon's escapades during their childhood days. He encouraged Devon and Mona to continue putting God first place in their lives.

I must have clapped the loudest at the end of his speech. "Great speech!" I told him proudly when he took his seat. He nodded and squeezed my hand.

At the end of the reception, Orane introduced me to Devon, Mona and a few other friends. Shortly thereafter, we left, totally exhausted and ready to 'hit the sack'.

CHAPTER 15: TEARS

The sun was just beginning to rise, when we waved goodbye to Aunt Joy, Uncle Ernest and Aunt Bee, to head back to MayPo. Half an hour later, Orane pulled into a homeless shelter bearing the sign "Lightway Family Center", to visit Perry Nattanay, his childhood friend.

"Babes, don't be alarmed," Orane said, before we exited the car. "Perry is a very wonderful person but he has many challenges in life."

"That's alright Honey," I said comfortingly.

Orane spoke to the receptionist and within minutes, Perry ran as best as he could through the reception area, laughing and dragging his left leg. His determination touched my heart. He was overjoyed to see Orane and greeted him loudly, thanking God.

When Orane could get a word in, he introduced me as his future wife. Perry screamed with joy, danced around and wished us well. He then promptly introduced Ola, his girlfriend who was waiting quietly in the wings.

"We met at the shelter. I want to marry her," he stated proudly.

Ola blushed and her small frame was wriggled with low laughter. It was obvious that Perry meant the world to her.

As we moved from the reception area and stood outside the building, Perry expressed his appreciation for the money and gifts that we had brought. While he continued to talk with Orane, my eyes drifted to several other residents of the shelter.

Sadness enveloped me!

There was a feeling of desolation and oppression in the atmosphere. I moved away from Orane and Perry, feeling the need to pray over the shelter. Yet, all I could say was "Jesus" as I moved around.

I fought back tears as Orane requested permission to pray. Perry and Ola agreed. With all heads bowed, Orane prayed for them and the shelter and sure enough, the heavy spirit was lifted from the atmosphere.

There was silence in the car as we continued our journey. I knew that Orane was thinking about Perry and so was I. Perry could barely walk and only one hand was functioning but he was filled with joy. I looked across at Orane, just in time to see tears welling up in the corner of his eyes. I reached into my purse and gave him a facial tissue and he dabbed his eyes as he drove. I waited for the right moment to speak.

"How did Perry end up in the shelter?"

Orane explained that Perry was raised in his neighborhood and that he was physically challenged from birth. When his parents died, Perry began living with a family member who migrated to the United States of America and left him in the care of another family member. Soon the task of taking care of him became burdensome so he was placed in the shelter. Orane kept in touch with him as much as possible and oftentimes visited him.

"God bless you Honey. You are doing what you can for Perry."

Orane nodded thoughtfully.

An hour later, I realized that our route would take us past Natasha's home so I called her.

"Natasha, how are you?" I greeted her.

"Baby sister," Natasha squealed.

"In the flesh, well almost." I giggled. "Orane and I are in the neighborhood. Can we pay you a short visit?"

"Oh yes. Let me give you directions."

"Hold on. Please give directions to Orane." Natasha and her family had since changed residence.

"Hi Natasha." Orane listened then laughed. "Yes. I have been hearing good things about you too. But we'll talk...Yes. Yes. I'll be able to find you."

We drove across a meadow and I called Natasha to confirm that we were on the right track. *Track indeed!* The car bumped and scraped as we slowly traveled on the endless make shift dirt road. Immediately, I understood why Natasha and Colin, her husband drove heavy duty trucks. I smiled apologetically and my eyes graciously thanked Orane. His gentle gaze told me that everything was alright. After what seemed like an eternity, we drove up a hill and into a Jamaican Georgian architectural style, two-story house with a wooden roof.

Natasha and Lori-Ann, her younger daughter, greeted us on the verandah. They were excited to meet Orane. "Let's go inside," Natasha said, ushering us into the living room.

The interior of the house was beautifully decorated with antique furniture. The Brazilian Cherry hardwood floor conveyed a feeling of happiness and warmth. We ate lunch in the dining room around a magnificent rectangular ten-seater mahogany dining table then left Orane to relax before the TV in the spacious living room.

Natasha and I entered her master bedroom and jumped on the bed, giggling like teenagers. She made crazy faces as she expressed her joy that Orane had proposed.

"I love him so much," I whispered, sitting in the middle of the bed.

"I can see." Natasha giggled. "It's all over you."

"Ahhh!" I flopped backwards on the pillows.

"I have a gift for you," Natasha beamed, swinging her legs over the side of the bed.

"Really?"

She reached for a gift bag beside the nightstand and handed it to me. I pulled out and gazed at a beautiful white cowl-neck jersey top.

"Thank you," I said, hugging her.

"Wait until you see this," she said, eagerly opening a drawer on the dresser. She pulled out a midnight blue sleeveless cotton blouse with two bronze toned chains that served as the straps.

"Wow! It's gorgeous."

"Go ahead, try it on."

I slipped into the blouse and admired myself in the full length mirror.

Natasha laughed enthusiastically as I modeled. "That's for your honeymoon."

"Oh sis, thank you," I said, hugging her.

A few minutes later with my new blouses in hand, Orane and I waved goodbye to Natasha and Lori-Ann.

The sun had begun its descent over MayPo when we arrived at Maydine's home, totally exhausted. Orane parked at the gate and took out my carry-on.

"Babes, get some rest," he said. "I'll see you later."

"Honey, you're exhausted and so am I," I said, touching his muscular arm. "Why don't you take a nap and we'll talk later."

Orane inhaled then exhaled deeply. "Okay."

"Hello lady and gentleman! Welcome back!" We turned and saw Maydine approaching the gate. Mr. Mohan watched from the verandah.

"Sister Maydine!" I gave her a big hug.

"Mrs. Mohan, good to see you," Orane said, hugging her.

"You too Orane," Maydine responded.

"Honey, I'll just pull my carry-on in the house." I winked at Orane before hugging him. "Bye."

"I will call you later," he said smiling. "Bye Mrs. Mohan."

"Bye Orane," Maydine said, her smile softened her pleasant features.

Orane waved at Mr. Mohan before sliding in the driver's seat and we watched his car disappear around the bend.

"Well, well!" I turned to see an animated Maydine dancing about. "I want all the details."

I laughed heartily. "We will be up all night."

CHAPTER 16: REQUEST GRANTED

"Forget it!"

That was Mr. Mohan's response when I requested permission to go on a date, back in the day. Maydine invited Orane to dinner which stirred up past memories of my meager dating life during my late teens. Mr. Mohan was a man of few words so conversations about dating during high school were not "pretty", not at all. To put it mildly, Mr. Mohan was all about school. "Your mother sent you here to complete your education," he said back then.

I decided to have a little chat with Mr. Mohan prior to dinner. So far, his interactions with Orane had been very courteous. I had not formally spoken to him about Orane but I was sure that Maydine filled in the blanks. Still, I would rather err on the side of caution. I found Mr. Mohan in the living room, reading the newspaper on the burgundy recliner

"Mr. Mohan," I called out to him.

"Yes ma'am." He shifted the newspaper to the side.

"Orane will be here shortly."

"Yes ma'am." A smile crept up the corners of his mouth as he peered at me over his reading glasses.

"Please don't give him a hard time," I pleaded gently.

He chuckled and folded the newspaper. "I wouldn't do that."

Immediately my eyebrows arched. "Please say yes to whatever he is asking."

Mr. Mohan smiled. "Okay ma'am."

Half an hour later, Orane arrived and we sat down at the rectangular six-seater mahogany dining table, spread with stewed curried goat, baked chicken, steamed rice and peas, macaroni and cheese, potato salad, tossed salad and fruit punch. Maydine brought out her finest plates and gold cutlery.

I playfully poked Maydine. "My sister, when I grow up, I'm going to cook just like you. This is simply divine."

Maydine smiled at me. "Glad that I still have the touch."

"Yes. Dinner tastes delicious!" Orane joined the conversation. "Mr. and Mrs. Mohan thanks for the invitation."

"You are always welcome," Maydine beamed while Mr. Mohan nodded.

Glancing at me, Orane decided to seize the moment. "Mr. and Mrs. Mohan, I have been meaning to talk with you." Maydine and Mr. Mohan perked up in anticipation. "Annalisa and I have been talking for a while. I love her. It's not every day that a man discovers a woman like her. She is beautiful on the inside as on the outside. I thank God for her and for blessing me with such a wonderful gift. We are considering marriage and I'm hoping that you will give me your blessing to marry her."

Go on Honey! You said that so well! It was my proudest moment. He was calm and self-assured. I felt like a rare and sacred treasure.

"Babes, would you like to say something?" Orane asked tenderly.

I looked up to see everyone staring at me. "No," I responded quickly. For some strange reason, his question caught me off guard.

"You have nothing to say." Maydine's mouth fell open. "Now that's a first."

Everyone laughed while they waited patiently for me to regain my power of speech.

"Nothing right now," I said bashfully. Bewildered by the sudden attention, I found myself uncharacteristically tongue-tied, rendered speechless.

Speechless! Me? This was a LOL (laugh out loud) moment.

Mr. Mohan turned to Orane and smiled proudly. "Annalisa has waited a long time to get married. I would not like her to be disappointed. Please take good care of her."

Ann Marie Bryan

OMG! (Oh My Gosh)
A veiled threat!
No, an open threat!
Awkward!

Maydine tried hard to look unconcerned. Her eyes focused on her plate then she burst into nervous laughter. As I anticipated, Orane took what was said with grace and confirmed that he would take care of me.

"You have our blessing," Mr. Mohan said and Maydine nodded approvingly.

Phew! That went well.

A gentle smile appeared on Mr. Mohan's face and remained there throughout the rest of the meal. The evening ended with Ariel Brut Cuvee non-alcoholic sparkling wine and lots of laughter. Mr. Mohan and Maydine gave us tips for keeping a great marriage. After all, they had over thirty years of experience.

CHAPTER 17: FAMILY TIES

New Year's Day, my family members and relatives who were in Jamaica decided to visit Mama at the family home in Litskel, a two-hour drive from Maydine's home. I was looking forward to seeing Mama who I had not seen for over six months so I woke up early to pack food for the trip.

"Anna, have you heard from Orane?" My eyes darted around the kitchen trying to locate Maydine.

"Sister Maydine, I called him but no response."

Maydine entered the kitchen from the living room. "It's almost time to go and Harriett is still waiting for him."

The mountainous terrain to visit Mama was more suited for sport utility vehicles so Orane decided to park his car at Harriett's home. Carpooling was the order of the day.

"Let me try again. I hope he's not asleep," I replied.

The house phone rang just as I was reaching for my cell phone. I hastened to answer it.

"Good morning, Orane Conway!"

"Good morning, Babes. I just woke up."

"Oops! Didn't your alarm go off?"

"Babes, I'm going to rest. I'll catch up with you when you return."

My jaw dropped. *He did not just say that.* My mind screamed in several different languages.

"Babes, are you there?"

"Yes," I responded through clenched teeth.

As though sensing my thoughts, he asked, "Do I still have time to get ready?"

"I believe so," I replied in a flat tone.

"Okay. I'll call Doc and let her know that I'm running late."

"Have you forgotten that you will be meeting my mother to-day?"

"Babes don't be upset. I'll see you in a bit."

"Okay. Bye." I felt so annoyed. *What was he thinking?*

Twenty minutes later, we left home in Maydine's gray Toyota Rav4 to meet Harriett and her family and Orane. The lush greenery and pleasant sunny day did little to allay my annoyance with Orane. I was still steaming. We were greeted with welcoming smiles and cheerful good mornings when we pulled up at the meeting spot, the residence of Uncle Joseph, Mr. Mohan's cousin.

"Hello," Orane greeted me with a soft stroke on my back.

My body stiffened in response and my slight glare warned him to stop. "Hello!" I said coolly.

Orane removed his sunglasses and flashed a charming smile. "Is it chilly or what?"

I shoved my hands into the pockets of my jeans and tipped my chin up defensively. "It's chilly."

He poked my side. "Babes, are you still upset?"

There was no holding back my annoyance. "I cannot believe that you were thinking of not coming."

"I am sorry Babes. I know this is important to us."

I did not respond.

"Babes!" He wrapped one arm around my shoulder. "I don't like it when you're angry with me."

I shrugged my shoulder. "I'm not angry with you."

"Yes you are." He tickled my side. "You are a beautiful angry bird."

Angry bird? I fought back giggles and instead pulled away from him. "Stop it! You know I'm ticklish."

"How can I make it up to you?"

"I am more annoyed than upset."

"There you are, communicating." He tugged at my sleeve but I was unrelenting. "Babes, love keeps no record of wrong."

118

I smiled at his last ditch effort. "So, you're going to throw the whole bible at me?"

"I know you'll respond to it. So talk to me."

"I'm annoyed because I really wanted you to meet my mom. It's important. You know she travels frequently. Plus, I don't know when I'll be back in Jamaica."

"I know it's important to meet your mother. I want to, I need to. It's just that I was feeling extremely tired."

I sighed softly. *Don't be too hard on him, I cautioned myself.* "I know that you're tired. We have been running around since I got here."

He gave me a slow smile, his eyes boring into mine. "Babes, my intention is to make you happy not sad."

"Okay." I managed a half smile. "My intention is to make you happy."

"Are you stealing my lyrics again?"

I grinned at him. "I'm preparing for oneness. What's yours is mine." I threw my hands around his waist and hugged him tightly, breathing in his familiar cologne.

"I love you!" he murmured, kissing my forehead.

"I love you too," I whispered.

"Let see how much." He poked a finger in my side and I pulled out of our embrace, laughing loudly with delight.

"Let's roll people," Mr. Mohan yelled and we all moved towards the sport utility vehicles.

"Travel with us." I pulled Orane by the hand. "We have space in our vehicle."

His face lit up with joy. "Great!"

Two hours later, we drove through the Main Street of Litskel, waving to passersby. Spontaneous shouts of greetings occurred between us and Mama's neighbors as we journeyed through the streets leading to her home. Our family grew up in Litskel, a small quiet town in the center of the island where everyone knew everyone. People lived in Litskel for generations, primarily because of the strong sense of community.

Warm hellos, friendly smiles and hugs, greeted us the moment we arrived at Mama's home. The beautiful sprawling off-white three-story house with a wooden roof had great views of the breathtaking landscape from all sides.

Curious glances were launched at Orane, the latest addition to the family, but he took it all in stride. Some family members and friends were excited and delighted about our relationship, while others were offended and even disappointed that they were not brought in the picture earlier. Nevertheless, in their words, I needed to "settle down" so that kept everyone happy.

Mama was in the living room, elegantly dressed in a royal blue cap sleeve sheath dress and matching sandal, when she met Orane. It was love at first sight. Mama held his hands then put him at arm's length.

"Let me look at you!" she exclaimed then hugged him.

Orane was equally exuberant. "Mrs. Jones, it's a pleasure to meet you, the mother to my beautiful Annalisa."

Joy filled my heart as I watched the exchange between them.

Half an hour later, Orane and I were admiring the beautiful landscape in the backyard, when my four brothers approached us. They looked like giants in the land, a mighty army and instinctively I wanted to protect Orane.

"My brothers," I murmured to Orane.

He chuckled softly, gazing at me. "Don't worry. I can handle this."

I introduced Orane to them and I could literally see them searching Orane's very being in a valiant attempt to protect me. While they were mostly pleasant, I could tell my brothers were wondering about this man who had quietly captured my heart.

"Welcome to the family!" Junior said.

"Thank you!" Orane responded as they shook hands.

Junior was born two years after me but like the rest of the family, he constantly referred to me as baby sister and took pleasure in giving me counsel.

"Welcome to the family my brother," Codel said as he shook Orane's hand. He was the second to last person born in our family.

"Thanks," Orane responded smiling.

Wayne, the youngest member of the family eyeballed me before saying, "It's great to see Annalisa finally settling down. I never knew this day would come." He laughed finding himself funny. "I was just about to ask her to put my name on her bank accounts."

I stifled a screech. *No, he didn't!*

Help!

I glanced around hoping to find Maydine or Harriett. Anyone! Wayne laughed out loudly as I gaped at him.

"I bet you would love that," I said, slapping him over the head. *Where is help when you need it most?*

Wayne hugged me playfully. "Come on baby sister, you know I have to mess with you. Take care of her Orane."

Orane nodded his agreement. He clearly understood the "situation".

"Orane, you are getting a great lady, the cream of the crop," Tahaime, my oldest brother chimed in. "She deserves everything good in life so please take care of her."

Orane hugged my shoulder. "Yes, I will. I couldn't ask for a better woman."

For a moment Tahaime looked sad as if he needed reassurance. "Sis, you will be alright," Tahaime said gently.

"Oh yes. I'll be alright." I gave him a high five.

"Lunch is ready," someone yelled.

The delicious scent of soul food met us as we entered the dining room. Orane and I took our food and sat in the gazebo in the backyard where we could continue to observe the layout of the landscape.

"Good thing I wore my armor today." Orane shuddered playfully.

"I'm sorry Honey." I nudged him. "I didn't realize that I am such a prized possession."

"I understand," he said gently.

"You're my prized possession."

"Thanks Babes. I know you'll protect me from the big bad wolves."

Orane's imitation of little red riding hood had me in stitches. "You are funny!"

"What's funny is me biting your chicken leg while you were laughing."

"No you didn't." I eyed him suspiciously then inspected my fried chicken leg.

"This is good food," he said, chewing his food.

I took a bite of the chicken leg and groaned in delight. "Yes, really good!"

"I see this is how it's going to be," Orane said in a dry voice.

"Yeah. Oooh delicious! I've already gained ten pounds."

"I didn't notice. Show me where you're hiding all that stuff." Mischief was written all over his face.

I winked at him. "I bet you would like to know."

Half an hour later...

"Seriously Babes, that was good. We're going to need seconds."

"Sounds like you're going to need thirds and fourths."

Orane winced. "Unkind. That's a brutal attack on me."

I was unrelenting. "I will still love you, even if you become a fat man."

His eyes widened then saddened as he dropped his head to the side. "Please stop hurting me," he pleaded, going for the Best Actor Academy Award.

"Oh stop." My grin turned to uncontrollable laughter as his eyes drooped like a wounded animal. He reminded me of Puss in Boots, the fictional cat in the Shrek film series. I was laughing so hard, that I doubled over. "I did say I would still love you."

Orane rolled his eyes. "Whatever!"

"Oh Beau, you should have seen your expression. It was price-less!"

"Right!" he retorted dryly.

"What can I do to make up for my bad behavior?"

Orane inhaled then exhaled deeply. "I don't know...if I can forgive you." He had mastered the wounded look. "Maybe you can start the healing process by getting me seconds." His head dropped to the side again. "I don't know." He sighed loudly.

"Look at you! You deserve an academy award."

His low laughter followed me as I left to get seconds.

"Hey cousins, good to see you!" I greeted Suzie and Josephine on my way to the dining area.

"Right back at you girl! I see you are handling business," Josephine said, and they laughed loudly and high-fived each other.

"Oh behave you two! Naughty, naughty," I playfully cautioned them.

"You wild thang!" Suzie hollered and they laughed even more. Chuckling, I waved them away. "Just naughty!"

No one was in the kitchen but I could hear conversation and laughter coming from one of the adjoining rooms. I fixed two plates with small portions of food and placed cling wrap over them. I caught sight of a sweet potato pudding and cut two slices. *Ohhh, this is good.* I savored the taste of a small piece of the pudding. *I need to take a piece...Did someone just say my name?* I paused for a moment to hear the conversation in the adjoining room.

"...yes, Annalisa should be in her thirties, maybe thirty five or so."

"She went to school with me so she's in her thirties," someone remarked.

"Do you think it's her age why she rushing to get married?" another person asked.

My pulse began to race and I propped myself up against the cupboard for support.

"I don't think so," someone responded. "People get married at any age these days."

"I hope she's not pregnant because she's in the church," another voiced chimed in.

I swallowed hard and my entire body stiffened at their insinuations.

"Annalisa pregnant! No way. Clearly, you don't know her." I recognized the voice of Vena, my cousin.

"Yeah right! So what's the rush?"

"Rush. Annalisa is not the type to rush anything," Vena stated calmly. "She must be very sure that Orane is the one."

"The little I know about Miss Annalisa is that she prays about everything," someone remarked.

"They are grown folks. How long does it take to realize that you have found your soul mate?" Vena challenged.

"Since I don't have one, I wouldn't know," someone responded and laughter erupted in the room. "Let me leave Annalisa alone," the same voice continued. "She must know. All I know, if I found Mr. Right, I would waste no time."

"I bet you wouldn't," someone yelled.

Much laughter followed the remark before the conversation shifted to another subject.

Their comments tore at something inside me. I pulled myself to full height as I took up the plates of food. I felt so offended. Blood rushed through my veins and I could feel the pressure building behind my eyes.

Calm down. You're getting angry.

Angry! Annoyed! Whatever!

Who are they to insinuate things about me or question my judgment?

I wanted to go in and tell them a thing or two. For a moment a heated battled raged in my mind, a tug of war between good and evil. That day, I was so glad that I had put on the whole armor of God. Using the word of God, I shut down all the negative external forces. There was nothing to explain. Even if I did explain, I doubted that they would have understood.

I smiled at the foolishness of it all.

Everything in me screamed, begging me to exit the same way I entered the kitchen but curiosity got the better of me. I smiled as I entered the adjoining room. "Hey everybody!"

The babble died immediately and then a chorus of "hellos" greeted me along with a few troubled looks and hypocritical smiles from my distant cousins and few other persons whom I did not recognize.

"Got seconds for us," I informed them.

"Go on girl. Do your thing," someone shouted and the others murmured, "Yes, yes."

"Anna, we need to chat," Vena yelled.

"Give me a buzz," I responded as I headed through the door. "I am staying at Sister Maydine."

"Sure will!" Vena replied.

As I made my way back to the gazebo, I recalled the idiom, *'Eavesdroppers never hear any good of themselves'*. A slight smile made its way onto my face. *Perhaps, who knows!*

Within minutes, I handed Orane his plate.

"Thank you my baby." He tipped my chin up and lightly kissed my lips. "You are a life saver."

I smiled at him. *Life saver! That's a first!*

As we ate, I momentarily reflected on what I had heard. A brief debate started in my mind, a part of me wanted to mention my jaw dropping moment to Orane. But, I decided not to. What purpose would it have served? How would that have added to my life or his? I smiled and encouraged myself in the Lord. Whose report did I believe? I believed the report of the Lord. My spirit soared. *Thank you, Lord. You are watching over me and nothing happens without Your providence.*

Orane gently patted my knees. "Babes, are you okay?"

I smiled and looked him straight in the eye. "You know I am." A gentle smile curled the corners of his mouth as he rested his head on mine.

Hours later, during our goodbyes, Orane asked Mama for my hand in marriage. She gave him her blessings but not before she dropped the "bomb". She had one wish. She pulled us aside and whispered in hushed tones. "Just one wish...no pressure. Please have a child after you are married." The request was so unexpected that Orane and I laughed feverishly. We promised to do what we could to fulfill her wishes.

On our way home, I snickered foolishly as Orane used his hands to form a large circle over my womb.

"Oh stop." I playfully pushed his hands away.

"The baby talk caught you off guard," he whispered. "Your reaction was hysterical. I had to help you lift your jaw off the ground."

"You're talking about my reaction. You should have seen yourself!" I grinned at him. "Your eyes stretched to their limit as if you had seen a ghost."

Orane laughed as I imitated his reaction, then insisted, "I was calm, cool and collected. You looked like a deer caught in the headlights."

"Whatever," I responded, pursing my lips.

"Psst! Come closer mommy!" he teased, poking my side.

I shook my head and pouted, mumbling, "No. No."

"Shhhh!" His voice fell into a whisper and he gently pulled me into his arms. "You will be a hot mama."

"Excellent prediction!" I chucked, nestling closer to him.

CHAPTER 18: PARTING AGAIN

My spirit registered, *"Peace be still"* as I caught sight of Riverdale Pentecostal church from the parking lot. Gospel music filled the air! Orane had picked me up at Maydine's home and I accompanied him to church and was so glad I did. I was feeling a bit sad as my time with him was rapidly coming to an end.

After greeting a few persons in the foyer, Orane and I entered the sanctuary. The sunlight spilling through the glass windows at the front of the church filled the altar with kaleidoscopic brilliance. Seated near the front rows, in full view of this splendor and radiance, I had to acknowledge the awe-inspiring presence of God. "Almighty God, you are great and mighty. You are worthy of all praise, honor and glory," I murmured.

My eyes wandered down the aisles, skimming over the persons already seated in the padded pews and finally rested on Orane. He looked great in a navy double breasted suit. I smiled as I reflected on the omniscience of God. He was at work even on the minute details of my life. God is awesome! He made sure that I became involved in an apostolic ministry knowing that my husband would have a Pentecostal background.

Thank you Lord, for watching over me.

Later that day, I met Samuel, Orane's father and Daphne, his wife, at their home. Samuel was an elderly gentleman of medium height with a slender build, narrow shoulders and a full head of gray hair. His grasp was warm and sincere and his eyes were extremely kind, missing nothing.

"So glad to meet you Annalisa. Welcome to the family!" he said.

"It's a pleasure to meet you sir," I responded with a comforting smile, taking in his easy going countenance.

"Make yourselves at home while I get drinks," Daphne said cheerfully, after hugging me. She then disappeared through a side door.

We sat in the living room and drank fruit punch while we chatted. Orane had a great relationship with Samuel and Daphne. Their love for him was obvious and Orane...he treated them with utmost love, kindness and affection.

I was extremely happy that Orane treated his parents with respect. He would certainly reap the great benefits outlined in Ephesians 6:2-3, *"Honor your father and mother," which is the first commandment with promise: "that it may be well with you and you may live long on the earth."*

Samuel's bold light brown eyes gleamed as he spoke about the Lord. We listened intently as Godly wisdom leaked out of his mouth. It was a breath of fresh air to meet this anointed man of God.

✳ ✳ ✳

Two days later, it was time to say goodbye...Again!

It was dawn when Orane picked me up from Maydine's home. We chatted and laughed along the way covering our true emotions. I was doing well until we were in the vicinity of the airport. Tears gushed down my face and I buried my face in my hands, sobbing uncontrollably.

"This is too hard," I muttered over and over again.

Orane patted my back, whispering words of comfort but I knew he was trying to keep it together.

I wanted to be brave.

I planned to be brave but I just didn't have the strength. I did not want us to part. Parting was just extremely sorrowful. It was hard emotionally, physically and mentally.

Orane pulled into the departure area and took out my suitcase and carry-on. I shook my head and stuck out my lips like a petulant child as he wrapped me in his arms.

"I love you," he said gently, mopping my eyes and fixing strands of my hair that had escaped during our embrace.

Tears continued to roll down my cheeks. "I love you too," I whispered, dabbing my eyes.

"Look at me!" he said softly. "It's not goodbye. I'll see you soon."

"Okay!" I murmured, trying to pull myself together.

"You'll be alright." I could tell Orane was making a valiant effort to remain strong for both of us. "I'll call you," he said reassuringly.

I dabbed my eyes. "Okay!"

He wrapped me in his arms and gently kissed my cheek. "Have a good flight."

My throat caught as I fought back tears. "I will." With that, I took hold of my suitcase and carry-on and walked away ... alone, through the revolving door of the airport. I never turned around, which was for the best. I walked until I knew Orane was no longer visible.

It was so hard!

In a blur, I dragged myself through the terminal and passed through security. By the time I entered the aircraft, life was sucked out of me. Snuggling back in my seat, I closed my eyes and prayed for strength. There was just no easy to say goodbye. *Goodbye...Goodbye seemed so permanent.* The paradox was that without my deep feelings for Orane, parting would not have been this difficult.

Twenty minutes later, I fastened my seat belt then gazed blindly out the window of the aircraft. *Could I handle the separation when we are married?* My eyes welled up with tears and I quickly dabbed them. I zoned in and out of the safety drill instructions from the monitor, combined with demonstration from the air hostesses. With the captain's call, the plane took up position and barreled down the runway and then we were airborne.

Think happy thoughts, I encouraged myself.

Happy thoughts!

My mind raced with expectations of my life with Orane. We were moving towards a more perfect union on a firm foundation, Jesus Christ. A smiled peeked at the corner of my mouth in anticipation of seeing him again. By then, goodbye would have been a distant memory. Soon, I succumbed to exhaustion from several busy days and late nights. I fell asleep.

CHAPTER 19: A SPECIAL BOX

Springtime!

Hope, joy and the promise of new birth!

I love spring, this beautiful, colorful and inspirational time of the year.

Spring brought me the blessings of change. I was on pins and needles in excitement. From all indications, I was about to be officially engaged.

How did I know?

Ah, a woman just knows these things.

Jamaica, here I come again! I nestled comfortably in my seat on the airplane.

Phew!

There was much to do before the trip. So much for my forward planning; I was running around like a chicken without a head. Thankfully, I got everything done including informing my Bishop and First Lady that I would be away for a few days. The man and woman of God were pleasantly surprised about my pending marriage. As expected, they gave me Godly counsel. I listened attentively and attempted to memorize all that they said.

A light touch on my shoulder, forced me back to the present and I looked up into the kind blue eyes of the air hostess. "Would you like something to drink?" she asked smiling.

"No, thank you." I returned her smile.

Time to catch up on my rest! I reclined my seat and fixed my pillow to support my neck. *Perfect time for a nap!* I exhaled softly and closed my eyes. Before I knew it, unconscious giggles slowly began to escape my lips then my face registered a permanent grin as pieces of my conversation with Orane floated through my mind.

Half an hour later, sleep was still nowhere in sight for my exhausted body, pushed even further away by the loud conversations from passengers around me. I stared out the window admiring the silky clouds then decided to flip through a Travelers' Guide magazine that was in the pocket of the seat before me.

My eyes were just beginning to get heavy when my thoughts drifted to Sandy, my office mate. We got along fabulously, right from the start. Sandy, a self-proclaimed fashion guru, gave me coupons and I purchased a few trendy tops and bottoms for my trip.

"Roomie, come back with the ring," Sandy threatened me playfully before I left the office yesterday.

"I shall return, with the ring." I giggled, making the peace sign.

"Bye," she grinned. "Have fun!"

I beamed. "You know I will."

Sandy wagged a finger at me. "Not too much now. Get the ring first!"

I grinned at her. "Okay roomie, will do!"

Sandy was on the spot when Roy struck, the previous day.

Roy! OMG!

That day, I must have looked like a deer caught in the headlights.

I was sitting with my team members in the office when Roy, another co-worker greeted us. He smiled at me then said, "Annalisa, are you getting married? Yesterday afternoon, I saw you and your friend going into Zandee's Bridal shop."

The spotlight was on me.

My insides jolted and a soft gasp escaped my lips. Time stood still as I navigated the corridors of my mind to tackle the situation. You could hear a pin drop as everyone digested his question and waited for the answer.

I looked Roy squarely in the eye. "You saw me, where?"

Oops! Not a good response!

I should have turned the table on him by asking, "What were you doing at the bridal shop?"

I could see everyone making mental notes of our conversation for future reference. This was a no win situation. Roy laughed and insisted that he saw me before moving on to speak with another co-worker.

Later that day, I saw Roy in the parking lot at work and felt an overwhelming desire to wring his neck. He laughed loudly as he approached me.

"Roy Hollington, how could you talk about my business like that?" I scolded him playfully.

After speaking with my Bishop and First Lady, Kay and I visited Zandee's Bridal Shop to look at bridal gowns.

"I knew it was you." Roy laughed heartily. "I'm sorry."

"Yes. It was me. Thanks for outing me like that."

Roy laughed and apologized again for his wicked ways.

As the plane landed, I was jolted out of my thoughts and began making preparation to deplane. The airport was not busy so I cleared immigration and customs with ease.

The warm afternoon air greeted me as I entered the bustling arrival area. Orane and I spotted each other in the distance and walked quickly towards each other.

He smiled at me with open arms. "Babes, welcome home!" His deep-set eyes pierced my soul.

With screams of joy, I threw myself in his arms. "Thanks my love! It's good to be home." My heart raced with love and happiness.

He gazed tenderly at me. "It's great to see you. You look beautiful."

He spun me around a few times to admire my forest green cotton pants suit with a cream colored tank top and sandals.

"Thank you Honey. It's great to see you too. You look wonderful." In fact, he looked quite handsome, dressed in a classic fit black Dockers pants, blue long sleeve shirt and black shoes.

Ann Marie Bryan

Orane eyed me with a slight smile. "These are your cases?"

"Yes and carry-on."

"I see you're not returning," he teased as he placed my luggage in the trunk of his car.

"I'm staying," I responded playfully.

"Yes, you are," he said, tickling my side as he held the car door for me to enter.

I giggled and quickly entered the car. "Thanks Honey."

"Buckle up pumpkin," he said, before closing the door.

I giggled even more.

"All set to go?" Orane asked as we pulled away from the curb.

"Yes Honey." I touched his shoulder. "It's so good to be here."

"Because of the food?"

I winced. "See, that's why you shouldn't let people know your business."

"And here I am, secretly wishing that I'm the reason for your joy."

I eyed him. "Not if you keep behaving badly."

"Pumpkin, I'll be good," he said smiling.

I grinned at him. "Pumpkin?"

"It's the best that I can do right now. I ran out of lyrics."

"You're so funny! And yes, you add a lot of joy to my life."

"I feel the love," he said smiling.

"You should." I giggled, dancing in my seat.

"Look at you!" he teased. "You look great and you are in a great mood."

"Thanks Honey. I am totally happy."

"Did you finish your list of things to do? I know you were running around."

"Yes." I sighed heavily. "Through blood, sweat and tears."

He chuckled loudly. "Thankfully, you survived."

"Is that the sound of sarcasm?"

"No," he insisted but laughter was in his eyes.

"I am going to let that one go."

"Babes, my heart was in the right place," he said, still attempting to convince me.

"I am going to take your word for it."

"Yes, you can." He smiled at me. "How is the preparation going for your Easter production?"

"Great. We are on top of things! Anaya is handling the dance classes for me."

"Your 'adopted baby sister'? Does Mama know that you have added Melissa, Kay, Anaya and countless others to the family?"

"Yes," I grinned. "I have a lot of 'sisters'. I cannot have enough sisters and I have always wanted a younger sister."

"Good for you. I can't wait to see you in action on the stage."

"Ah. I'm okay."

"I bet you're more than okay. You're very talented."

A gentle smiled blossomed on my face. "God has blessed me with a beautiful gift. It's my getaway!"

"Getaway?"

"Yes. When I dance, it consumes me." I smiled as his eyes widened. "In a positive way. I become the vessel to transmit the message that God is sending to His people."

"That's ministry. That's powerful."

"Yes. It's..." The car suddenly wobbled and made a very strange noise. "What's happening?" I asked with some amount of trepidation.

"Sounds like we have a flat tire." Orane slowed down and brought the car to a halt.

Flat tire indeed!

Immediately, I thanked God that the punctured tire was on the side away from the traffic on the busy highway. I began to pray quietly as Orane removed the tire. I made myself handy by helping to remove the screws then watched the traffic as Orane replaced the tire.

Soon, we were on our way again, singing our rendition of the gospel song *"Praise is what I do"* by Shekinah Glory Ministry. We stopped briefly by Orane's home to greet his mother then headed to

Harriett's home. I had decided to stay at Harriett's home instead of Maydine's because of the proximity to Orane's home. Harriett and Everton welcomed us with open arms.

❋ ❋ ❋

The next day, I slept late attempting to recover from jet lag. Orane picked me up for lunch and we spent the rest of the afternoon hanging out in the town. I had arranged for Simon to take professional photos of us in the evening at Maydine's home because of the beautiful flowers and trees surrounding the property. When we arrived, Melissa and Simon were seated on the verandah talking to Mr. Mohan.

"Hello my 'sister'!" I greeted Melissa with a hug. She looked great. Melissa's 5' 8", slightly medium frame was all bright in a yellow sleeveless cotton dress and matching sandals. Her dark brown hair was short and layered with light brown streaks.

"Hellooo. You look like love," she teased.

"Oh stop girl! Simon, great to see you!" I hugged him.

"Melissa, you remember Orane." Orane hugged Melissa as they murmured "Hello, good to see you again."

"And this is Simon, Melissa's husband."

"Great to meet you Simon."

"Likewise!"

Simon and Orane shook hands.

"Mr. Mohan, good evening." I greeted him with a hug.

"How are you doing sir?" Orane asked as he shook Mr. Mohan's hand.

"Good to see you Orane. I'm doing great. Everything going well with you?"

"Yes, very well." Orane chuckled and everyone laughed.

"Annalisa," Simon called for my attention, "I don't mean to rush you but we have to take the pictures before it gets dark."

"Yes. Back in a flash," I responded, pulling Orane into the living room.

"Hello! Anyone home," I shouted.

"I'll be with you in a minute," Maydine called out. My eyes roved around the room trying to locate the direction of her voice.

"Hello you two." Maydine entered from the kitchen. "Awww! My children are here," she smiled and group hugged us.

"How are you Mrs. Mohan?" Orane asked.

"I'm very well Orane. It's great to see you both. Now, don't be a stranger after Anna leaves."

Orane smiled at her. "No Mrs. Mohan, never that."

"Mother dear, I have to change so I'll be in the front room. Please show Orane where he can freshen up."

"Okay Anna! Orane please come with me."

A few minutes later, I left the room in an elegant sleeveless stretch denim sheath dress with a narrow boat neckline and a tiny gold belt at the waist. To complement my outfit, I donned gold evening sandals and accessories. My hair was brushed straight and sleek.

"Orane!" I called out from the living room.

"Yes Babes." He entered the living room from the verandah. "Wow! You look beautiful. Are you...?"

I saw his lips moving but did not hear a word that was coming out. I was distracted by his disarming good looks. He was wearing black pants, a long sleeve aqua shirt and black dress shoes. His wavy black hair seemed even darker as it glistened under the lighting. He looked at me, awaiting a response. I smiled tenderly at him. "You look very handsome. What were you asking?"

"Thank you," he said, taking me by the hand. "Are you ready for our photo shoot?"

"Yes, I am," I said softly as we moved towards the verandah.

Within minutes, I was in a fit of girlish giggles as Simon took the photos. With everyone watching, a bout of shyness overtook me. Orane's soothing words caused me to relax and yielded to my artistic nature so that the model within me emerged.

An hour later, Harriett walked in and greeted us when we were seated at the dining table.

"Look at you, can't stay away!" I teased her mercilessly.

She waved me away. "Glad to be right on time," she declared, as she sat in the vacant chair at the end of the dining table across from Mr. Mohan. Orane and I sat facing Melissa and Simon.

"Is this Maydine's seat?" Harriett asked.

Maydine emerged from the kitchen and smiled at Harriett. "Welcome Sis. You can have that seat." She then pulled up a chair next to Mr. Mohan.

Maydine, always the perfect hostess.

The dinner table was decorated with white dinner plates, gold cutlery and gold trimmed wine glasses. It was Christmas all over again. Mr. Mohan prayed and we started on a splendid meal of baked chicken, stewed curried goat, roast beef, macaroni and cheese, potato salad, baked plantains, steamed rice and peas, tossed salad and carrot juice.

I took a bite of my chicken leg. *Mmmm! Delicious! I'll probably gain ten pounds before I leave Jamaica.* I looked up just in time to see Harriett eyeballing me with pursed lips. I gave her a wide grin and mouthed, "Shhhh!" Her light brown eyes were filled with laughter as she gently shook her head at me.

"How was the drive to get here?" I asked looking towards Simon and Melissa.

"Nice drive out," Simon responded, before sipping his carrot juice.

"It was okay. Good to be out of Kingston," Melissa remarked. "I have not been in this area in a long while."

"Glad you made it safe and sound," Maydine said joyfully. "Wonderful to see you both."

"Thanks Sister Maydine. Great to be here," Simon said smiling.

"Yes!" Melissa murmured, chewing her food.

"Annalisa you look totally smitten," Simon teased. His dark brown eyes were wickedly amused.

I glared at him piercingly to shut him up. "What do you mean?" I asked innocently to everyone's amusement.

Simon chuckled. "You are beside yourself."

"Shush!" I pretended to hit him, sending much laugher around the table.

Maydine and Melissa cleared some of the empty plates from the table and Melissa emerged from the kitchen with a strawberry cheesecake.

"Oooh nice!" I said, licking my lips. "Who baked it?"

Melissa smiled as she sliced the cake. "Simon and I purchased it for dessert."

"Wonderful. Let's have the cake plates!" I said, handing Melissa my cake plate.

"Give me your wine glasses," Mr. Mohan called out as he opened a bottle of Chateau de Fleur non-alcoholic sparkling wine.

"Here's mine!" I handed him my wine glass then Orane's.

"This is yours." I gave Orane a slice of cake.

"Thank you wife," he whispered.

I giggled softly then groaned with pleasure as I tasted the cake. *Oops!* A crumb fell on my blouse.

"Will this stain...?"

I glanced up to find everyone looking at Orane. He was absorbed, looking at a small box in his hand. My heart hammered; the pulsating sound filled my ears.

Isn't that a box?

Yes, it is a box!

That's a ring box!

My teeth rattled and adrenaline surged throughout my body as I tried to get my bearings. I giggled self-consciously and everyone giggled right back.

"Glory!" Harriett cried out, followed by laughter and applause from everyone.

Orane was on his feet, smiling confidently amidst the joyful atmosphere. Simon's camera started rolling as Orane turned to face

139

me. His dark brown eyes pierced mine as he took hold of my hand and encouraged me to stand. My heart fluttered and my stomach must have performed a thousand cartwheels as I stood on wobbly legs by his side.

"Before I propose," Orane drawled smiling, "I know this is not the official wedding ceremony but I would like God to be a part of this occasion and for Him to be in the center of our marriage. I am going to ask the lovely Dr. Selby to pray over this ring."

Murmurs of agreement echoed throughout the dining room.

"To God be the Glory!" Orane concluded. He hugged me and I buried my head in his shoulder as Harriett stood up beaming.

"Let us pray!" Harriett stated boldly.

"Oh God, we give you praise, honor and glory because you are so awesome. Eternal God, we come to you because we know that unless you build the house, we labor in vain.

Lord, we present to you this couple. Father, we know that it is by divine intervention that they were brought together, not by our hands but your hands. Therefore, we thank you Lord for the blessings that you have brought to their lives.

Even as we are gathered here, to witness this special occasion, we know that what you have done in heaven, you have now done here on earth and therefore we call on you right now to bless this ring that will be presented to Annalisa. Lord, let it be a circle of love that keeps Orane and Annalisa together. Let it be a symbol of their love.

Thank you Lord, in the name of Jesus Christ I pray, Amen!"

Loud amens erupted after Harriett's prayer.

"Oh my God!" Melissa shouted, followed by laughter from everyone.

Then, a hush fell in the room.

I blushed as Orane gazed at me as if I was the most beautiful thing he had ever seen. "Annalisa, will you marry me," he asked tenderly.

Celestial songs played in my head and butterflies danced in my heart...the greatest thrill of my life as I choked out a jubilant, "Yes, I will."

Screams of delights, applause and cheers mixed with high praises to God filled the atmosphere as he slipped the beautiful diamond engagement ring on my finger then wrapped me in his arms and kissed me.

Exuberantly, I extended my left hand to the group and their shouts of joy rang out in the dining room. Ohhhs, ahhhs and loud outburst of laughter echoed as they gathered around to inspect my engagement ring.

A few minutes later, we gathered in the living room and Orane and I sat on the sofa and listened to congratulatory speeches and toasts, amidst joyful laughter.

That same night, news of our engagement spread like wild fire among our family members and friends. My ears were hot from taking phone calls about our engagement and upcoming nuptials. Exuberance and laughter filled the air waves as many experienced God's love and faithfulness in our lives.

My heart was still palpitating with excitement as I lay in bed that night. I could hardly sleep. I kept staring at my engagement ring and reliving the moment, that wonderful moment when Orane slipped it on my finger. Unforgettable...in so many ways.

CHAPTER 20: MAKE IT HAPPEN

It's a new season!

Life certainly brings many seasons, some more enjoyable than others. This was my season of unlimited celebrations and all the delightful feelings that accompany them.

Immediately following our engagement, Orane and I began an intense period of wedding planning. But, planning a wedding is not for the faint hearted. I was horrified at the amount of work involved in achieving a seamless wedding ceremony and reception. So, like any well thinking bride, I appointed my perfect team of worker bees—Maydine, Bella, Harriett and Melissa, to be our wedding coordinators.

Orane and I felt deeply convicted that our nuptials should be a celebration for God's faithfulness in our lives. Our theme *"Two hearts celebrating God's faithfulness"* was a symbolic representation of God joining our hearts.

Elegance, beauty and grace would epitomize our wedding.

The selection of our wedding colors was my baby. I selected colors that were timeless and representative of the love that Orane and I shared. Red represented the presence of God, the blood of Jesus Christ, covenant of grace, sin atonement, redemption and love. Gold symbolized the majestic and celebratory tone of our delightful season.

Two days after our engagement, Orane and I sat on Maydine's verandah, deep in wedding planning.

"You did what?" Orane asked, with raised eyebrows.

I gazed at him apologetically. Our vibrant discussion about which of our current pastors would fill the role of marriage officer was not going well. I had just informed him that back in the day,

I had assigned this important task to Reverend Richard Fuller, my former pastor at Laybrook Presbyterian Church.

"I'm sorry Honey," I pleaded, gently touching his hand.

He released a harsh sigh. "I see you took care of that all on your own."

My shoulder drooped and I smiled sheepishly. "I forgot that marriage includes two people."

He ignored my explanation. "I take it Reverend Fuller had a significant impact on your life."

"Yes, great impact. He is a faithful and gifted man of God. Remember that I served as the artistic director of the dance ministry at Laybrook."

Orane exhaled slowly.

I flashed him a disarming smile and held his hand. "I love you."

He shook his head and eyed me. "I love you too but I am not falling for your feminine wiles."

I gazed at him for a moment in silence before quietly saying, "Do you remember, the topic of your Pastor's message this morning? He spoke about...love. Love 'bears all things, believes all things, hopes all things, endures all things'."

Orane chuckled at my attempt to sway him. Nevertheless, after a few more of my "feminine wiles", he conceded. Immediately, I contacted Reverend Fuller who was delighted to serve as our marriage officer. He informed me that he had already received the news of our engagement.

"Thanks Honey." I smiled at Orane after hanging up from my call with Reverend Fuller.

His mouth curled into a smile. "As if, I would say no."

I grinned at him. "You put up a good fight though. We are to see Reverend Fuller as soon as possible."

"Okay!"

"Can you think of anything that we left out of the plan?" I asked, stifling a yawn.

143

Orane drummed his finger on the arm of his chair. "You need to get in bed."

"We still have a lot of planning to do," I protested, resting the laptop on the small table before us.

"Your eyes are looking tired," he insisted, scowling as I yawned again.

"Oh stop." I lightly slapped his hand then quickly moved away from him. He chased me around the verandah and caught up with me. "Help!" I screamed with delight as he wrapped his arms around my stomach and pulled my feet off the ground. I screamed even more as he twirled me around. "Put me down!" I yelled.

"Do you promise to get in bed?" he asked, still twirling me.

"I promise," I said breathlessly. "Put me down."

"Good girl," he chuckled as he set me back on the ground.

I sighed heavily, putting a hand on my heart as I rested my head against his strong shoulder. He gently kissed my forehead.

"I love you Annalisa." His voice was filled with raw emotion.

I swallowed hard, reining in strong feelings as I caressed his face. "I know you do. I love you too."

"Off to bed now," he said tenderly.

"Okay Honey."

He smiled triumphantly. "I will find my way out."

With that, he left and shortly thereafter, I hopped into bed.

❋ ❋ ❋

Early the next morning, the search was on for a suitable venue for our wedding reception. While Orane attended to business in Kingston, Maydine, Harriett and I checked out possible venues. We all agreed that Genova All Suite Hotel, a popular wedding site, was the perfect setting for an unforgettable celebration. Located in the heart of Kingston, Genova All Suite Hotel had colonial architect surrounded by beautiful lush gardens, absolutely suitable for a momentous occasion.

Orane joined us at the selected venue for a meeting with the Banqueting and Catering Manager who gave us relevant information to make plans for our reception. The option to have our reception at the poolside was tempting but the possibility of rain made us opt for an indoor location, the Grand Persian Hall.

After lunch, Orane left for another business engagement and we joined Melissa at Pedora Bridal Shop where I tried on a lovely white sweetheart neckline, fitted bodice Organza gown. Amidst squeals of delight from my entourage, I gazed at my reflection in the huge wall mirror and announced, "Not the vision I have in mind."

"I have just the gown for your special day," declared Peggy, the jovial store manager.

"Where is it?" we asked in unison.

"There, it's the latest rage." Peggy pointed to a display case with a white V neck Taffeta gown with a layered tulle skirt. We dashed over to it for a closer inspection.

"No thanks! It's not what I envisioned," I politely declined her suggestion.

"It's gor...ge...ous!" Peggy exclaimed. "You should try it."

"Okay. I guess so. Mel, please help me with the dress."

"We'll sit out here," Harriett said as Melissa and I entered that changing room.

Suddenly, I felt agitated. "Mel, I changed my mind. It's a waste of time to fit it."

"Okay!" Melissa gently removed the gown from my hand.

"I cannot see myself going down the aisle in it," I murmured.

"Let me take it out," she said calmly.

We thanked the not too happy Peggy for her assistance and quickly left the bridal shop for our appointment with Kris Martin, a renowned wedding photographer.

The vehicle was noticeably quiet as we made our way home. Mental and physical fatigue had set in from our hectic schedule. Notwithstanding, I declared it—*Mission accomplished*! Our wedding plans were well on the way.

CHAPTER 21: HEART TO HEART

"Babes," Orane called out gently.

I was absorbed in recording the names of the persons on our bridal party. It was midday and we were on our way to Kingston for pre-marital counseling.

"Yes Honey."

His face was taut. "I'm curious. Has anyone asked you why we are getting married, so quickly?"

I leaned my head to the side, searching his expression as I recalled the incident at my mother's home. "Look at you! You have a question." I touched his arm playfully.

He took his eyes off the road and glanced at me earnestly. "Babes...I'm serious, your sisters?"

"No, no one asked. But, why would they?"

He exhaled. "Just wanted to know."

I grinned. "You do know, I'm a grown woman, right!"

He chuckled softly. "That I know. Just making sure you're ready for the ride of your lifetime."

"I'm ready husband-to-be!" I smiled, gently touching his shoulder.

In Reverend Fuller's study, we settled the dates and times for our counseling sessions then explored our spiritual beliefs, family backgrounds and expectations of marriage. Before he wrapped up the session, Reverend Fuller expressed his concerns about our living arrangements after our wedding day. It was a pleasant experience to hear us articulate our feelings publicly and obtain feedback and Godly counsel.

"It was great to see Reverend Fuller again," I remarked as Orane pulled away.

"I could see that," he responded smiling. "You have a great relationship with him."

"Yes. I have known him forever," I said thoughtfully. "You were very honest in the session."

"I was," he stated candidly. "There is no point in holding back if you want an honest feedback."

"So true!" I exhaled looking ahead. "Where are we going?"

Orane took his eyes off the road for a second to smile at me. "We are going on a date."

"Oooh, that's nice." I was tempted to ask where but I decided that a surprise would be more to my liking.

Nearly an hour later, I was happily surprised when Orane parked on a street in Port Royal, a historic town located in southeastern Jamaica.

"Honey, thank you." I grinned at him. "I have not been here in ages."

He smiled at me. "I knew you would like it, Miss Archeologist."

"You remembered that I wanted to be an archeologist." I smiled at him proudly. "Ohhh, I get to visit the Giddy House again. I remember going there as a child."

"Look at you! You've come alive." He chuckled softly as we strolled, hand in hand down the main street. "What's the Giddy House?"

I peered at him through the rays of the warm afternoon sun, my right hand shading my eyes. "All I know is that it is a lopsided, half sunken, red brick building. I remember feeling as if I would topple over when I stood in it."

"That's the idea of the Giddy House," he said. "It was an artillery store house that was tilted by an earthquake in the 1900's."

I gently squeezed his hand. "So history buff, what else do you know about Port Royal?"

"A lot," he replied confidently, slipping one arm around my shoulder.

"It was partly buried in the sea by an earthquake in 1692 and hit by other natural disasters including another earthquake in…"

"You forgot?" With my hands on my hip, I stopped on the side walk to eyeball him quizzically.

He crossed his arms in front of his chest and I could see his brain working. "It was in the 1900s," he remarked.

"Yes. 1907."

"I was going to say that," he chuckled.

With its prominent landmarks, monuments and structures, Port Royal was being restored to operate as a major tourist attraction. We toured the city and had fun taking pictures at the Giddy House and Fort Charles, one of six forts that guarded the town, centuries ago.

Later that day, we ate dinner in a private booth at the unique Kenstowana Hotel in a relaxing ambience overlooking the Kingston Harbour.

"Annalisa," Orane looked at me poignantly during our meal, "sometimes, I wonder if I gave you enough time to consider my proposal."

With a spoon of my pistachio ice cream in hand, I looked directly in his eyes. "Are you having second thoughts?"

"No! I want to marry you. Right now, if I had my way. You know that."

I swallowed the ice cream then held his hand. "We placed everything on the table from the beginning of our friendship when our hearts were not yet committed…unless there is something else."

He looked thoughtful. "Just making sure, that you are sure."

"I'm good. I have prayed and fasted about marrying you. I know the Lord is leading me in this direction."

"Me too," he said quietly.

I eyeballed him, knitting my eyebrows. "I am still sensing hesitation."

"Our session with Reverend Fuller made me wonder if I am doing you an injustice by marrying you when we both live in different countries."

I exhaled. "It will be hard on both of us...very hard but not impossible. I think we can make it work."

He smiled tenderly, thankful for my response. "Our love, devotion and commitment to each other will be tested but we will make it work under the direction and guidance of the Holy Spirit."

I nodded. "We will make it work. Let's continue to keep in touch daily. We should not give each other any reason to...we must absolutely trust each other."

Orane wiped his mouth with his napkin. "Yes. Definitely! Do you promise to be brutally honest with me?" He laughed softly. "Not that you need any encouragement."

"Oh yes, brutally honest." I grinned at him. "Our prayer times will be even more important."

He nodded vigorously. "There will be financial sacrifices but because of my occupation, I will visit more often."

"Thanks Honey, that's very thoughtful of you. We will prepare a schedule for our visits."

He took bite of his chocolate cake before saying, "It will take some time for my visa to be processed and that will give me enough time to wrap up my business ventures here."

"Have you thought about living in the United States?"

"No. Like I told you before, I never thought of living anywhere except Jamaica. I am going to leave that to the Holy Spirit."

A soft sighed escaped my lips.

"No. It's not a bad thing," he said reassuringly. "I trust the Lord."

"Thanks Honey. You know, I'll be praying."

"We will be praying," he corrected me.

"Yes," I nodded in agreement.

"Our times together will be precious," he said. "So, when we are together..." I blushed as he paused and gazed into my eyes. "We must to take advantage of those special times."

I felt my cheeks burning so I looked away. "Yes," I murmured coyly.

My whole world flipped as I felt his fingertips softly stroking my cheek, infusing my mind with thoughts that could not be expressed. I sensed that he could see what was going on within me, deep within me.

He held my hand then kissed it. "I love you," he said passionately. "I have never come across anyone like you in my entire life. Our relationship is a special gift from God and I will cherish it forever."

I smiled tenderly at him and agreed. "Forever."

"Amen," he declared.

❋ ❋ ❋

At dawn two days later, Orane and I travelled to the airport in silence. Parting again! He reached over and held my hand as I wept. "Babes, don't cry. It's going to be alright. Please don't cry."

I sobbed even louder.

He was on autopilot, trying to hold it together. Soon, he too was teary eyed. I stared through the window into the darkness knowing that many more days like this were ahead.

"Babes, it's going to be alright," he consoled me as we pulled up to the departure area.

"I'm sorry, I don't mean to," I said, clutching his hand and putting my head on his shoulder.

He kissed me on my forehead and wrapped me in his arms.

I exhaled loudly.

"Look at me," he said holding my shoulders. "This is not goodbye. It's see you later." He made a funny face and soft giggles escaped me. "There's my baby. Let's move before they tow us."

Orane took out my suitcases and carry-on from the trunk and we hugged.

"I'm not going," I whispered.

He kissed my cheek tenderly. "I love you. See you soon."

"I love you too. See you soon."

With that, I disengaged from our embrace and moved quickly towards the revolving door, resisting the urge to look back. Walking away from him was one of the hardest things I had ever experienced. I gritted my teeth to hold back the tears as I checked in.

A few minutes later, I boarded the aircraft with everything in me screaming, *No! I do not want to do this.* A strangled sob escaped me as the aircraft taxied down the runway and I gazed blindly out the window trying to hide my tears. A light touch on my hand disrupted my despair. "Are you okay?" I glanced to my right, into the concerned eyes of the passenger sitting next to me. I nodded avoiding her eyes.

"It's going to be alright," she said reassuringly. "It's going to be alright."

Later during the flight, she introduced herself as Sherry and our conversation flowed naturally even though at the beginning, I was somewhat reserved. However, as our conversation progressed, I felt comfortable enough to tell her about my engagement. A bright smile lit her face as she clapped her hands and exclaimed, "Congratulations!"

"Thank you!" I responded with a half-smile.

Sherry eyed me. "Now I understand your tears."

She informed me that her husband resided in Jamaica but she worked in Miami. Our common situation laid the foundation for the rest of our conversation. "It will get easier," Sherry said knowingly.

I thanked God for providing Sherry, a comforting angel at a time when I needed one most.

CHAPTER 22: SHOPPING TIME

"Come on Annalisa, let's see the hand."

I could not recall who made that statement as I entered my office but my cover was blown. Soon, my co-workers heard the news of my engagement. Some offered assistance with planning while others offered tips on married life. Sandy was particularly elated to see that her labor was not in vain. "Way to go Annalisa." She grinned at me. "You're back with the ring. High Five!"

Lyn, a wonderful friend and co-worker, emailed me a link to access a free wedding planner. This detailed planner turned out to be just what I needed. Lyn and I started taking walks during lunch, just to keep me fit and trim for all my upcoming wifely duties and activities.

Enough said!

Support came from many quarters as news of our upcoming nuptials spread. Our wedding coordinators worked tirelessly to ensure that our vision became a reality. We could not have asked for a better team, they exuded much care in the process. Emails flew back and forth with suggestions and new ideas.

Melissa had waited patiently for this day to come and I could not have asked for a better maid of honor. Night after night, she and I ironed out the fine details of the wedding plan.

Melissa emailed me during this period:

My sister, my friend,
How great is our God, sing with me! How great is our God, Hallelujah! How great, how great is our God!

I love you so much. I admire and appreciate you. I am overjoyed for you and God's obvious pleasure over you, His precious, faithful daughter. Ah indeed, great is His faithfulness.

It was a great and special day when God brought us together...and kept us together. Thank you Lord, for your grace and goodness to us.

I responded:

Right back at you! God makes no mistakes. As I look over my life, God has truly blessed me with the gift of friends who are more like sisters. I am truly honored that you are my sister, my friend and my maid of honor. I could not have asked God for a more perfect friendship.

Even Orane noticed that we have a special friendship. It is not only you but your entire household and extended family. You have all been a blessing to me. God is faithful and I am humbled by the love and support that Orane and I are receiving as we get married. We have brought joy to a lot of people, including our families. We seek to use our marriage as a testimony of God's faithfulness.

Thank you my sister! You have been a great example to me in your walk with the Lord and your married life. I love you with all my heart and will always be there for you and your family. Thanks for touching my life with good things from day one and forever. Have a wonderful day!

My sisters pulled out all the stops so that their baby sister could have it all.

All of it!

Nothing was off limit as they shared their love, time, talents and money.

Orane joyfully embraced his role to attire the groomsmen. I solicited the help of the bridesmaids with the selection of their gowns. However, since none of the bridesmaids lived in Tallahassee, Anaya and I spent countless hours at different bridal stores in search of the perfect gown. Anaya fitted several gowns and I took pictures with my cell phone and emailed them to our bridesmaids. After numerous fittings and several emails, we all agreed to purchase the gorgeous apple red gowns from Zandee Bridal Shop.

"How's your gown shopping going?" Maydine asked, during our telephone conversation.

"More like not going," I grimaced, reclining in the sofa at home.

"I thought you had worked through your issues."

I sighed deeply. "Still working."

This may sound a little bit strange but it's the truth.

Shopping for my bridal gown was not the ultimate experience that I envisioned.

I was astonished by my own reaction.

But...I am still learning about me.

I visited a few bridal shops with friends to look at bridal gowns and I was scared stiff. Yes! Scared stiff! The task was extremely daunting. Half of the store looked like a 'sea of whiteness" so I literally fled from the bridal section. I calmed my nerves by looking at potential bridesmaids' dresses and accessories.

Phew! An overwhelming sense of relief would hit me after leaving the bridal shops.

I contemplated browsing the internet to view gowns but fitting would be an issue. So, I did what any well thinking Christian woman would do. I took the situation to God Almighty who knows me best. I asked the Lord to show me the right wedding gown.

As I anticipated, God did not disappoint. Harriett visited for a few days and I made another visit to Zandee Bridal Shop. *Without warning, my inner warrior arose.*

"I am interested in looking at bridal gowns," I said to the store clerk.

"Great! This way please. I will get you a wedding consultant."

"Thank you!"

A few minutes later, the store clerk returned with a smiling lady who introduced herself as Sally Henderson." Sally took us to her desk and I completed a form which captured information about our wedding.

"We have a process to select your gown," Sally said enthusiastically. "Please look through this catalog and identify the gowns you would like to fit."

"Thanks! I will," I responded.

"I'll be back shortly to answer any questions that you may have," Sally said as she handed me a post-it pad.

"Thank you." *This was even better than I thought.* Suddenly, the selection of my wedding gown was not so overwhelming. I should have asked for assistance on my first visit but I was too busy running scared.

Harriett looked over my shoulder as I marked my few choices. My spirit quickened as I laid eyes on a white satin A-line gown. This was the vision that I had in mind.

I fitted my other selections before fitting that particular gown. *What do you know?* The gown fitted like a glove, no adjustment needed.

"Wow! You look gorgeous!" Harriett clapped her hands enthusiastically as I exited the changing room. "It's perfect."

"Thank you!" I was dizzy with excitement as I glanced at myself in the full length mirror. *Stunning!*

And just like that, I found my wedding gown.

As I slipped out of the gown, my eyes caught sight of its size.

"Sally, what is the meaning of this?" I asked playfully. "I usually wear a size six or at most a size eight."

"Not to worry, the size of your bridal gown would be one size up from your regular dress size." I looked deep into Sally's eyes to see if she was pulling a fast one on me. She grinned. "I'm not kidding. It's the truth."

I smiled at her. "Okay. I'll take your word for it."

It turned out that Sally was right.

CHAPTER 23: GOOD NEWS

Orane arrived in Tallahassee in late spring. With our big day set for summer and tons of preparations still going on, we took on the task of compiling our guest list. Reality kicked in quickly! Our budgetary constraints gave us much needed perspective, so we settled our guest list at immediate family members and close friends.

Two days after Orane arrived, we took on the task of purchasing a wedding band for him. Eventually, after making trips to several jewelry stores, we found bands that suited our budget and taste. Orane wanted a plain band but I convinced him that a unique band with three perfect diamonds was a better bang for the buck.

The search to purchase a tuxedo for him became a little troublesome and time consuming. While tuxedos were available, the tuxedo we wanted had to be ordered in advance and Orane would no longer be in Tallahassee, to fit it. In the end, we decided to rent.

"We are making progress," Orane remarked as he browsed our wedding plan. We were seated on the sofa at my home, still knee deep in wedding planning. I placed the copy of Modern Bride that I was reading on the stack of bridal magazines on the coffee table.

"Great progress. Everyone has been so supportive."

"Yes," he agreed. "Did you receive the invitations?" he asked.

"Yes. I told you. You forgot." I had purchased beautiful pearl colored wedding invitations written in brilliant gold ink and assigned Maydine the duties of calligrapher and Aunt Joy as her assistant.

Orane gave me his full attention. "I believe you did...mention it."

"Hmm!" I chuckled. "You're at the age when you need to start keeping notes, not mental ones." He threw a cushion at me and I squealed, "Help! I'm being abused."

"Naughty woman!" he chuckled, tickling my side.

"Behave!" I giggled, escaping his fingers.

"What's next?" he asked.

"I'm about to email the members of our wedding party so that they are clear about their roles. You can finalize the list of your family members and friends."

"I noticed how conscientious you are about planning."

"I am." I eyed him. "And I'm about to be super conscientious about this, because on that day, I'll have eyes only for you."

Orane chuckled. "Only on that day!"

I knitted my eyebrows cutting into his hilarity. "You better pray not."

He winced. "We wouldn't want that now."

My face dissolved in a smile and he laughed softly, shaking his head before gently patting my knee.

"I am marrying a Godly woman."

I pouted innocently. "I will always have eyes for you."

He picked up my hand and toyed with my fingers. "Mmmm. I like the sound of that."

We gazed at each other smiling and in a flash, we found ourselves leaning in until our noses were almost touching. My heart hammered and my lips parted eagerly in anticipation. *Phew!* The intensity was broken by the ringing of the phone. Orane exhaled slowly as we eyeballed each other.

"There is time," he said softly, brushing his hand across my cheek.

"I...I'm going to get that," I mumbled, still shaken from the adrenalin rush.

An angel to save the day!

I took the cordless phone from its cradle on the counter, absentmindedly playing with my hair.

"Hello!"

"Hey Annalisa, sorry to disturb you guys but I have good news."

"Arianna, how is it going? I could do with good news," I responded, moving back to the sofa.

"Great! The honeymoon spot you guys wanted has worked out. I will…"

"Thank you Lord! Thanks Ari! Wait a minute Ari." I grabbed Orane's hand and my eyes bulged with excitement as I animatedly told him the good news.

"That's wonderful!" he said enthusiastically.

The selection of the honeymoon spot was Orane's baby. At first, it was top secret then he ran the location by me. He was bent on traveling to Europe but I persuaded him to let us spend our honeymoon in Jamaica. So, we narrowed our choices to three 5-star luxury hotels on the western side of Jamaica. Enter Arianna with hotel connections plus the desire to make a significant contribution to our wedding.

"Ari, thanks so much!" I beamed.

"You're welcome. Call the hotel and ask for Matthez Zichy. Give him your exact dates."

"I sure will. Thank you!"

"No problem. I will send you a check as we discussed. The outstanding amount won't be much for you guys to cover."

"Thanks. You're a blessing!"

"Anytime! I'll see you soon."

"Bye and thanks again."

I set the phone back on its cradle.

Wonderful! Just wonderful!

"God is good!" Orane said when I rejoined him on the sofa.

I nodded vigorously. "Yes, He is!"

"Annalisa!" Orane's voice was calm and soothing, but there was an edge in it.

"Yes," I responded, wondering what could possibly be wrong.

His face was somber. "Change is coming," he declared in a deep dramatic voice.

I could not help but laugh. "You are funny."

"Admit it, I had you fooled," he said, tickling my side.

"Stop," I giggled, begging for mercy.

Orane smiled as he leaned back on the sofa.

I nudged him. "Are you ready for the change?"

"Like never before," he said joyfully.

"Marriage will be quite a change!" I remarked.

"Yep! I hope you don't want your toothpaste squeezed in a particular way."

"Of course!" I poked his side. "But, I plan to choose my battles."

"That's your strategy going in? I have none."

"Yes you do." I grinned at him. "Live one day at a time."

He chuckled softly. "Yes, that's it. And place everything at the foot of the cross."

"Is that a hint for me?" I questioned with raised eyebrows.

"No. Noooo," he replied, chuckling softly.

"I know it will be a great change for us but we will give ourselves time to adjust. I'm ready."

He gazed at me, just the way my heart wanted him to, and replied, "So am I."

CHAPTER 24: SHOWERS OF JOY

Orane was still in Tallahassee when my coworkers rocked my world by throwing a lingerie shower in my honor. Sandy was 'head cook and bottle washer' (*Jamaican phrase meaning person in charge*). She sent Evite invitations to the ladies at work and coordinated all the activities surrounding the shower.

I arrived at Bellaire Restaurant and Lounge on that scheduled Saturday afternoon to find several smiling faces gathered around a long rectangular table. The ambience was perfect. We laughed at anything and everything in a relaxed and pleasant environment.

The fun was amplified when we went on a picture taking frenzy. Anaya took on the all-important role of photographer. A few minutes later, I leaned back in my chair feeling the absolutely divine effects from eating grilled chicken breast, baked potato and steamed vegetables. I sighed and closed my eyes. *Ohhh! They may need to call Orane to roll me out of here.*

"Come Annalisa, it's time to open your gifts." Sandy motioned me to a round table stacked with gift bags.

"I am afraid. Is it safe?" I laughed, moving to the table.

"Be very afraid!" Sandy teased.

She read the name of each giver then handed me the gift while Kay took notes. Screams of joy erupted from my lips as I read each card and opened the gift. I received couple's games, gifts cards and unique appealing lingerie of all types, colors, shapes and descriptions.

Then it happened!

Sharp intakes of breath and gasping sounds filled the air.

I felt hot and bothered just by looking at them—a black lace spaghetti strap body suit and edible underwear. I made a loud gasping sound, creating hysterical laughter in the room. Some of the ladies laughed so hard that they clutched their chests while others collapsed in their chairs.

Then, we were hit again with another shock and awe moment!

Spontaneous outbursts of "Noooooo" and groans came from the group as I displayed a home wrecker—a ghastly multicolored floral flannel housedress.

"Check the pockets," Renita called out amidst the laughter.

"Pheeeew," I exhaled. Thankfully, a pink sheer bikini along with the matching bra was hidden in one of the pockets. Chuckles broke out as I gazed in amazement at them. The pieces were so tiny that I deliberated where to tie them on my body.

"Where am I going to put these?" I asked, totally bewildered, bringing much laughter to the group.

"Anna, this is what you do." Renita stood up and explained dramatically. "After an argument with Orane, slip this housedress over the lingerie. Then say, "Goodnight Orane" and let the housedress fall to the ground."

Girlish giggles welled up in me and raucous laughter erupted all over the room.

After all the gifts were opened, I cut a beautiful cake labeled *"Congratulations Annalisa"* and then I insisted that I served the cake to the lovely ladies. While we ate, I listened to their advice on relationship and marriage.

- *Be happy*
- *Don't start anything in the relationship that you do not plan to continue*
- *Do not go to bed angry*
- *Never say no to sex*
- *Buy a chandelier*
- *Don't keep the same routine*
- *Be flexible*
- *Keep it spicy*

"Thank you ladies!" I beamed. "I appreciate all that you have done and all your gifts. I am eternally grateful to you and I feel highly favored. God bless you all."

I was surprised by the thought that went into each gift. The ladies did not only give me an enjoyable bridal shower and much needed gifts but memories that I will cherish forever.

Half an hour later, I arrived home. Orane was nowhere in sight. "Orane, where are you?" I called out.

"I'm coming." He ran down the stairs. "Mrs. Conway, you're back?"

"Yes I am, Mr. Conway," I grinned at him. "I need help. The trunk is full."

"Not a problem. Is it open?"

"Yes! But don't look at my goodies."

"Why not?" Mischief was written all over his face. "My bad!" He chuckled at my expression then disappeared into the garage.

I held the door as he entered with a stack of my gifts. "Honey, please put them on the washing machine," I requested, opening the door of washing area, near the stairs.

In a few trips, all my gifts were packed away. "Thanks love." I patted his back as he closed the door leading to the wash room.

"Come on, give me a hug," he said, pulling me in his arms. "Mmm! This feels so good."

"Yes it does."

His head angled as he leaned in for a kiss. I pointed to my cheek and he began to trail soft kisses towards my lips.

"Naughty, naughty!" I scolded him playfully.

"No. Want more," he murmured, reaching for me as I pulled away.

"Look at you!" I teased. "You're biting off more than you can chew."

"Not nice, after all the work I did."

"You will be duly compensated."

"Yes!" he jumped in the air. "I am counting. There were a few times…"

"Yes love." I winked at him. "We have a life time to take care of all of that."

"Oh come on!" he teased with open arms.

"Tempting but no!"

"Fine! I'm going upstairs. You'll be begging me to come down," he said proudly, marching up the stairs.

"You know I will Honey. You know I will," I said, grinning at his back.

✴ ✴ ✴

Two days later, Orane and I drove to the airport in the early morning light, sometimes talking and at other times silent, just enjoying each other. We knew that our times together would always be precious.

"I will call you later," he said, reassuringly as we stood on the curb in the departure area.

"Okay Honey." I managed a half smile. We had devised a departure strategy; albeit, not an exciting one—I would leave him in the departure area and keep going.

"Come here my baby," he said smiling and I walked into his open arms. "I love you."

"I love you too," I purred softly, almost giddy from his light kisses on my forehead. Reluctantly, I pulled away but not before reaching forward and brushing my lips lightly against his. "Bye. Have a good flight."

"Bye Babes, see you soon," he said, gazing tenderly at me.

I smiled at him. "See you soon!"

He exhaled loudly. It was the smile he wanted to see.

With that, I mustered up all my courage and jumped in my car. My heart clenched and my throat closed as I drove away. Tears flowed and I just allowed them to...until my tear ducts were dry.

✴ ✴ ✴

Ann Marie Bryan

Equally excited about our upcoming nuptials, the ladies at my church hosted a second bridal shower for me. I arrived at the church hall on a cool Sunday afternoon to find a large rectangular table laden with all kinds of goodies and a beautiful cake labeled *"Congratulations, Annalisa & Orane"*.

It was fun to be surrounded by great women of God, playing games, laughing and eating. Anaya took on the role of moderator and once again, Kay took notes as I opened each amazing gift. Orane and I scored some pretty sweet loot. Our kitchen and bathrooms were perfectly outfitted because of the generosity of these ladies.

Later, Kay recorded as I listened to their advice.

- *Leave and cleave*
- *Establish home rules first using God's word*
- *Marriage is a journey. Put God first always and trust him*
- *Always remember the three Cs—Communicate, Compromise and Cuddle*
- *In all you do, seek the Lord first so that He can direct your path*
- *Enjoy each other, love each other and spend time with each other*
- *As you get closer to God, you will get closer to each other*
- *Keep God in the center of your relationship*
- *Stay away from divorce court*
- *Read Psalm 71*
- *Pray together every day and love God more than each other*
- *Make each other the focus and never say no...*
- *Do not tell all your girlfriends about your marital problems*
- *Keep your own individuality*
- *Love one another and be good to each other*
- *Talk about finances*
- *Pick your battles*
- *Cleanliness is next to Godliness*
- *Rest*
- *Love never hurts especially after the honeymoon*
- *Set the rules from day one, for example prayer times*
- *Protect your husband*
- *Practice patience*

- *Communicate*
- *Support your husband in his calling*
- *Never have a comfort zone*
- *Watch your tongue*
- *Pray, have faith and love*

Later that evening, I was floating on air from an absolutely delightful time spent with the wonderful spirit-filled ladies. Orane and I were certainly blessed by their extraordinary love and tremendous support.

CHAPTER 25: JUST NERVES

I am getting married!

It suddenly hit me like a sack of cold potatoes on my last day at work before leaving for my wedding. I sat at my desk way past my departure time. My nerves were shot and I felt terrified. Eventually, I pulled myself away and begged my co-workers not to say goodbye or any mushy stuff.

I walked to my car feeling a sense of loss as if I was leaving everything behind. During my mental anguish, I wrestled with returning to the office because I had not said bye to Sandy. She had not returned from an early morning meeting. As I contemplated calling her cell phone, I saw Renita walking towards me.

"Hey Anna!"

"Renita!" I greeted her with a half-smile.

She looked at me excitedly. "Leaving for your big day? Let me accompany you to your car."

"Thanks," I responded half-heartedly.

"Why are you looking like that?"

"I don't know. I just feel so…emotional."

"It can't be Orane because I know you love him. Are you sad because you are leaving us?"

"I don't know. I…" Tears welled up in my eyes as we entered my car. I did not utter a word as I drove Renita back to the office.

She gently patted my shoulder. "Don't worry! You'll be alright. Think happy thoughts."

I stopped the car and gave her a slight smile. "I didn't say goodbye to Sandy."

"She knows you're leaving but you can call her."

I called Sandy but I could barely speak, tears began to flow.

"Anna, where are you?" Sandy asked.

"I am outside the office."

"Wait, I'm coming."

In a matter of minutes, Sandy was standing at my car door. Her light brown eyes were filled with concern as she gently rubbed my shoulder. "Why are you crying?"

I dabbed my eyes then looked at her. "I don't know.'

"It just nerves, don't worry. You'll be alright. You will have an amazing time," Sandy said comfortingly.

I gave her a slight smile. "Yes, I will. I wanted to say goodbye."

"Have a safe trip." Sandy smiled at me then proceeded to dance around. "It's time for fun! Have a blast!"

A soft giggle escaped me. "I will try." I exited the car and gave her a hug. "Thanks. I am going to make it."

"Yes, you will," she said reassuringly.

"Have fun Anna." Renita hugged me.

"I will," I said, climbing back into the driver's seat. I managed a half smile. "Thank you, ladies. Bye!"

"Bye!" they responded cheerfully.

I drove off with the memories of their smiling faces.

Just Nerves!

I smiled widely. *Indeed, just nerves!*

A sense of relief hit me as I thought of my loving supportive family, friends and coworkers. I knew that prayers were going up. I recalled my email to our bridal party, family members and friends, nearly two weeks ago.

My Prayer Warrior Family Members & Friends!

Happy Monday! Hope all is well with you and your families.

I need your assistance with respect to fasting and praying for our (Orane & I) wedding and marriage. I know many of you have been praying and fasting but I would like to dedicate this week (Sunday—Saturday) to prayer and fasting. In particular, this Wednesday is a day of fasting. Let's send our praises up to heaven so that what is established in heaven will be done on earth in our marriage.

Thank You! Have a blessed week!

Later at home, I took a break from packing and stretched out on my bed. A smile broke out on my face as I thought of my delightful season; a beautiful time, perhaps the most beautiful season I had been through. Granted, I had been through many wonderful seasons but this season was far different from anything I had experienced. God was awesome, showing up in every little detail of our wedding plans.

Everything was lined up to perfection.

A strange phenomenon?

No. I call it miraculous.

And speaking of the miraculous, I must confess that at this point, being single seemed but a distant memory. How could it be? Did God design it this way? I was single and happy. Yet, getting married added a new dimension to my happiness. I was happy, undeniably happy.

I surprised myself with the mature approach I took towards my relationship with Orane. Evidently, the days of waiting for my husband taught me valuable lessons. I was so glad that I waited. The time was right and I was ready for the newness. All my dreams and desires were about to be fulfilled on a whole new level.

Secretly in my heart, I was looking forward to the novelty of being a wife. *Wife!* That would definitely be a new title. *What kind of wife would I be?* I had set my mind to be a great wife. I had asked for God's help in this regard. I had to. This was all new territory and I preferred to cover all my bases. I planned to enter my marriage fully equipped. I had set my mind to stay committed and in love with my husband.

So, full steam ahead!

CHAPTER 26: LET IT RAIN

I woke in a daze, to the heat of the morning and sounds outside my bedroom window. May melted into June producing a stream of hot days and warm nights. It was summertime! Jamaica's climate was hot, very hot and humid. I peeked through my bedroom window and saw Maydine raking leaves and Mr. Mohan feeding the dogs in the distance.

"Good morning, Sister Maydine," I called out.

Maydine looked startled then a bright smile appeared on her face. "Anna, good morning! Sorry to disturb your beauty rest."

My nose tickled. "Not a problem. Ah…achoo!"

"Bless you, Mrs. Conway!" Maydine smiled at me.

I grinned at her coyly. "Thank you mother. I'll be out shortly."

Reaching for the bible on the bedside table, I meditated on Psalm 23 and prayed. Twenty minutes later, I kicked off the sheets, hit the shower and dressed in a pair of red cotton capris and white tank top with a splash of red hearts on the front.

Prior to my arrival, I had made a list of things to do, so after breakfast I immediately started on the list. Wedding paraphernalia were laid out all over Maydine's guest room.

Humming, I took up the stack of unfinished wedding programs and began to glue red ribbon with a tiny red bow at the center, across the top of each. Maydine sat on the bed and folded the programs.

"You are all about love." Maydine smiled, pointing at my tank top.

I smiled at her. "All about love."

"The programs are beautiful," she commented.

"Thanks. Anaya did a great job." I paused for a moment from my labor to peruse one of the folded programs. Anaya had spent hours designing them and the menu cards. *My 'baby sister' was extremely creative.*

My eyes widened.

Do not panic, I cautioned myself.

Too late!

"Noooo!" I shrieked, pointing to the error on the program then falling backwards on the bed. The words had shifted on the back page.

"Okay, let's see," Maydine said calmly, ignoring my melodrama. She inspected the programs. "Half of them have the error," she concluded.

"I am not panicking," I said in a dry voice.

"We can reprint."

"Yes. I have the program in my email or on my jump drive."

"You need special paper," Maydine remarked. "Let me call Harriett and see if she can help." After a quick call to Harriett, the situation was resolved.

At midday, Orane joined us for lunch and later we used the time to firm up our schedule. From the sofa in Maydine's living room, we confirmed transportation for our bridal party, immediate family members and overseas guests. In the midst of the planning, I began to cough excessively. I freaked out at the thought of getting sick, now, of all times. Sensing that I was catching the flu, Maydine gave me a homemade remedy before leaving for a church event with Mr. Mohan.

"Babes, you don't look yourself," Orane said, feeling my neck with his hand.

I exhaled loudly. "I'm feeling exhausted and a little off balance."

"Not good. Come, let's pray."

After he prayed, Orane fell backward onto the cushions, arms flopping loosely over his head. "Annalisa, you need rest." He eyed me with concern. "Come here," he said, hugging me close. "Please rest. I don't want you to be sick."

"Yes, Honey," I said comfortingly, running my hands gently down his chest. "I'll get in bed early."

Orane gazed at me, capturing my chin between his thumb and forefinger. He briefly ran the pad of his index finger over my eyebrows. I closed my eyes and took a deep breath as I shuddered under the onslaught of his touch. He planted a kiss on my forehead before standing.

"I am leaving. You need to hit the sack now," he announced.

"Noooo!" I groaned pouting. "I know you're tired," he insisted halfway through the door.

I followed closely on his heels. "Not that tired!"

"Come here!" He gently kissed me and I sighed contentedly. "Be a good girl while I am gone," he said softly.

"I'll try," I responded with childlike innocence.

The low sound of his laughter followed him as he entered his car.

An hour later, I climbed into bed, hoping to ward off the flu like symptoms. Sleep did not come as quickly as I anticipated. I was not accustomed to going to bed this early and my intermittent coughing did not help. Nevertheless, thoughts of Orane and our wedding day skittered through my mind as I tossed and turned.

"Sickness is not a part of the plan. Lord, I receive my healing," I declared boldly.

Turning on the lamp on the nightstand, I began to read a novel which I found in Maydine's study. I made it through a few chapters before my eyes grew watery and heavy. Laying the book on the nightstand, I dimmed the lamp and snuggled into my pillow. Thankfully my coughing had somewhat subsided.

"Anna, Anna," Maydine called out.

"Yes....yes, Sister Maydine."

"Did I disturb your rest? I saw your light on," Maydine poked her head through the door of my bedroom.

"It's okay. What is it?"

"V is on the phone. She would like to speak with you."

"V?"

Maydine knitted her eyebrows. "Vena, your cousin."

"Vena, yes sure. We do need to chat. Thanks." I waved at Maydine before she exited my bedroom.

Grabbing the cordless phone from its cradle on the nightstand, I greeted Vena with a smile. "Vena, how are you doing?"

"Hey Anna! I'm good. Hope I did not disturb your beauty rest. I wanted to pop by but figured that you would be busy."

"Busy is an understatement," I said dramatically, "but you know that I would make time for you."

Vena chuckled. "I know. I remembered how we use to communicate frequently before you migrated."

"Yes. Life happened. It's great to hear from you at this very, very happy time in my life."

"Lucky you!" she blurted out. "I am still single."

"That's alright. Your blessing is on the way," I reassured her, trying to ignore the bitterness in her voice.

"Are you sure you want to get married?" she asked pointedly.

My brows knitted at the skepticism in her voice but I quickly shook off the nagging feeling that was rising in my mind. "Oh yes, very sure," I responded lightly.

She gave a hollow laugh, before saying in a measured tone, "I remember you saying that God has to send you someone special. Is he special?"

"Vena, are you okay? Put my cousin Vena on the phone," I teased, uncomfortable with the turn of the conversation. But, Vena did not respond. "Yes. He is special," I said quietly. "So what have you been...?"

"They say marriage is hard work," she said testily. "At this age, you should remain..."

Good grief! What is this? I tried to keep the edge out of my voice as I interrupted her. "Vena, are you okay? Is there something you need to tell me?"

"Not really. I am defending you everywhere I go. They say you're pregnant so that's why you are rushing to get married."

I did not respond immediately. There was a throbbing beneath my jaw as a mixture of revulsion and apprehension washed over me. "Vena, I have to go."

Vena exploded. "You did not invite me to your wedding. I cannot believe it. I thought that I would be on your bridal ...." She was unrelenting and angry.

"Stop talking like that. You know..."

"Anna, I have known you forever. I first heard through the grapevine that you are getting married."

I exhaled deeply and tried to reason with her. "Yes Vena, we have known each other for a long while but we have been out of touch. I'm sorry that you are taking it so personal."

"Am I not family?" she exclaimed emphatically. "How can you not invite me to your wedding? The times when you were down and out, I was the one who..."

I held the cordless phone at arm's length and swallowed the lump in my throat, before urging, "Vena stop...'

She raged on. "You're acting all high and mighty. I have testimonies..."

Help me Jesus! I really don't need this right now.

"Vena, I'll talk with you another time. Have a goodnight." With that, I disconnected the call.

Phew!

I shut my eyes for a moment; the situation was too difficult for me to process. "Lord help me! This does not make sense," I murmured, placing the phone back in its cradle.

They thought I was pregnant.

They?

I struggled between anger and curiosity. Curiosity was eating away at me, yet at the same time I did not want to know...did not care. *Here I am, fiercely guarding my 'chastity belt' to honor the Lord and all this crazy talk going on behind my back.*

My conversation with Vena left me numb, like someone had punched me in the stomach. I did not want to face the fact that Vena was acting more than a little strange…perhaps even a little jealous. I did not understand her actions or reactions.

My spirit sagged as I burrowed into the bed and pulled the sheets closer to my chin. That conversation was not good, and not at all promising for the future of our relationship. Disconnecting the call did not add to the health of our relationship but I had to stop the insanity. I exhaled deeply in a vain attempt to extinguish my anxiety. Moments later, I found encouragement in the word of God and committed the situation to Him.

I heaved a sigh of relief as I pressed play on the small CD player beside the nightstand. The words of Michael W. Smith's worship song *"Let It Rain"* filled my room. Shortly thereafter, I fell asleep.

CHAPTER 27: BED REST

The sounds of laughter and a familiar voice woke me up. I jumped out of bed and ran to the living room to see Maydine, Mr. Mohan, Harriett and Bella.

"Sister Bella," I yelled happily.

"Annalisa," she smiled warmly at me.

I threw my arms around her and hugged her tightly. "I'm so glad to see you. It has been a while."

A bright smile lit Bella's face. "Yes, way too long." Her medium, 5' 5" frame and long black hair swayed in rhythmic harmony as she joyfully danced around. "My baby sister is getting married. Bring out the bubbly. Time to raise the roof. Oh, Oh, Oh!"

We all laughed.

"Too early for that." Maydine slapped Bella on the shoulder. "You need to eat."

Bella gave a sheepish smile, before saying, "Fine!" She tilted her head then linked her arm with mine as we moved towards the dining room.

While Bella ate, we chatted about the days of old. Mr. Mohan left us at the table to attend a meeting at his church.

"Oh no. We cannot have that!" Belle frowned at my coughing. "You don't look well."

Maydine glanced at me then informed Bella. "Orane told her to stay in bed but noooo."

I grabbed a napkin and dabbed my watery eyes, then protested, "I have been in bed all day. I even had dinner in bed."

Bella, a registered nurse, looked thoughtful. "I have just what you need for that cough." She rummaged through her large red purse, pulled out a sachet and handed it to me.

"Will I live?" I asked, reading the packet.

Bella pursed her lips while Maydine and Harriett chuckled softly.

I grinned at her before swallowing the pills. "Yes, I will."

"Mrs. Conway," Bella smiled mischievously, "I purchased a few goodies for you."

"Bella, behave yourself," Maydine warned her.

"I'm too young for this," Harriett declared smiling.

"Thanks Sister Bella." I smiled at her. "I know I could count on you."

Bella's dark eyes narrowed. "I'll give them to you later. Away from these two." She then playfully wagged her index finger at Maydine and Harriett as they began to protest. "I don't want to hear it."

I broke into giggles as I watched and listened to the banter of my three eldest sisters, three peas in a pod, their laughter filled the air, pulling me in. I adored all my sisters. We had a visceral connection. Our different personalities, individual disappointments, loves and passions, had caused us to journey through periods of tears, shock, joy, amazement and triumph. *A great epic movie!* No matter the distance between us, we were never far apart, always within reach.

After she ate dinner, Bella, a decorator at heart went to work. From under the comforter, I watched her decorate my plain white satin shoes with clear rhinestones and then continue to decorate the programs. Her masterpiece was the decoration of the three transparent vases to be used in our sand ceremony. The three vases were decorated with clear rhinestones, white ribbon and tiny white bows.

When Orane stopped by to check on me, he met Bella. I watched in amazement as they chatted on the sofa in the living room about anything and everything. By the way they were conversing; you would think that they had known each other for years.

"Sister Bella, I will see you tomorrow," Orane said smiling. "Please make sure Annalisa stays in bed."

"What?" I interjected pouting on the sofa.

He leaned forward with serious eyes. "Stay in bed."

"Orane, I will make sure she stays in bed," Bella remarked, eyeballing me.

"Okay, bed it will be," I conceded, wiping the sweat from my forehead. "I'll accompany you to your car."

On the way to his car, Orane waved goodbye to Maydine who was raking the yard in the distance, with much joy in each rake. My second mother was totally overjoyed about my upcoming wedding.

"Annalisa." The seriousness in Orane voice drew my attention. "It's time for you to see a doctor."

I gazed into worried eyes. "Don't worry Honey. I'll go to bed right after you leave and I'll make an appointment to see my former doctor."

"Promise?" he asked softly, hugging me.

"Yes, I promise." I hugged him tightly. I could see concern in his eyes as he closed the gate behind him.

"Sister Maydine," I called out.

"Yes Anna."

"I'm heading to bed. I will see you tomorrow."

"Oh Anna! I know that you're still not feeling well." The care in her voice made me feel better.

"I'll be alright. I'm going to make an appointment to see Dr. Thompson."

"That would be good. Do you need anything now?"

"No. Thank you."

"Okay. Call me if you need anything," she said comfortingly. "I will check on you later."

I smiled and gave her a grateful nod. "Thanks Mother dearest."

As the MayPo sky gave way to night fall, another coughing spell hit me. *Was I becoming some kind of nocturnal creature? This was becoming very weird.* I noticed that I coughed sporadically during the day but as nightfall approached, the coughing spells increased.

Sickness was not a part of the plan, I continued to declare.

I flopped back against the pillows on my bed, wiggling to find a comfortable position. I felt more exhausted than I ever felt in my

177

life. Running my hands over my face, I could feel the soreness in my cheeks. My throat was aching and my eyes stung and were puffy from the constant coughing. I exhaled loudly, hoping that the medication would kick in soon.

Two hours later, I was still tossing around in my bed, willing myself to sleep. I snatched a bit of sleep between my coughing spells and must have fallen fully sleep in the wee hours of the morning.

CHAPTER 28: BOUNCING BACK

Ouch! I need a new body!

I woke up the next day feeling extremely tired. I fell back in bed, feeling like I needed to just lie under the covers. My head weighed a ton, too much for my shoulders and my eyes were burning from lack of sleep. I must have fallen asleep again because an incessant knocking woke me up.

"Anna, wake up," Maydine called out, behind the closed door.

"Okay," I murmured, trying to ignore the throbbing in my throat.

I dragged myself out of bed and glanced in the bathroom mirror. The night's turmoil was evident. I looked a fright, like something that the cat dragged in. After showering, I used concealer to hide the dark circles under my eyes but I could not hide the wounded feeling in my body. The lack of sleep was certainly taking an effect.

Orane picked me up after breakfast and we traveled to Kingston for my appointment with Dr. Toby Thompson. Thankfully, Dr. Thompson's receptionist was able to squeeze me into his tight schedule, after I told her about my big day, which was four days away.

Orane was quiet for most of the journey; his dark brown eyes were filled with concern.

"I'll be alright," I comforted him.

After updating my records at the doctor's office, the nurse showed me to an examination room. As I lay on the bed, I glanced around the room and attempted to read the health tips on the light blue walls but my aching eyes made reading difficult. I could not wait to find out what was ailing me.

Within minutes, Dr. Thompson entered with his winning smile. He was a ruggedly handsome, tall man, perhaps well over six feet with broad shoulders and curly black hair.

After a thorough inspection, he sat back in his swivel chair and smiled at me. I looked at him curiously. "You do not have the flu," he informed me.

My mouth fell open as the diagnosis ricocheted in my head. I was taking every flu medication in the book. "What is...?"

"You have an allergy, possibly to dust."

"Dust!"

"Strong possibility. Not to worry. A few antibiotics will take care of it."

"Will I be ready for...?"

Dr. Thompson smiled at me with understanding eyes. "Yes. You will be ready for your big day."

"Thanks, Dr. Thompson."

My thoughts swirled as he wrote the prescription.

Dust?

I would never have guessed that I had an allergic reaction to dust. Very strange! But, may be not so strange! Maydine raked the yard in the mornings and sometimes in the evening. Still, I continued to extend my faith. *Sickness was not a part of my plan or God's plan for me.* I continued to declare good health for my wedding day.

Orane filled my prescription and I took one pill before we joined Mr. Mohan, Maydine, Bella, Aunt Joy and Harriett for lunch at the exquisite Vosacana Japanese Restaurant. Thankfully, Orane made reservations because the restaurant was packed with patrons who clearly shared his views on the desirability of the Japanese meals.

I couldn't wait to taste the food and I was not disappointed. It was simply divine! Cooked to perfection! I was so full that I dare not take another bite.

"Your ailment has not affected your eating habits," Orane said, laughing softly as he wiped his mouth with a napkin.

I knitted my brows and ignored him.

"Do I need to roll you out of here?" he teased quietly. "I saw you..."

"Shush, that's my secret shame." I had quietly unbuttoned my jeans beneath the table.

He chuckled softly as I playfully glared at him. "We have company," he whispered, still chuckling.

Half an hour later, Orane and I waved goodbye to the group and headed for counseling. In Reverend Fuller's study, we discussed scriptures regarding the role of a husband and wife. We explored and assessed our personalities, personal goals and individual differences. Conflict resolution, communication styles, sexuality and intimacy were topics that created exciting frameworks for discussions. Orane and I also articulated our feelings about living apart at the initial stage of our marriage. Reverend Fuller gave us home work to develop a long-term plan of action to keep our marriage alive. I left the session freshly energized and fully prepared to constructively tackle future challenges and conflicts that may arise in our marriage.

That evening, as Orane and I journeyed back to MayPo, I began coughing again.

"I hope the medication kicks in soon," I murmured.

"Yes," he agreed.

"I would hate to be coughing on our wedding day."

"I just need my baby up and running," he said, adjusting the radio channel from the news to jazz music.

"I know you do," I said softly.

"You are..." His voice cracked and he cleared his throat. "You are very special to me."

I smiled contentedly. "Honey, you are a blessing to me...my treasure. I love you."

Warmth radiated from his eyes as he smiled at me. "The feeling is mutual. I love you too."

After we pulled up at Maydine's home, Orane touched my hand. "Let us pray," he said caringly. We thanked the Lord for my full recovery and an unforgettable wedding day.

An hour later, I pulled the comforter tightly around me as the cool breeze blew through the window. I was still coughing but that did not prevent me from having sweet dreams about my husband-to-be and our wedding day.

✳ ✳ ✳

The following day, Melissa and I headed to see Alaine Burgess, my hair stylist at Reflections Beauty Salon in Kingston. We laughed incessantly as we reflected on the days gone by, chatting at several miles per hour as only good friends do.

Alaine greeted us with hugs as we entered the salon. "Annalisa, the day is finally here!" Back in the day, Alaine had many visions of my wedding day and her role in it.

"Yes. Finally," I declared amidst laughter.

"Hello everyone," I greeted her employees.

It was always a pleasure to visit Alaine's hair salon. She gave true meaning to the term 'customer service'. Simply breathtaking would aptly describe the salon's décor. The mint green, rectangular room had a large mirror lining the entire length of one wall. The patterns on this mirror captured the elegance of stalagmites and stalactites. Large beautifully framed photos and green plants were stationed strategically to enhance the décor.

"Did you get the makeup?" Alaine asked, interrupting my gaze.

"Yes," I responded.

She perked up. "Let's go to my office."

Alaine observed with glee as Melissa and I laid out my personal effects on the round wooden table—jewelry sets, veil, gloves, make-up, pictures of my wedding gown and suggested hairstyles.

"Looking great!" Alaine beamed. "You have everything that I will need. I'm going to relax your hair and then do styling and make-up tomorrow."

"Sounds great," I responded.

"So, when will I meet this Mr. Conway?" Alaine asked with arched eyebrows.

"Today is your lucky day!" I grinned at her.

"Al...righty then!" she said enthusiastically. Melissa and I laughed as she performed a victory dance.

Two hours later as Alaine was putting on the finishing touches on my hair, Orane arrived, looking like the man about town.

"Has anyone seen my lovely bride?" He pretended not to see me.

Alaine responded in an English accent. "She is here sir, almost ready to go!"

Laughter erupted in the salon.

"Ah yes! There she is! So beautiful!" Orane said exuberantly.

"Yes, here I am." I giggled, participating in this bit of melodrama.

"I will wait for my queen in the foyer." Orane bowed like a knight of days gone by, then withdrew, amidst sustained laughter.

"Nice gentleman, Miss Annalisa!" Alaine giggled.

"Totally!" I grinned.

An hour later, Orane and I arrived at Maydine's home.

"I am so glad that your coughing has subsided," he said, breathing a sigh of relief.

"Yes, me too. Thanks so much Honey." He stared at me with knitted brows. "I appreciate all that you're doing."

"You are welcome." He smiled at me, and our eyes stayed lock for a moment.

"But, how are you really doing?" I asked, touching his hand.

"I'm good but a little tired. I'm trying to wrap up loose ends so that we won't be disturbed on our honeymoon." He chuckled loudly. "We cannot be disturbed."

"No disturbance!" I giggled.

He eyeballed me. "Mrs. Conway, are you ready for all things new?"

My heart skipped a beat. "Mrs. Conway! That has a nice ring to it Mr. Conway." I lightly brushed his cheek with my hand. "You know I am."

"Hmmm!" he murmured with contentment and we both chuckled softly.

"How's the nuptials speech coming?" I asked.

"It's coming! I'm still working on it." His expression softened and he reached for my hand and kissed it. "I love you."

"I love you too Honey." I lifted my hand to his jawline and gently traced it then kissed him lightly, something he did not expect. "O...kay!" I murmured, pulling slightly away from him. "We will pick up on Saturday night."

He exhaled deeply. "Yes. Be gone woman before I take you away," he said, caressing my arm.

I smiled softly and untangled myself from him. "Okay, if you insist."

Orane accompanied me to the front door and greeted Maydine.

"I have a surprise for you both!" Maydine grinned. "Life size surprise!"

"What?" I asked suspiciously as Orane looked on.

"Come out surprise!" Maydine yelled, looking towards the living room door.

"Idalyn!" I screamed and hugged her.

"So glad to see you," Idalyn said. She had arrived from Tampa, Florida earlier that day.

"This is my Orane!" I beamed.

"Orane!" Idalyn hugged him.

"Nice to meet you Idalyn," he responded. "Let me guess, you are sister number five."

"Sister number four. Natasha is number five," I informed him.

"I see this will take a while," he drawled.

Everyone laughed.

"You have not yet met Verona. She is the sixth sister," Maydine said comfortingly. "But don't worry, take it in stride."

Shortly after that, Orane left and I chatted with Idalyn until midnight as she took on the task of making alterations to two of the bridesmaids' gowns. I hoped that the gowns would look great and classy on all the bridesmaids.

CHAPTER 29: GREAT CHOICE

Orane whistled exuberantly, as I made my way down the "catwalk" towards him. He was leaning against his car in Maydine's driveway. In a smooth sweep of one hand, he locked me in a warm embrace. My heart pounded against my rib cage as he stared down at me.

"You look very elegant!" he said softly, adding butterfly kisses to my cheek. I was decked out in a white sleeveless scoop neck dress with pleats. A bow accent at the waist added to my feminine flair.

I kissed him gently. "Thanks. I feel fabulous. You're not looking too shabby yourself." He was wearing gray pants, a long sleeve burgundy shirt and gray dress shoes.

He tickled my side and I giggled even more. "Look at you Mrs. Conway!" he smiled, leaning toward me with one hand on either side of my hips. "Ready to roll?"

I tenderly caressed his face. "Yes Honey," I said, not too steadily.

He winked at me; his eyes were filled with excitement. I smiled, watching as he hurried around to the driver's side and hopped in.

It was an exceptionally cool and scenic Wednesday morning and we were off to meet with Reverend Fuller. I smiled happily at Orane and he returned the smile. Some days just seemed to begin right, specially sent to us, holding warmth, promise and potential. This was one of those beautiful days.

Our final premarital counseling session covered finances, children and parenting. We also examined our commitment level to our marriage and reviewed our long-term plan of action to keep our marriage alive.

Later that day, Orane and I dined at Abernay, a fast food establishment while I waited for Melissa to continue wedding planning.

"Hope I'm not disturbing anything." Melissa beamed.

"Hey Mel! I did not see you come in." Orane and I were playfully gazing at each other.

"How could you?" Mel grinned as we hugged.

"Good to see you Melissa," Orane chuckled and hugged her.

"Likewise Orane!'

"I'll see you both later," Orane said, pushing his chair under the table.

I gently touched his face as he kissed my cheek. "See you later Honey," I whispered.

"See you in a bit Orane," Melissa smiled.

I opened my purse and took out a notepad. "We pretty much have everything covered," I said to a smiling Melissa.

She leaned forward animatedly. "Are you ready?"

"Ready! Ohhh yes. I'm so ready." I giggled. "I'm going to walk the aisle as if it was custom made for me."

"I bet you will." Melissa grinned at me. "Just don't start crying."

"Crying!" I dramatically rolled my eyes to the sky then pursed my lips, before saying, "That is not a part of the plan.

"No crying?"

"I will be the happiest bride in the whole wide world. I'm leaving the crying to my family."

"Imagine the tears as baby sister walks down the aisle."

"Baby sister!" I exclaimed. "I am so far from baby age."

"Stop pretending! You know how your sisters feel about you."

"Yes. My fabulous sisters! I am so blessed to have them in my life."

"The most amazing thing is that you're all so close."

I smiled at her. "Mama and Papa would not have it any other way."

"Yes." Melissa agreed.

"Mel, you do know that we consider you a real sister."

Melissa nodded. "Yes. I get that feeling."

"Yes Mel, you are our sister." I looked at her seriously. "My relationship with you and Simon means a lot to me. In fact, your whole family means a lot to me. Orane and I are forever grateful..." Melissa raised her hand to protest and I knitted my eyebrows. "I am not finished. Can't you tell that I'm giving a speech? Anyway, as I was saying, thank you for setting a great example of a Godly marriage. Orane and I love..." My voice cracked and I paused to get my emotions under control. "We love and appreciate you and Simon very much."

"See all this emotional stuff. You're getting teary eyed already." Melissa smiled as I winced. "The feeling is mutual," she said quietly. "Simon and I wish you and Orane all the very best. We are glad that you both know the Lord and we are confident that your marriage will be all that God has ordained it to be."

"Thanks. Orane and I are very optimistic and confident about our marriage."

"Simon seems quite comfortable with your choice."

My lips curled in a smile. "Yes. I remembered how scared he was when I decided to accommodate Orane at home."

Melissa chuckled loudly. "Yes. He was so concerned."

I raised one eyebrow. "So he's no longer concerned?"

"Of course, he has concerns," Melissa laughed mischievously, "for Orane."

"Oh, it's like that. Simon has no loyalty. You tell him I said so."

"He knows how it can be when two people love each other."

"Raging passion!" I smiled knowingly. "As you know, Orane and I wanted to honor the Lord by waiting."

"Thank God that you are both on the same page," Melissa exclaimed, throwing her hands in the air.

"It's been a struggle but we are holding on."

"I understand," she nodded, pursing her lips.

"We put that on the table from the beginning. According to Mr. Conway, he wants to give his testimony with a straight face."

Melissa smiled perceptively. "I realized his deep commitment to God the first time I met him."

"Yep! He's committed," I concurred.

"Have you packed for the honeymoon?" Melisa's pursed her lips and her eyebrows rose to their maximum level. "Saturday night is approaching."

"Oh yeah! Victoria's Secret lingerie will be on display," I said dramatically.

"Nice, very nice," she said in hushed tones and we burst into girlish giggles.

Suddenly, Melissa grew quiet. Something was brewing. "We have a surprise for you," she said nonchalantly.

"We? What's the surprise?" I eyed her suspiciously.

"Some of the ladies who are attending your shower tomorrow...," she paused and playfully rolled her eyes, "your final shower, pooled..."

I giggled loudly. "Final? You're all trying to get rid of me."

With arms folded across her chest, Melissa asked, "*Three* bridal showers? Who does that?"

I chuckled softly.

"Anyway,' she continued, "we pooled our resources and we are giving you a spa treatment, manicure and pedicure."

My eyes bulged with excitement. "Wow, that's so nice! Thank you."

"Let's get out of here. We are heading to the spa right now before we go to the hair salon."

Great choice ladies!

Almost three hours later, I stood in the foyer of Crescent Day Spa feeling rejuvenated and relaxed in mind, body, soul and spirit. I was treated to a superb upper body massage utilizing essential oils with long soothing strokes and therapeutic techniques to relax my muscles and improve my circulation.

My manicure and pedicure included exfoliation, moisture mask, massage and polish. For the first time...drum rolls please...I wore acrylic nails.

At Reflections Beauty Salon, Alaine applied different shades of make-up to my face and successfully discovered the best color combination to use for my big day. After that, we reached a consensus on my hair do and she styled my hair.

Orane picked me up from the hair salon and we made our way home.

"Thank you husband-to-be," I said as Orane pulled up at Maydine's home.

"You are welcome wife-to-be," he responded smiling. "I must tell you again. You look beautiful."

"Thank you Honey. Are you packed and ready to roll?"

"Packed? Who needs clothes?" He threw back his head and laughed loudly.

I knitted my brows and playfully slapped him on his shoulder. "Naughty man!"

He reached for my hand and kissed it then placed it back on my lap. "I'm packing tomorrow when you are having your *third* bridal shower or is it your *fourth?*"

"Ah, my third, but I'll take a fourth."

"If I might borrow your phrase, 'look at you'!" He chuckled. "What time should I take Aunt Joy to the shower?"

"7:00 pm is good. Are you sure you don't want to attend?"

"Positive!" He grimaced. "Permit me to sit this out."

"I heard that you declined to go out with the guys too."

"Yes. I need to rest and get myself ready to handle the challenges of having a wife."

"Funny!" I said, poking his side. "Consider this. Having a wife is a good thing, plus, you will obtain favor from the Lord. Isn't that something?"

"It sure is." He exhaled softly, relaxing against the seat. "You are my wonderful gift from God."

"You are my wonderful gift..."

He chuckled. "Babes, I'm going to start charging you. You can't just use my lyrics."

"No lyrics," I said tenderly. "It's the truth."

Our eyes locked knowingly. I swallowed hard as he smiled and tenderly caressed my face, rubbing my cheek with his fingers. My lips parted under his hand and I closed my eyes. It felt good...so good, that I zealously wrapped my arms around his body and pulled him closer. His strong fingers traveled up the small of my back and I could feel his breath on my face. As our bodies merged, I kissed him and he responded in kind, deeply and passionately.

"I love you," he said, shuddering softly as he buried his head into my neck.

I choked back a whimper as I felt warmth quickly rising within me. "I love you too."

Breathing heavily, Orane turned me to face him. Streams of shivers rolled down my spine as I gazed into his incredible dark brown eyes. "You are beautiful," he said, mustering up all of his self-control.

Help me Lord! I looked away from him as I valiantly attempted to control my desires. "Thanks Honey!" I murmured breathlessly. "We will honor God."

He was quiet for a moment before saying, "Yes, we will."

"We are going to make it. We can do this," I reassured him gently, pushing my hair away from my face.

"Babes," he looked at me apologetically. 'I'm..."

"Don't say a word," I said softly, caressing his cheeks. "Let's ask the Lord to help us."

With that we held hands and sought the Lord in prayer.

He heard our cries.

CHAPTER 30: DREADFUL NEWS

I woke up to the warm rays of the morning sun across my bed. Time was drawing nigh. I threw my hands in the air and burst into girlish giggles then rolled out of bed to my usual routine. The scent of pancakes greeted me as I entered the dining room.

"Good morning everyone."

"Good morning," responded Maydine, Bella and Idalyn.

"Here comes the bride, here comes the bride," Bella sang as I took my place at the breakfast table. "Are you nervous?"

"Oh nooo, no wedding jitters." I shivered and everyone laughed.

"You are in a great mood," Maydine remarked smiling.

"I feel great and I feel blessed to be surrounded...*(my voice broke)* by family and people who love and care for me. Thank you all so much. Words cannot express how much I appreciate all that you have done and continue to do."

"Stop! You're going make us cry," Bella said. "You know that we cry for everything in this family."

"Yes. But no crying at our wedding, please," I told her.

"You heard that?" Bella playfully pointed at Maydine.

"Did you hear that?" Maydine responded, threatening Bella with her eyes.

I threw my hands in the air. "It's a happy time. A time of celee...bration."

"Ce...lebrate good times, come on!" Bella sang.

"O...kay! Are you going to sing about everything?" I slapped Bella lightly on the shoulder. "Stop it."

She chuckled and began to sing. "I sing because I'm happy."

"No you didn't!" I said, eyeballing her.

Maydine and Idalyn joined in. "I sing because I am free. His eye is on the sparrow, and I know."

"Yes I know," Maydine sang in soprano.

"I know," Idalyn echoed in alto.

"Yes, I know," I sang in high pitched soprano.

"He watches over me," we sang in unison and clapped enthusiastically.

The phone rang and I could hear Mr. Mohan answering. He called out for Maydine to pick up.

"Hello!" Maydine answered joyfully. "I can't hear, what are you saying? Shush, shush," she motioned to us. "Harriett, take your time! What's going on?...Oh no, I'm so sorry to hear that? Oh Lord, help the parents!" Maydine exclaimed.

We became extremely quiet trying to make sense of the conversation and waiting for Maydine to conclude.

Well, that's what we should have done.

Instead, we eyed Maydine impatiently.

"What going on?" we asked loudly. Bella pushed her ear next to the phone as Maydine continued the conversation with Harriett.

"Stop!" Maydine said to Bella. "Wait a moment Harriett!" Maydine turned to us. "A couple of students who attends Harriett's school were in an accident while traveling in a taxi. They all died."

Sounds of sharp intakes of breath, followed by "Oh no! No! No!" shattered the air and we groaned at different level! A wave of sadness enveloped the room as we grieved for the parents who heard this dreadful news.

Maydine informed us that Harriett, as the school's principal would have to deal with the students, parent and media along with other personnel, so Bella and Idalyn needed to help with the preparation for my shower. Maydine then walked to the verandah to finish her conversation with Harriett.

Later that day, I called Harriett at home to offer my condolences. She was still in tears from the painful experience. "Annalisa, no parent should have to bury a child. I cannot imagine what these parents are going through." As the day dragged on, we managed to revive our spirits with psalms, hymns and spiritual songs.

CHAPTER 31: SHOWER ME

I looked superb, very much like the bride to be in a hot pink Calvin Klein empire cocktail cotton/spandex dress with a scoop neck, ruched panels at the fitted bodice and a slightly flared skirt.

The cool evening air greeted me as I step out of Maydine's Toyota RAV4 at Harriett's home. As we walked up the driveway, I could hear music, soft chatter and laughter.

"Surprise!"

"Welcome!"

And other screams of delight rang out as I entered the living room to attend my final bridal shower which was organized by my family, wedding coordinators and bridal party. I ran around the room yelling words of endearment as I hugged everyone.

Standing in the middle of the room, I hollered, "People, people, my loves, my doves, my turtle doves."

"Annalisa no tears, okay," exclaimed Janay, a friend and former member of Laybrook Presbyterian Church Dance Ministry.

"No. No tears today," I responded cheerfully.

"But Anna you've actually gained weight," Allera, another friend chuckled.

"Yes, but I plan to work it off, " I responded, dancing around.

Spontaneous outburst of laughter filled the air and someone shouted, "Go on girl."

"Oh yes, that's the plan." I smiled at them. "Everyone, this is Aunt Joy, Orane's mother."

Several hellos greeted Aunt Joy who smiled and nodded.

"Annalisa, come here!" Melissa called out. She was holding a hot pink sash with the word 'bride' written in black.

I beamed. "That's for me?"

"Yes!" Melissa responded jubilantly.

Amidst fanfare, she draped the sash across my shoulder then led me to the "bridal" chair.

"Anna your hair is still neat," Allera said, as I used my hands to smooth my hair.

I smiled sheepishly at her.

"Everything is in place," she whispered confidentially, before saying in a loud voice, "Good evening ladies! Welcome to Annalisa's bridal shower! Let's take a few minutes to recognize the very special bride, Annalisa."

I smiled and bowed as applause erupted around the room which was fabulously decorated in red, gold and white. All bells and whistles were on display. *Great job Nichelle!* While Harriet was dealing with the crisis at her school, Nichelle, Harriett's daughter took over the preparations for my bridal shower.

At Allera's bidding, we each selected a bible character and gave reasons for the selection. I chose Esther, a woman of faith, courage, love and devotion. Esther operated in her season and became an instrument that God used to prevent the destruction of her people.

Next, Anaya and I were blindfolded to play *"Pin the leaf"* on Adam, a job we completed successfully, amidst squealing noises from the ladies.

"Question time!" Allera yelled, grinning mischievously.

"Anna be careful, they will hold your answers against you," Janay begged dramatically.

"Anna," Allera smiled at me, ignoring Janay, "A little birdie asked Orane these questions and got the answers."

"Plead the fifth," someone hollered and giggles broke out in the room.

"I can do this," I declared grinning. "Shoot".

"Now ladies, Annalisa is answering these questions about Orane but you are to answer them about her," Allera informed the group. "Whosoever gets the highest score will receive a gift."

Murmurs of okay echoed around the room.

"Write all your answers to the questions then we will discuss them," Allera said, when we were all armed with sheets of paper and pencils. "Here we go! What is his favorite color?...Who is his favorite girl?...Name his favorite musical instrument...Name his favorite song."

"Annalisa don't commit yourself. Be careful," Arianna shouted, to everyone's amusement.

"Annalisa it's okay!" Alaine yelled. "We won't tell."

"Ladies, ladies!" Allera cautioned playfully. "What is his favorite bible verse?...What is his favorite juice?...What is his favorite cologne?...Name his favorite bible character."

In the end, Janay won the round with answers regarding me and received her gift enthusiastically. The ladies were quite tickled that I knew all the answer to the questions about Orane.

"Ladies," I declared spiritedly, "the moral of this little game is, you are to know your man."

Spontaneous laughter erupted and I found myself grinning at my own bit of melodrama.

"Let's eat," Allera said smiling. She blessed the food and we were treated to baked chicken, an assortment of sandwiches and salads, fruits, pastries and cold beverages. While we ate, I chatted with the ladies, some of whom I had not seen in years.

Creative juices flowed when we resumed and Allera divided the ladies into two teams. Each team dressed their selected bride using white tissue paper and tulle, then I carefully determined the winner.

"It's time for gifts," Allera declared. Her eyes stretched to their limit.

"Ladies," I said smiling. "Thank you so much for the spa treatment and the mani and pedi."

"You're welcome," they responded in unison.

"We still have more gifts for you," Allera said, handing me a gift bag.

It was from Bella. "I am afraid," I said, covering my eyes. "I will just take this home."

"Noooooo," they shouted animatedly.

Screams of delight echoed around the room as I pulled out a private party kit and short sheer pink lingerie with pink fur at the neckline.

"Fire," someone shouted.

"Anna, that's like floss," Arianna yelled.

"Now, don't come knocking," Janay shouted as I held up the matching pink fur stiletto heels.

I opened several other gifts while the ladies hollered ohhhs and ahhhs along the way. After laughter subsided, Allera was back on the job.

"For being such a wonderful bride, we have an extra present for you." She handed me a large package.

"What is this?" I beamed, peeling away the red wrapping paper to reveal a beautiful gold framed canvas photo of Orane and me. "Oh my word!" I screamed, hugging the photo over and over again before showing it to the ladies.

"Awww!" they responded at different levels.

"It's beautiful," I said, gazing at the photo with love. "Melissa, I know that you are responsible for this. Thank you."

Melissa smiled and mouthed, "You're welcome."

Naturally, I refused to let the photo out of my sight.

Just a few minutes later, advice came:

- *Pray together*
- *Always listen*
- *Always be happy*
- *Never let the sun go down on your wrath*
- *Always be tactful, the male ego is very fragile*
- *Never lose his trust*
- *Get to know your husband, do things that will uplift him.*
- *Always smile, it makes a difference*
- *Always be honest with your husband*

- *Do not try to have the last word*
- *Always be the bride he married*
- *Never say I am done or I quit*
- *Always give thanks in everything*
- *Never make decisions when angry*
- *Never say I am frustrated*
- *Never stay hungry in the name of love*
- *Always share*
- *Never nag*
- *Show appreciation always*
- *Never "close shop"*
- *Always hug and kiss your husband goodnight and good-bye*
- *Always write love notes for your man*
- *Never go to bed angry*
- *Never take gossip about your partner*
- *Always be honest about how you feel*
- *Stay in love*
- *Make time for each other*
- *Never bring up things already addressed in the past*
- *Always be your husband's girlfriend.*
- *Keep looking hot*
- *When you are upset, never say things you don't mean*
- *Never use the retirement money*
- *Always have fun*

"Speech! Speech!" the ladies chanted.

"Sing instead Annalisa, sing!" Janay shouted and everyone laughed.

"No. I'll sing at the wedding," I joked. "Thank you so much guys. I really appreciate this. This is my *third* bridal shower!" I beamed, clapping my hands.

"Your third bridal shower?" Janay exclaimed.

"Can you believe it?" Melissa said, bringing laughter to the room.

Smiling I continued, "Everywhere I go, I leave with bags. Everybody is so excited. It's like, oh yeah, finally, let's get it done quickly."

The ladies laughed at my dramatic skills.

"Thank you so much. Most of you have been with me forever. You have seen the trials, the temptations, the ins and outs, the struggles and the mountain tops. Most of you know that marriage is something I have been praying about, on and off for years. I did not want to get married just to wear a ring. Seriously, I didn't! I wanted to marry somebody who I could love, somebody who I could be myself with, somebody who I could pray with and somebody who would support me emotionally."

The ladies were all ears!

"Proverbs 31 talks about a virtuous woman buying assets and attending to her household. She's just a beautiful woman, wearing fine linen and so on. Her husband praises her. He told her, many daughters have done virtuously, but thou excellest them all. Then, the bible states that her children would rise up and call her blessed. One day, after reading this scripture, I said, 'God that's the only part of the scripture that has not been fulfilled in my life and I'm looking forward to it'.

Nevertheless, whether married or single, I would be okay. It's not that I feel that marriage would complete me. I think that marriage is something that God desires for me at this time. I know that with Orane, I am not coming off the path. You and I have been in relationships where we have struggled to keep on the path because we tried to pull the other person along. With Orane, it was a natural flow. He came along and we just kept moving on the same path. I really love that."

Murmurs of agreement came from the ladies, followed by girlish giggles.

"I like him a lot and I also love him," I said smiling. "We chat and have fun together. He allows me to be me. I can be playful at times but he knows when I get serious."

I rolled my eyes and an avalanche of giggles erupted from the group, before I continued.

"For instance, I may say, 'the world is a bad place today' and he understands what I mean. He's a really good guy and he appreciates me. The best part is that Orane is a praying man." I beamed. "I love it, love it, love it. In fact, I hate to say this, but he's the one that's always saying, let us pray or let's have devotion. He believes in prayer; he really does."

Silence descended on the room as we paused to digest this.

It was a defining moment.

"Annalisa, I appreciate you," Mrs. Sallue, an older friend and prayer warrior interjected. "I know this is genuine because I feel it in my spirit. Your marriage is something that we are happy about. Be encouraged because we are encouraged by your testimony."

Strong murmurs of yes, echoed around the room.

"I am never alone," I declared. "I have a family with lots of sisters, brothers, nieces and nephews plus tons of friends who really care."

Agreement came from the group, "Yes, love and care!"

"I do not pressure myself," I said smiling. "I wanted a ring," I extended my left hand, "but, it had to be from someone special. I wanted a male figure in my life who would impact my life in a positive way; someone who I could help to grow and fulfill his God-given purpose. We will have goals as a couple but we will also have individual goals. So, I feel this relationship is a blessing."

"Yes, yes," they murmured.

I smiled and continued, "Everything happened very quickly. But, I've always felt that God would move quickly when the time was right. I know Orane enough. I do not know him one hundred percent because that's an ongoing process and he is evolving. But, I know that he has a kind heart and I always wanted that." I broke out in giggles then declared, "It's NOT about the money."

Pockets of snickering and chuckles broke out in the room.

I playfully batted a hand. "He has a gentle spirit. His mind… oh, he has a beautiful mind. I love his mind. He has the regular perspective but he's always coming from another angle and I'm just, ah …"

"He keeps you on your feet," Melissa filled in.

"Yes," I grinned. "He keeps me alert and makes me think. Sometimes, he will ask questions just to hear my thoughts. He desires a helpmate so we will make decisions together. I really love that."

"And if you hear from him," Mrs. Sallue said quietly, "he will say the same."

"I know." I beamed shamelessly. "I heard him talk to Reverend Fuller about me and I was so blessed. It was beautiful." I paused then informed them. "We quarrel sometimes. Yes, we do."

The ladies were in agreement.

"Yes!"

"Healthy relationship!"

"It's natural!"

I eyed them sheepishly. "The first time we pretended to quarrel."

Uncontrollable laughter broke out and I could not help but laugh too.

"To be honest, Orane and I cannot be annoyed with each other for too long because we are very good friends. Our first quarrel was about devotion. He felt that I was stronger when he first met me. You know, the cares of life happened, so I kind of slipped off the straight and narrow road. He desires a strong Christian woman, that's first and foremost so he wants me to maintain my Godly spirit and spirituality. It's NOT about the body," I gave them my model pose, "or the looks." I exhaled, cupping my face.

Hysterical laughter exploded around the room and someone shouted, "Anna, behave yourself."

I smiled pleasantly at them. "Orane and I are growing and we are learning about each other, day by day and we have so much help. You guys are so awesome. I thank God for the support of my family and friends. Let's talk about my sisters. They are all different so they fulfill different roles in my life."

"You always say that Annalisa," Janay hollered and I snickered.

"Sister Bella will tell me about the sweet little things, the little to-to-too," I touched my lingerie bag, "and the guys. Sister Maydine plays the mothering role and Sister Harri just keeps me on the path. And, all you guys have been just wonderful. Thank you!" I clapped my hands enthusiastically and they smiled at me.

"Annalisa, show them what you did in the store," Bella called out, doubling over with laugher.

"Share it," the ladies exclaimed, their eyes pleaded with me.

I laughed then innocently explained. "I heard a gospel song playing in a store, while we were searching for a gown for Aunt Joy and I started to dance. I wanted to worship. It was just beautiful."

Howls of laughter broke and Bella hollered, "Just show us a little piece of the dance."

"Annalisa, what if there were cameras in the store?" Janay asked, with laugher in her voice.

"Oops!" I responded grinning. "I just danced."

Bella chuckled. "I laughed so hard in the store. The people in the store just stopped and were like...in disbelief."

I grinned sheepishly. "Naughty me!"

"Very naughty," someone shouted.

"Let's change the topic because, I'm curious," Mrs. Sallue interjected. "How did you meet 'Mr. Right', Orane?"

I grinned at her. "O...kay! Story time! Let me start at the beginning. Sister Harri, may God bless you! I know, I was a little stubborn but I came around, didn't I? For those of you who don't know, Sister Harri knew Orane for a while and had been telling me about this nice gentleman. I am like, Sister Harri please." I lifted my hands in frustration. "She could not even tell me his first name. Okay, if he is that great, what is his first name? Silence!" I threw my hand in the air again in exasperation. "But eventually, we were introduced and we took it from there."

"The rest is history," Melissa squealed.

Giggling, I continued, "I have been introduced to quite a few guys and nothing worked out, so I didn't think that this was going to be any different. Plus, Orane lived so far away." I rolled my eyes to the sky and giggled. "So far away! But, I am looking forward to my wedding day and I am looking forward to my honeymoon. Oh yeah! Oh yeah!" I danced around, grinning from ear to ear.

"We'll be there," Arianna yelled as the group clapped and cheered wildly.

Allera beamed in admiration. "Thank God for you sister."

A thoughtful lull came over the group and no one moved.

"Let's recite Isaiah 40:31," Allera said intuitively.

Together, we said, "But those who wait on the Lord shall renew their strength; they shall mount up with wings like eagles, they shall run and not be weary, they shall walk and not faint."

"That's the word of the Lord," Allera said quietly. "The Psalmist emphasized this—teach me Lord how to wait. Annalisa is a living testimony of this. In the book of Samuel, the word of the Lord states that when we honor God, He honors us in return. This is God's character. He is a covenant keeping God. Annalisa, you have been honoring God. It's a continuous thing and this is just the tip of the iceberg of God honoring you. Yes, this is just the tip of the iceberg," Allera declared joyfully. "Eye has not seen, nor ear heard, nor have entered into the heart of man the things which God has prepared for those who love Him." She smiled at me. "Just continue to honor God.

The Lord bless you and keep you. Saturday is going to be beautiful. Beautiful!"

We held hands and prayed to end an enjoyable evening of ministry, entertainment and fun. I was showered with love from my circle of love.

CHAPTER 32: LET'S REHEARSE

It's wedding rehearsal day!

A serene smile stretched across my face and youthful exuberance filled my being. I rolled from side to side muffling my squeals of delight before jumping out of bed to perform a spontaneous thanksgiving dance to the Lord. Rushing to my bedroom window, I inhaled then exhaled the crisp morning air. *A gorgeous day!* The sky was pale blue and wide sunbeams played lazily across the trees. "This is the day that the Lord has made. I will rejoice and be glad in it," I declared, grinning from ear to ear.

A familiar aroma greeted me when I entered the dining room for breakfast. Mr. Mohan, Maydine, Idalyn and Bella were already seated and eating boiled green bananas, steamed ackee and saltfish and fried ripe plantains.

"Ohhhh, I will not be able to fit into my dress." I winced, taking my seat at the dining table.

"We'll make sure you do!" Bella said mischievously and the others laughed.

"Yes, we will," Maydine playfully reassured me.

"Your shower was beautiful," Idalyn remarked, smiling as she stirred milk into her coffee.

"Yes," Maydine acquiesced and Bella nodded.

"We had a great time. It was really great to see everyone," I replied, biting into the fried plantains.

"For the next leg of your journey," Mr. Mohan said, looking at his watch, "we plan to leave for Kingston at 12 noon."

"Sounds good," I responded. "That should give us enough time to check in prior to rehearsal." Most of our family members, friends and guests were staying at the Parsion Kingston Hotel because of its proximity to the Genova All Suite Hotel.

"Yes, that time should be okay," Maydine agreed, before turning to face me. "Are you finished packing?"

"No. I have a few more items to pack."

"You won't need that much clothes for where you're going," she teased nonchalantly. Totally unexpected from Maydine!

Time stood still as everyone waited for my reaction. I blushed and my mouth fell open as I looked around the table for an ally. It was me against the world. Idalyn snickered while Mr. Mohan chuckled and excused himself from the table.

"I am way too young for this kind of conversation," Bella declared. A wide grin stretched across her face.

"Naughty mommy!" I pursed my lips and wagged my index finger at Maydine. "You will be in the naughty corner all day and I am taking away your mothering rights."

She giggled and patted my back.

Half an hour later, Orane popped by to drop off Aunt Joy while I was scurrying around and packing. Hurriedly, he blew me a kiss and was on his way. He was travelling to Kingston with the groomsmen to pick up their suits before checking into the Genova All Suite Hotel.

I had just zipped my suitcase when Maydine entered my room, wearing a troubled expression.

"Is everything okay?" I asked comfortingly.

Maydine's light brown eyes stared into mine. "Vena is here to see you."

My heart sank at the mention of her name. "Why?" I stiffened. "Hasn't she done enough?" Of all the people I might have imagined seeing today, Vena was not even in the distance. I plopped myself on the bed, recalling our last conversation.

"Talk with her," Maydine encouraged. "You did say that you had committed the situation to the Lord."

I sighed heavily, glancing towards the window. "Okay, I will be out shortly." *I silently cried out to the Lord. God help me! Strengthen my inner man so that I will communicate with Vena in a manner that represents you. I have no desire to give the enemy a foothold in my life...not now...not ever.*

Vena was sitting quietly on the sofa in the living room. She gave me a quick, uncertain look. "Hi Vena," I greeted her.

"Hey Anna. I know that you are busy but I needed to speak with you."

"Sure," I responded, "we do need to talk."

"Can we talk in your bedroom?"

Oh Lord! Will I be safe? Maybe I could take a chance, I pondered, assessing the situation.

"Okay."

I escorted her to my room and motioned for her to sit in a chair near the window. I sat on the edge of the bed, away from her. *Truthfully*...I opted to sit on the bed because it was nearest to the door, just in case I needed to make a run for it.

"I see you're finished packing," Vena commented, trying to start a difficult conversation.

"Pretty much! You look great Vena. How are you?" I asked quietly. Vena aged well. At thirty-four years old, she could easily pass for a woman in her early twenties. Her petite frame looked very fashionable in a pair of denim capris and a red sleeveless cotton wrap blouse. Her long black hair bounced around her shoulder as she spoke.

"I'm good," she said, avoiding eye contact. "Anna, I just wanted to apologize for..."

"Vena, it's okay. I know you..."

"No Anna. I know I was out of place." She shot me a penitently glance. "I apologize for my behavior."

"That's alright. I am sorry too that I disconnected the call." I moved and sat on the side of the bed across from her. "How are things otherwise?"

She was quiet for a moment before saying, "I thought that I would be married by now."

"Vena, look at me," I said quietly. My request must have stunned her because she quickly looked at me. "I understand what you are going through but I don't have an easy answer for you. I know you love the Lord and His love for you is immeasurable. You must continue to trust Him with this area of your life."

Vena nodded, then exhaled loudly. "It's been so hard. I thought I met Mr. Right the other day but things just turned sour."

I gently touch her hand. "This is no consolation but we have all been there." Shock filled her eyes. "Yes, even me. In due time, in God's appointed season, you will meet your husband."

Agonizing, she said, "Sometimes, I'm afraid that it will not happen."

"I thought so too at one time or the other, even though in my heart, I knew that I would be married." I paused to ask the Holy Spirit for guidance. "You can trust God with your life. He will not disappoint you."

Vena smiled coyly. "I know. But, I still have that little fear that He will not come through for me in this area."

"Remember, fear is not of God. That is the enemy's way of keeping you in chains, to hold you hostage. Even if you don't get married, God will give you the grace to handle it."

Vena sighed deeply, the lines on her face softening. "I need to spend more time with the Lord. This has been a rough season."

I smiled at her. "I'm glad to hear, has been a rough season. That's the way to go, keep your mind on the word of God and just continue to cry out to Him. He can hear through the fog, the rain, the darkness, through all your circumstances and situations. When you can't pray just utter His name, Jesus...Jesus."

Reverent silence filled the room.

"Thanks so much. I needed to hear that," Vena said softly.

"I'm just glad that you're okay." I got up and grinned at her with open arms. "Come here, give me a hug."

We hugged then prayed for each other. Vena wished me well before she departed.

Then, it was time to roll!

"Let's go people," Mr. Mohan said, signaling for everyone to enter Maydine's Toyota RAV4.

Our journey into Kingston was excruciatingly slow. Traffic was heavy on this very humid Friday afternoon. Two hours later, we checked into the Parsion Kingston Hotel. Orane called several times to check on our location. He had already informed Reverend Fuller that we were running late.

Hurry was the name of the game as I freshened up for our wedding rehearsal. My family members had already gathered, when I arrived in the hotel's reception area. "You look great!" Bella said, amidst the pleasantries, totally impressed by my deliberate transformation.

"Thank you." I smiled at her. I had created a chic chignon and donned grey accessories to complement my aqua blue Calvin Klein pleated bodice knee length dress with a sweetheart neckline and wide straps that crossed in the back.

Half an hour later, we were greeted with hugs and squeals of delight from our wedding party, family and friends when we exited the vehicle in the church yard. Orane smiled and beckoned to me in the distance. He was surrounded by a group of men.

"I shall return," I said to Maydine.

"Okay dear," Maydine replied.

I made my way to Orane and greeted the group. "Good evening gentlemen."

"Good evening," they responded smiling.

Face to face with Orane, I laid my head on his shoulder and he hugged my waist comfortingly. I moved even closer to him as he kissed the top of my head. A feeling of utter contentment came over me.

"You okay?" he asked tenderly.

"I am now," I murmured, enjoying the warmth emanating from his body.

"Great!" he said. "There are people here who can't wait to meet you."

"Really?" I asked innocently, moving out of his arms.

"Babes, meet the best man for the job."

"Ridley, so nice to finally meet you!" I smiled extending my hand. Ridley and I had spoken a few times on the telephone.

"The pleasure is mine, Mrs. Conway," he drawled.

Cheers went up from the group and I giggled with joy.

Orane smiled and continued the introductions. "This is Pero and you remember Rayton. You met Ray at Mona and Devon's wedding in Ocho Rios."

"Nice to meet you Inspector Pero."

"The pleasure is mine Annalisa." Pero's handshake was warm and sincere.

"Ray, great to see you again."

Ray smiled and hugged me. "Great to see you too Annalisa, on this great occasion."

"Yes ma'am," a familiar voice said. "You're finally here."

I turned and was pleasantly surprised to see Petra, my prayer partner, 'sister' and friend of umpteen years, who resided in New Jersey.

"P, what are you doing here?" I squealed hugging her. "I thought I wouldn't see you until tomorrow."

"My BFF (*best friend forever*) has me on ushering duties. I need the details of my responsibilities face to face. Tomorrow is not an option." Petra smiled happily at me. "It's good to see you."

"Good to see you too P. This is my darling, Orane. Honey, this is Petra."

Orane shook Petra's hand and in a deep exaggerated voice, "Pleasure to meet you, Petra."

We all laughed.

"Nice to meet you Orane," Petra grinned.

"We are going to see the Pastor," Orane announced to the group. "We'll be back shortly."

"See you in a bit," I said as Orane took me by the hand, our fingers intertwined.

Ann Marie Bryan

As we walked towards the church office, I glanced in the sanctuary and thought of all the worship services, weddings and other events that I had attended there; the many times that I had ministered in dance on the altar. *Thirty two steps would take me from the entrance door to the altar. Happy, very happy memories!* I looked forward to taking the long walk up the aisle.

We entered a narrow passageway behind the sanctuary and knocked on the main office door.

"Come in," Reverend Fuller called out.

"Good evening Reverend Fuller," Orane said. "We apologize again for being late sir."

"Good evening Orane," Reverend Fuller shook his hand and smiled. "I understand."

"How is the bride?" he asked, smiling as he hugged me.

"I am wonderful Rev. How are you?"

"I am doing great. Come this way please."

We followed Reverend Fuller to an adjoining office. "Please be seated." He motioned us to two chairs before his desk. "Are you ready?" he asked, leaning back in his chair.

"Yes!" Orane and I said in unison.

We all chuckled.

After Reverend Fuller's final words of counsel, we discussed the step-by-step procedure for the wedding ceremony including our positions at different times during the ceremony.

"All minds clear," Reverend Fuller asked.

"Yes," Orane and I responded.

"Great! Gather the bridal party and I will join you in a few minutes."

We thanked Reverend Fuller and exited his office to be greeted by more family members and friends.

"Let's meet in the sanctuary," Orane shouted.

"Let's all sit together!" I told the group as we moved to the sanctuary. "Over here please." I motioned to the pews at the front right hand section.

210

"Well hello!" said a familiar voice.

"Verona!" I screamed, moving towards her. She dropped in a minicurtsy and danced about before joyfully hugging me. I smiled at her. "It's so great to see you. You look fabulous." With her thick long dark hair, tall slender frame and large dark brown eyes, Verona looked striking in a polka dot denim bustier dress and matching sandals.

Verona hugged me again. "Thanks! Great to see you too! Are you ready?" she whispered.

"Oh yes," I snickered.

She nudged me, giggling. "Go on with your bad self!"

"Girl behave," I chortled, pulling her towards Orane. "This is Orane. Orane this is Verona, the sister that you haven't met."

"Hi Verona, nice to meet you." Orane greeted her with a hug.

"Great to meet you Orane," Verona responded. "Welcome to the family."

"Thank you," Orane said smiling.

"Anna, we'll catch up," Verona said mischievously as she took her seat.

"Hello everybody," I said enthusiastically, "so good to see you."

Murmurs of "you too", "yippee" and other cheers greeted us as Orane and I stood before the group.

"Go Annalisa!" someone yelled and laughter erupted.

"Hey, I feel you!" I said smiling. "For those of you who don't know him, this is Orane Conway, my husband-to-be and the love of my life."

"Hi Orane!" the group roared.

"And, for those of you who don't know me, I am Annalisa. I am the bride," I said cheekily.

"Alright now!" someone yelled bringing much laughter.

I giggled and took out my little notepad. "We have a few things to discuss before we proceed with the rehearsal. First of all, thank you all so much for coming out and celebrating with us on this very special, ah my bad...let me say, this auspicious..."

Hysterical laughter broke out with some yelling, "aus what?" I ignored their calls and continued "auspicious occasion. Okay, keep it holy." I grinned at them. "Where are our groomsmen and best man?"

"Over here." The five men raised their hands.

"Great."

"And where are our bridesmaids and maid of honor?"

"Here! Over here!" they shouted joyfully.

I introduced the members of our bridal party and went straight to business.

"Let's talk about our positions during the ceremony. Orane, Ridley and the groomsmen will be standing on the right side of the altar." I pointed towards the altar indicating the spot. "The grooms-men will meet the bridesmaids half way down the aisle and present the ladies with beautiful bouquets of flowers. You will escort them to their places on the left side of the altar before returning to your spots. Are we clear?"

Murmurs of "Say it again" came from the group. I demon-strated further and clarity came along with several "Oh I see".

I glanced towards the front of the church and saw Kevin Bassick, Simon's brother and a longtime friend heading towards me. Kevin was in charge of finding appropriate songs for the bridal par-ty's march. I trusted Kevin's judgment and musical abilities. He was the former musical director for Laybrook Presbyterian Church Dance Ministry and I knew he had a sound understanding of my taste in music. Kevin greeted us and assured me that he had found appropri-ate music.

"Reverend Fuller is here," Orane informed me.

I introduced Reverend Fuller to the group and he walked us through the ceremony from start to finish. "You may now take up you positions," Reverend Fuller said, moving to the altar.

My spirit soared with excitement as the music started for the procession of the bridal party but that was short-lived. I watched as the bridesmaids walked up the aisle, some walking unsteadily. They definitely needed another rehearsal and the somewhat distracted groomsmen did not help. I stared at them, stunned by their unexpected frivolous behaviors.

Lord help me to keep it together! You know I like things to be done excellently.

My disgruntled thoughts were interrupted when Reverend Fuller signaled for me to walk up the aisle. I forced myself to focus and tune out all the distractions. My heart somersaulted several times as I walked with my hand tucked in the crook of Mr. Mohan's arm. Before long, Orane and I stood before Reverend Fuller, listening to further instructions.

A strange giggle caused me to look towards the bridesmaids and immediately I became discontented. They seemed very self-absorbed and unfocused. I was getting "hotter" by the minute as their level of response during the rehearsal was not what I anticipated.

As if that was not enough, the reading of the sand ceremony and scripture lessons lacked expression, the dancers needed more rehearsal and the ring bearer discovered a new toy, our ring pillow.

This was not how I visualized our wedding rehearsal. I felt like I was running around screaming fire and no one was paying attention. I wanted to yell, "Stop! Everybody STOP!"

Orane detected that I was incensed but his gentle nudges and encouraging words did little to allay my annoyance.

By the time Reverend Fuller concluded the rehearsal, I was furious and just itching to speak with the bridal party.

"Reverend Fuller can we do another rehearsal?" I asked.

"Yes. But you will have to proceed without me. I have another engagement."

"That's okay Rev. We can do it."

"When you are finished, please inform the church's caretaker," Reverend Fuller said.

"We will. Thanks Reverend Fuller!" Orane replied.

"Thanks Rev," I echoed.

Reverend Fuller smiled. "You are both very welcome. Have a good night and don't stay out too late."

"We won't," I replied.

I quickly gathered our bridal party at the front pews. I was having a hard time being anything but annoyed.

"Babes, it's going to be alright," Orane whispered reassuringly as he hugged me. I gently rolled out of his embrace and planted a hand on my hip.

Lord help! I feel like I am about to go Bridezilla any moment.

I exhaled loudly and decided not to play around. "My bridesmaids," I began, "what's going on with you? You are acting very self-conscious. I am not feeling you. You are my cheerleaders. What's going on?"

Orane squeezed my waist and I glanced at him. His arched eyebrows and eyes reminded me to play nice. I sighed loudly.

Nichelle spoke up on behalf of the bridesmaids. "We'll get it."

My eyebrows rose and I inhaled sharply then exhaled slowly to press for details. She continued, "We were working it as we go along but now we have it."

"Are we all good?" I asked boldly.

"Yes. We're good," they responded in unison.

"Okay. Let's do another run but before we do, let's get our timing right for tomorrow."

"Orane, Ridley and the groomsmen are to be here at 3:30 pm. The bridesmaids are to be here at 3:40 pm. Melissa and I will be here at 3:50 pm. Our celebration begins at..."

"4:00 pm," they hollered in unison.

"4:00 pm it is," I grinned.

Yeah right! You're going to be here on time?" Petra teased.

"Yes," Orane said as I giggled. "You are my witnesses. My wife-to-be promised to be early."

"Yes dear. I'll be early," I said sheepishly and laughter broke out. "Okay people, let's do this." I headed for the aisle.

"Okay missy, you sit down. Let me handle this," Petra said joining me.

"Okay." I gave her a thankful look.

Petra grabbed her head. "I don't want my friend to be Bridezilla!"

I giggled, "Nope. Noooo that would not be…" We both grabbed each other laughing and concluded, "a good look."

No! Definitely not the look I hoped to achieve or the memory I wanted to hold.

Thankfully, our second rehearsal went off without a hitch and shortly thereafter, we headed to the wedding party's get-together, hosted by Melissa and Simon at their home, a five minute drive from the church. Hellos, hugs and the familiar aroma of Jamaican food greeted us as we entered the festive atmosphere.

The sense of unity and lighthearted mood set the tone for the success of our wedding day. We presented gifts to our bridal party and thanked everyone for making this season extra special. Of course, the night would not have been completed without thanking our wonderful hosts, Simon and Melissa.

Orane and I smiled perceptively at each other as we waved goodbye. *Tomorrow would be a day of celebration.* My heart danced in the intensity of the moment, as I journeyed to the hotel with members of my family. Within a few hours, my new reality would unfold. Deep within me, my exuberant spirit declared, *I am ready for this.*

CHAPTER 33: READY SET GO

My cell phone alarmed and I reached for it with a wide grin. Today, we say "I do". I often thought of this day wondering who would be the man standing next to me.

A wide smile broke out on my face. The mystery was over.

Throwing back the sheets, I excitedly climbed out of bed, absolutely ready for my new beginning. Within minutes, I emerged from the bathroom and slipped into my navy jeans, red sleeveless ruffled neck polyester blouse and red sandals. Cheerful good mornings rang out from family members and friends as I entered the breakfast area in the hotel.

"Good morning to you all!" I responded happily. "What special day is this?" I asked looking nonchalant.

"Your wedding day," they responded with much fanfare.

A bright smile lit my face. "Just making sure you remembered."

"As if we could forget," someone hollered.

Verona nudged me playfully. "My baby sister is getting married!"

"Oh yeah!" I danced around and everyone cheered.

"You are way 'off the chain'," Verona grinned, taking me by the hand. "Breakfast is this way."

Breakfast was buffet style, a choice between continental or Jamaican cuisines. We prayed and ate heartily. After breakfast, my family members left for hair appointments and I returned to my room.

A beautiful sunny day greeted me as I opened the balcony door. Brilliant sunlight filled the room with warmth and promise. Joyfully, I threw myself on the bed and read Psalm 91. God, my focal point brought me peace so soothing and comforting, for our tranquil and perfect day. God will forever be, at the center of our relationship.

Half an hour later, I took my *"Queen Esther"* bath!

At least, that's what I called it; my luxurious warm bath in therapeutic organic lavender essential oil and natural mineral salts. With an added gentle cleanser, the lightly foaming soak softened my skin. I sighed as the intoxicating aroma filled the bathroom, transforming it into a calming sanctuary for my body and senses. Fixing my bath pillow, I reclined comfortably. Moments later, the scent of the oil lingered, leaving my skin lightly fragrant.

As I dressed, Simon called to inform me that he had picked up my wedding gown from Dana, Melissa's sister and was on his way to transport me to Genova All Suite Hotel. I packed my bags and headed for the reception area. While I waited, Orane called to whisper sweet nothings in my ear. I was laughing so hard that I had to beg him to stop.

Some fifteen minutes later, I checked into my assigned suite, decorated with antique furniture and a plush multicolored carpet. Simon laid my wedding gown on the bed while I arranged my accessories for easy access. Before leaving for my hair appointment, Simon and I peeped in the Grand Persian Hall.

It was a sight to behold.

My spirit soared with excitement and it was hard to drag myself away. A team of "little elves" were feverishly preparing for the reception.

I arrived at Reflections Beauty Salon to find some members of our bridal party still getting their hair styled. *Being early for our wedding would definitely be a stretch for me.* The arrangement was that only Melissa and I would be at the salon that time. I sat in the reception area and talked with family members until Alaine was ready for me. In the interest of time, Alaine asked one of her assistants to style Melissa's hair.

"Anna, I am ready for you," Alaine beckoned.

"Yes ma'am." I smiled at her.

I prayed quietly as she created her masterpiece. Forty five minutes later, I beamed with radiance when I inspected my hair and light

Ann Marie Bryan

makeup. Alaine created an updo with distinctive ties to form a high stylish bun in the center. At the back, my hair was brush straight and sleek, falling gently past my shoulder. My sparkling silver tiara was placed in front of the bun and my veil draped behind the bun.

"Wow! It is fabulous. Thanks Alaine."

"Very Nice!" Melissa added.

"Glad you like it," Alaine said smiling. "Now, get out of here."

"Yes, got to run," I said, grabbing my purse. "How much do I owe for this bit of pleasure?"

"Anna go on! You owe nothing."

"Alaine!"

"Go on, we're good," she said, waving me away. "I'll meet you back at the hotel."

I hugged her. "Thank you so much."

"Anytime! Now go!"

Melissa and I dashed out of the salon. On our way to the hotel, Arianna called to inform us that Mr. Somers, my driver had arrived. She paused to strike the right tone, before telling me that Orane, his dad, best man and groomsmen were standing in the hotel's reception area waiting on their drivers. Melissa and I prayed that they would be gone by the time we arrived.

We cautiously approached the hotel while Melissa called Arianna. Thankfully, the group had left. Sighs of relief and groans of "Thank you Jesus" were uttered as Melissa and I rushed to my room.

Getting dressed was my priority.

Dressing in a hurry, not my forte!

But today, yes. I intended to impress myself.

I had no intention of keeping our guests waiting. Not today!

I rushed to the bathroom and within minutes freshened up, pulled on my accessories, stockings and bra then left the bathroom to find help to zip my bulky slip. In the bedroom, Melissa, Arianna, Anaya and Alaine were waiting to doll me up.

Melissa smiled at me. "Let's get your gown on."

218

"Ready when you are," I beamed, gazing at my beautiful wedding gown, a priceless gift from my mother. I sat on the bed and the ladies slipped my dress on by way of my feet. After much effort, my feet emerged and I stood up.

As they zipped my gown, they murmured to each other, pulling and tugging the gown to set it in place. I closed my eyes for a moment and thanked God for sending them.

"Time for shoes! Lift your right foot," someone said and I obeyed.

"Left foot!"

"Thank you," I responded as I felt my shoes in place.

Melissa assisted me with my white elbow length gloves while Alaine refreshed my makeup. I giggled as squeals of admiration erupted and the ladies stood back to admire their handiwork.

"Wow!"

"Nice!"

"Fabulous!"

"You look wonderful!"

I flashed them a grateful look. "Thank you ladies. You have been a blessing."

"You are welcome," they said in unison.

While Melissa dressed, I sauntered to the full length mirror. My face was flushed from excitement and my eyes sparkled with anticipation.

Gorgeous! I looked stunning in my white satin strapless A-line gown with its beaded embroidered metallic bodice, inverted V empire waist and cathedral train.

Hold that thought.

"Help please!" I called out. "I need to change my bra, sagging bodice." I had loss a little weight, most likely the result of my past ailment.

Not a problem!

The solution—A long line push up bra.

"Where is the bra?' Melissa asked.

"In my carry-on please."

"Let me unzip you," Anaya said.

"Thanks, thanks so much," I responded gratefully.

Anaya smiled at me. "Not a problem."

"Look away, let me get it on," I squealed.

The ladies giggled and gave me privacy.

"Okay. You can button me up."

We all stared happily at my reflection in the mirror.

Perfect!

"Problem solved!" Anaya said.

I smiled widely. "Yes, very nicely too."

Melissa handed me my beautiful bouquet of fresh red roses and baby's breath. She secured the rings then opened the door for Michael Kennedy, the photographer's assistant, who started clicking away. I became a model, moving to his every command. He was still clicking as I descended the stairs and entered the reception area. I paused for a few shots along the way.

Mr. Somers pulled up in his iridium silver metallic Mercedes-Benz and I wondered how to successfully enter the car. Sensing my dilemma, Melissa and the other ladies assisted me and I carefully sat on the back seat. Someone handed me my bouquet and put the rest of my train in, before closing the door. I made myself comfortable as Melissa slipped in the passenger seat.

"Hello Mr. Somers! How are you?" I asked smiling.

"Annalisa I'm great. I don't have to ask how you are doing."

Melissa and I burst out laughing.

"Ready!" Mr. Somers smiled at me.

"I sure am."

My heart was glad as I smiled and gazed through the window. *Let the celebrations begin.*

CHAPTER 34: WITH THIS RING

My arrival at Laybrook Presbyterian Church set off a flurry of activities. I could see family members smiling, waving and mouthing, "She is here." I smiled and waved vigorously.

I caught sight of our four groomsmen, Aldane, Jamie, Pero and Rayton, each decked out in a classic two-button black tuxedo, white wing collar shirt, apple red vest and tie and black dress shoes. White rose boutonnières matched their outfits superbly. Ridley was dressed in a similar outfit except he wore a gold vest and tie. The gold rose boutonniere pinned to his lapel completed his sharp look.

When Mr. Somers stopped the car at the main entrance of the church, Mr. Jalee, the videographer, signaled for me to roll the window down.

"Hello Annalisa," Mr. Jalee greeted me with his video tape rolling.

I smiled at him. "Hello Mr. J, good to see you."

"Thank you. You may take the window up," he said smiling. "I'm already set up in the sanctuary."

"Thank you Mr. J!"

"Anna, Anna," Petra called out, running from the door of the church.

"Hey P."

"Wow! You look beautiful, my friend."

I giggled at her. "A little something I threw on. You looked great yourself." Petra looked striking in a red sleeveless form fitting gown.

"Thanks! Are you ready?"

"Rock and roll baby!"

"Girl behave yourself. Ah, forget that, have a blast." Petra laughed as she moved away. "We are ready to begin," she informed the bridal party.

Thankfully, I was able to view the proceedings as the church had an open foyer. Instrumental music started and I caught a glimpse of Everton escorting Aunt Joy and Mama up the aisle. Mama looked amazing in a formal aqua blue skirt suit with a matching hat and silver accessories. Aunt Joy was adorned in a beautiful lilac beaded bodice evening gown and matching shawl. For an added touch of elegance, they both wore white rose corsages with sprinklings of baby's breath.

Our four bridesmaids, Dace, Nichelle and Shadae, my three nieces and Verona gracefully entered the sanctuary one at a time. We clearly hit the mark. They looked superb in apple red strapless satin evening gowns. The fitted bodice accentuated their graceful feminine figures. To complement their gowns, their bouquets were a beautiful mixture of gold, white and red roses.

Melissa's bright smile lit up the foyer as Petra signaled for her to proceed. She looked gorgeous in a lovely gold strapless light satin evening gown. She carried a bouquet of white and gold roses.

My heart beat quickened when Petra signaled for me to exit the car. With the assistance of Anaya and Arianna, who were dressed in gorgeous hot pink evening gowns, I made it to the foyer. They murmured compliments as they fixed my wedding gown and train in place. My heart fluttered even more as Petra adjusted the veil over my face.

"Looking wonderful my friend," Petra murmured.

I smiled at her. "Thanks P."

I glanced in the sanctuary then exhaled loudly as an overwhelming desire to cry hit me when I caught sight of Orane standing before Reverend Fuller. *It's a happy day! No tears, I cautioned myself.* My heart was full, full of unspeakable joy. There was tranquility and splendor everywhere my eyes could see in this jubilant atmosphere. The sanctuary was breathtakingly beautiful. The aisle was lined on either side with impressive free-standing floral arrangements with cascading orchids and huge center candles. Each stand was elegantly draped with white tulle and a gold bow.

A beautiful fresh floral arrangement dominated by red roses with sprinklings of baby's breath, sat in the center of the communion table on the altar. Two lovely large free-standing floral arrangements with red roses, carnations and white larkspur, graced either side of the altar near the bridal party. Palms and other green plants were placed strategically to add to the elegant setting.

I was brought out of my daze by a gentle tugging on my gown. I smiled as I looked down and saw Alcia, our mini-bride, touching my gown with childlike curiosity. I touched her shoulder and she smiled confidently at me. Alcia epitomized grace and elegance, dressed in a white spaghetti strap gown, silver tiara and white elbow gloves, stockings and shoes. She carried a miniature bouquet of red roses.

Anaya signaled for Alcia to join Dalen, our ring bearer, at the entrance of the aisle. Dalen was decked out in a black three-button suit, white shirt, red bow tie and black shoes. A white rose boutonniere with a sprig of baby's breath was pinned to his lapel.

I could see trouble brewing when Alcia took a hold of Dalen's hand. He began fussing at her, only to be restrained by Anaya. I could not hear what Dalen's troubles were but he was vehemently pointing outside. A bathroom break I suspected! Anaya was not fazed by his little tirade; she would have none of it, and so she held him in place.

After what seemed like an eternity, the music started for Alcia and Dalen to proceed. The guests cheered loudly as they walked up the aisle.

Then it happened.

A moment fit only for reality TV. My eyes widened and I placed my hand over my mouth to keep from laughing aloud.

Half way up the aisle, Dalen began to drag one foot, only to be pulled along by Alcia. He dropped the pillow with the rings on the ground and refused to budge. *Phew!* Thankfully, the real rings were not on the pillow. A cold hard stare from Alcia gave him the much needed jolt to pick up the pillow but he began dragging his foot again. Alcia refused to be daunted by what was happening and kept moving up the aisle. The guests were totally tickled but encouraged them along. Finally, the pair made it to the top of the aisle and took their places with the assistance of two members of the bridal party.

At the sound of Michael W Smith's praise song *"Joyful, Joyful, We Adore Thee"*, two female dancers dressed in long sleeve white leotards and long gold satin skirts with red satin belts, leaped down the aisle towards me.

"Yeah!" I shouted, clapping unreservedly.

They danced for a few minutes then grabbed a hold of the white aisle runner which was being held to the ground by Melissa and Simon's two sons. The dancers took the runner to the top of the aisle and laid it on the ground before gracefully exiting through the side doors.

Our guests applauded enthusiastically.

Next, the pretty flower girls graced the aisle as if they were on the red carpet! Crystalee and Tajay, my nieces, smiled proudly as they dropped white, red and gold petals on the runner from their small white baskets, before taking their places. The little princesses wore knee length off white dresses trimmed with gold, short gold gloves and white stockings and shoes.

Finally, the moment I've been waiting for.

This special moment!

I have read about it, watched it in movies, seen it at weddings and heard fascinating stories about it. Now, it was my turn to write my own beautiful memory.

I slipped my hand into the waiting arm of Mr. Mohan. He looked so proud, all dressed up in a single breasted navy suit, gold shirt, gold and blue striped tie and black dress shoes. A striking single white rose boutonniere rested on his lapel.

I was all set to work the aisle when I was pleasantly surprised!

My eyes stretched to their limit then a wide grin broke out across my face. Instead of hearing the recorded instrumental of

Luther Vandross' song, *"So Amazing (to be loved)"*, a flutist began to play the song.

Here I began my walk of a lifetime.

My eyes were on Orane, well, his back. He was still standing before Reverend Fuller.

I urged him in my spirit to look at me…to steal a glance down the aisle.

He knew my music. He wanted to look down the aisle. It was in his posture, a slight turn, even slight impatience. But, he did not! In the briefing session prior to our wedding rehearsal, Reverend Fuller told Orane that he would be the last to see the bride. Reverend Fuller stood erect making sure that Orane kept his end of the bargain.

The aisle seemed longer than I had imagined it.

Smiling, I walked through many happy faces, all smiling and mouthing words of encouragement. The images of their smiling faces are etched in my memory forever. I made spontaneous outbursts of greetings as I laid eyes on guests whom I had not seen in years.

Then, three-quarters of the way up the aisle…

Orane turned, smiled at me and began to walk towards me. I returned his smile, swept up and consumed by his gaze. My heart skipped a beat, many beats. He mouthed, "Wow!" and my smile widened. He was completely captivated by my graceful beauty. I was impressed by his debonair good looks. He was impeccably dressed in a double-breasted, non-vented, black tuxedo, quintessential white tuxedo shirt, black bow tie and black dress shoes. A white satin pocket piece and red rose boutonniere completed his dashing attire.

Orane acknowledged Mr. Mohan and then smiled at me. Mr. Mohan seemed more than ready to give me away. It could have been my imagination but I detected a bit of joyful eagerness as he shook Orane's hand.

"You are beautiful," Orane whispered. Our eyes pierced each other as I enthusiastically slipped my hand through his arm.

"So are you," I mouthed, giggling softly as he took a steadying breath.

We moved forward in unison, passing the bridal party and their welcoming smiles and came face to face with Reverend Fuller. He was dressed in a black shirt, gray pastoral robe and accompanying red scarf.

Reverend Fuller smiled, acknowledging us.

"Let us worship God," he declared. "I welcome you to this celebration, the marriage ceremony of Orane and Annalisa. We give thanks to the Lord, Maker of heaven and earth. Except the Lord build the house, they labor in vain that build it."

Reverend Fuller prayed and we sang *"Great is Thy Faithfulness,"* a hymn written by Thomas Obediah Chisholm. Orane and I smiled through the entire song, remembering God's faithfulness to us. During the singing of the hymn, Melissa was in full flight in her role as maid of honor. She mopped away sweat from my face and shoulders.

The first scripture reading, Psalm 91, reminded us of God's love, covering and protection. During the second scripture reading, Psalm 136:1-6 and 23-26, the congregation read, the end of each verse, *"For His mercy endures forever"*.

Reverend Fuller asked our guests to be seated before continuing. "We have come together this afternoon to witness and bless the union of Orane and Annalisa as they are joined in marriage. In marriage, they will share their dreams and goals, and their weaknesses and strengths. In marriage, they will share the joys and sorrows of life. In marriage, they will share all their emotions and feelings..."

Stillness aptly described the change of pace in the sanctuary; a reverent silence to appreciate the significance of the moment.

"Who gives this woman to be married?" Reverend Fuller asked.

"I do." Mr. Mohan joyfully stepped forward from the pew. He had a noticeable bounce in his steps. I eyeballed him crazily, warning him, that this was the moment to be choked up. His eyes widened followed by a blank expression and we both burst into laughter. Our guests cheered as he gladly placed my right hand in Orane's hand.

At Reverend Fuller's prompting, Orane and I turned to face each other, holding hands and smiling.

"Orane and Annalisa, as you seek to be joined in marriage," Reverend Fuller said, "I am required by law to ask you—Is there any reason why you should not both be joined in marriage? Please declare it now."

Reverend Fuller paused.

We smiled and held our peace.

Reverend Fuller turned his attention to our guests. "Also, if there is anyone who can show just reason, why Orane and Annalisa should not be married, declare it now or forever hold your peace."

Everyone held their peace!

Reverend Fuller smiled at Orane. "Do you Orane take Annalisa to be your wife, to love and cherish, to respect and care for, in sadness and in joy, in sickness and in health, to have and to hold from this day forward?"

"I do!" Orane responded smiling.

"Do you Annalisa take Orane to be your husband, to love and cherish, to respect and care for, in sadness and in joy, in sickness and in health, to have and to hold from this day forward?"

"I do!" I eyeballed Orane then broke into a wide grin.

"We can't hear you," someone yelled.

I looked toward our guests and said loudly, "I do."

Laughter erupted and our guests cheered heartily.

Reverend Fuller smiled broadly, before saying, "Orane, please repeat after me," he said.

With a gentle smile, Orane gazed at me and declared, "I, Orane, take you, Annalisa to be my wife. And these things I promise. I will be faithful to you and honest with you. I will respect, trust, help and care for you. I will pledge my love and devotion to you through the best and worst of what is to come for as long as I live."

Led by Reverend Fuller, I made my declaration. "I, Annalisa, take you, Orane to be my husband. And these things I promise. I will be faithful to you and honest with you. I will respect, trust, help and care for you. I will pledge my love and devotion to you through the best and worst of what is to come for as long as I live."

Melissa eagerly presented our rings.

Before blessing the rings, Reverend Fuller boldly declared, "These rings are symbols of the vows that you have taken. They are circles of wholeness, perfectly formed. These rings mark the beginning of a long journey together, filled with wonder, surprise, laughter, tears, celebration, grief and joy. May these rings glow in reflection of the warmth that flow through the wearers, Orane and Annalisa."

My heart fluttered and I felt weightless as Reverend Fuller asked Orane to place the ring at the tip of my ring finger. Under his guidance, Orane thoughtfully stated, "I give you this ring as a token and pledge of my constant love and of my fidelity."

I smiled pleasantly at him and responded, "I accept this ring as a token and pledge of your love. I will wear it proudly as your wife."

With that, Orane slipped the ring on my finger. My entire body felt warm and glowing as I glanced at the symbol of our love and union.

The sanctuary was noticeably quiet.

Then it was my turn.

I placed the ring at the tip of Orane's ring finger and boldly declared, "I give you this ring as a token and pledge of my constant love and of my fidelity."

Orane sounded a tad bit choked as he responded, "I accept this ring as a token and pledge of your love. I will wear it proudly as your husband."

No tears, my eyes cautioned him before I gently pushed the ring on his finger. He smiled perceptively while our guests applauded.

Warmth radiated from us and our hearts were glad as we held hands and faced Reverend Fuller, who encouraged us to grow together in love.

Now for my favorite part of a marriage ceremony!

This time it was my marriage ceremony.

I smiled at Orane as Reverend Fuller uttered the words, "Let us pray."

228

We kneeled on the long cushion provided at the altar and Reverend Fuller rested his hands on our heads and prayed for God's blessing on our union.

We stood up and faced our guests, as husband and wife.

Reverend Fuller joyfully declared, "As you have pledged your commitment to each other in the presence of God and this congregation, according to the laws of Jamaica, I do by virtue of the authority vested in me, pronounce you man and wife."

Sounds of joy resounded in the church as our guests clapped, shouted and hooted. Orane pressed his forehead to mine and we smiled excitedly at each other. *Hmm, we've come a long way.*

Reverend Fuller declared with fervor, "Who God has joined together, let no one separate. Orane...you may kiss your wife."

Silence descended!

Orane was all smiles! Man about town!

Me!

Shyness overtook me and my eyes pleaded with Orane to play nice as my heart thudded in my chest. His eyes twinkled with mischief as he slowly and deliberately lifted my veil. He was totally amused and so were our guests. A thousand goose bumps hit me as his eyes dropped to my lips. His arms formed a bow around my waist as his lips brushed mine gently but passionately.

We grinned at each other and hugged.

As if that was not enough, Orane took hold of my veil and began to cover then uncover my face for another kiss.

Laughter exploded from our guests.

Reverend Fuller smiled at us. "Submit to each other, love and respect each other. God gave Christ as the foundation for your marriage. Accept each other, just as you are. Let your marriage be for the praise and glory of God. Let your marriage be a blessing to the two families that have come together. May God bless you."

He then invited us to join him on the altar, announcing, "Today Annalisa and Orane have decided to commemorate their marriage through the celebration of the Sand Ceremony. This ceremony symbolizes their inseparable union into a new and eternal relationship, sealed with the love and blessing of our Lord and Savior Jesus Christ."

At the communion table on the altar, Orane stood before the vase containing red sand and I took up position before the vase with the gold sand. The red and gold sand represented our wedding colors and the white sand in the center vase symbolized Jesus Christ, the rock of our salvation and the solid foundation that would hold our marriage together.

Simon and Anaya read as Orane and I poured sand from our individual vases into the center vase.

Simon:	*"Today as Annalisa and Orane chose to represent their love in this special ceremony, they will each take their separate glass of sand and together pour the sand into the center glass, declaring to each other."*
Anaya:	*"You are my love for eternity."*
Simon:	*"You are my love for eternity."*
Anaya:	*"My heart is like these grains of sand merging together with yours."*
Simon:	*"My heart is like these grains of sand merging together with yours."*
Anaya:	*"I am yours."*
Simon:	*"You are mine."*
Together:	*"Just as these grains of sand can never be separated, so they symbolize the eternal bond in Christ that will hold them together. They are together like the sand and together they are ONE!"*

Our guest clapped enthusiastically, appreciating the dramatic reading.

"It's time for your signatures," Reverend Fuller said, placing the marriage register on the communion table.

Orane and I signed the marriage register, witnessed by Ridley and Melissa. During the signing, the pianist and flutist, beautifully played *"The Prayer,"* a song by Donnie McClurkin and Yolanda Adams. Then, sounds of joy reverberated in the sanctuary as Davidic Performing Arts Ensemble, danced superbly to the song, *"You Remain Faithful"* by the Omega Forbes Family and Friends Chorale.

Our guests broke in loud applause and cheers as Reverend Fuller congratulated us and I joyfully accepted our marriage certificate. I grinned and gave it to Orane for safe keeping.

With great fanfare Reverend Fuller announced, "Ladies and Gentlemen, I present to you, Mr. and Mrs. Orane Conway."

Amidst cheers of joy and laughter, the recessional music started. Orane and I proceeded down the aisle followed by our smiling bridal party. We exited the church and formed a receiving line to greet our enthusiastic guests.

Screams of joys and laughter echoed as we accepted the hugs, kisses, words of congratulations and blessings that came from the interaction with our guests.

CHAPTER 35: THE RECEPTION

Heavenly Bliss!

As we drove from the church yard, I nestled comfortably in Orane's arms, basking in the enchanting moment.

"Mr. Somers, please close your ears." Orane's request forced me back to earth.

"Never mind me Sir," Mr. Somers said, chuckling with understanding.

With arched eyebrows, I turned to face Orane. His molten chocolate eyes locked into mine. We were nose to nose.

"You're Mrs. Conway now," he whispered softly. "It's time to do good things." My lips parted softly to respond but no words came. Leaning forward, he pressed his lips to mine for a quick kiss. Blood rushed to my cheeks as he lifted his head. I could feel his breath on my lips as he whispered passionately, "We'll pick up later."

A soft smile pulled at the corners of my mouth as I touched his face with not-too-steady hands. "You are a bad man, Orane Conway."

"Bad? Take it back," he said, tickling me.

"Help!" I screamed with delight, begging for mercy. "You're ruining my dress."

He would not let up. "Take it back."

I squealed even more. "I take it back."

"Good!" He chuckled softly. "Your veil is..."

"Don't even mention it." I pursed my lips. "I'm going out there looking all tattered."

He caressed my cheek. "I don't know what came over me. I'll be a good husband."

"Yes you will! Stop!" I yelled, grinning as he began tickling me again. "Keep your hands to yourself."

He laughed softly. "You won't be saying that later!"

I pointed a finger at him. "You're a bad, oops I mean, great man."

"Let me help you," he offered smiling. "I do not want anyone to think you couldn't wait to handle your business."

"You mean, you couldn't wait," I grinned, moving away as he reached for me.

"Your veil needs fixing."

"I wonder why."

"Come over here woman." He chuckled and pulled me in his arms.

"Okay!" I said with childlike innocence.

I burrowed into his side and snuggled comfortably. *Awww! I like it here.*

The evening was warm but beautiful as we began our photography session. Shortly thereafter, I was literally asking the Lord for patience. With all of his amazing talent and careful set up, Mr. Kennedy took too long to take each picture. My smile turned into a grimace by the time the picture was taken.

Kris Martin better arrive sooner than later! Kris, our initial photographer, indicated that he had another event on that day but promised that he would be with us by the time of the reception.

"Mr. Kennedy, I know we need formal pictures but please take spontaneous shots too," I volunteered mildly.

"Yes Mrs. Conway."

We all chuckled. All understanding.

Mr. Kennedy was bent on doing his own thing. He promptly asked me to fall into Orane's arms for a kiss while the bridal party reacted spontaneously. *Cool idea!* After our photography session, we freshened up then headed to our reception.

Lush greenery was everywhere as we approached the Grand Persian Hall. Beautiful large floral arrangements stood on the steps leading to the Garden Terrace, overlooking the property, where our guests were treated to hors d'oeuvres—smoked marlin pate on toast points, miniature fruit kebabs and an assortment of cold beverages.

As our guests mingled, they were entertained by Mr. Joseph Devon, a pianist.

I exchanged pleasantries with our bridal party and a few family members then glanced inside the hall.

Magnificent and super romantic, aptly described the postcard-perfect decor of the Grand Persian Hall. My vision had become a reality through the talented hands of Suzanne Hugg, our decorator. *Definitely worth her weight in gold!*

The architectural style of the hall brought the desired lightness, grace and splendor for our celebration. Its huge white columns set the scene for grandeur. The walls were draped with white sheer material, mixed appropriately with panels of sheer apple red and gold fabrics.

Behind the head table was a backdrop made of gold fabric layered with panels of apple red, gold and white sheer fabrics. These panels were tied at the center with gold and red heart-shaped metallic accents that glowed from the lighting behind the backdrop.

Our guest book rested on a table just outside the entrance of the Hall. On the right side of the entrance door was a cascading waterfall with lights that gave the lush greenery several different shades. Across from the waterfall, the canvas painting from my bridal shower was mounted on an easel. Green palms with miniature white lights were well placed.

"Good evening ladies and gentlemen, I am Selvin Bassick. I am your capable Master of Ceremonies for this wonderful occasion. Welcome to..."

My happy grin froze as Selvin's voice jolted me back to the present. He introduced the bridal party and each couple entered amidst great fanfare.

"Ladies and gentlemen, please stand and welcome, Mr. and Mrs. Orane Conway."

We entered smiling, amidst applause, shouts of joy and happy faces then took our places at a round table slightly elevated between the two rectangular tables seating our groomsmen and bridesmaids.

The tables were beautifully decorated with gold and white table cloths. A beautiful large fresh floral arrangement dominated by red and gold roses, rested at the top of our table.

We were hardly seated before our guests started knocking their wine glasses.

"Orane and Annalisa," Selvin called out to us as we tried to ignore the request, "You know what that means."

We gave in and kissed, much to the delight of our guests.

Bishop Jonathan Barker blessed the dinner and cake and we were treated to cream of pumpkin soup and bread roll. The tasty entrée included chicken florentine stuffed with callaloo, snapper fillet in spicy cream sauce, seasoned rice and a medley of steamed vegetables. An assortment of cold beverages, sparkling wine, blue mountain coffee and a variety of gourmet teas were made available to our guests.

While Orane and I chatted during dinner, I took in the elegantly decorated round tables, covered with white table cloths and apple red sheer overlays. Each table displayed gold chargers, white dinnerware set, white napkins, silverwares, wine glasses and water goblets. The chairs were adorned with white covers and gold tiebacks. Tall modern centerpieces made of fresh flowers with huge center candles looked sharp in the stylish setting.

Great job Suzanne Hugg!

I stopped chewing and waved at Mama who was sitting at a table directly before us. She smiled, blew me a kiss then patted her heart.

I quickly swallowed the piece of chicken that I was working on. "I love you too," I mouthed.

Orane and I giggled through dessert—tropical fruit salad with a scoop of sorbet, reliving the moments as we watched a video presentation of us, titled *"Two Hearts Together"*, showing pictures from our dating life to engagement.

A few minutes later, Selvin was back on the job.

"Ladies and gentlemen, it's time to unveil this lovely cake. I now invite the mothers of the bride and groom to do so."

Ann Marie Bryan

Oops! Not so!

Mama and Maydine were on the program to unveil the cake. In spite of the mistake, the lovely ladies did not hesitate. They smiled and walked confidently to the cake table. Maydine's bronze sleeveless light satin evening gown looked chic on her petite, 5' 3" frame. Sequins highlighted the fitted bodice and her hair was all curls. Gold toned accessories completed her eye-catching look. They held the corners of the veil and Mama declared, "Ladies and gentlemen, on behalf of Mr. and Mrs. Conway, we unveil this cake."

Loud applause followed.

"Mr. and Mrs. Conway, please come to cake table," Selvin requested.

Lovely cake indeed!

I had browsed the internet and discovered that stacked wedding cakes were the latest rage. At the base of the four-decker cake were red roses. The first cake was separated from the second by four white pillars. Each cake was decorated with white and gold roses and wrapped at the bottom with white satin ribbon. The last cake was topped with a white ceramic bride and groom. Harriett and Natasha made and decorated our wedding cake as a gift to us.

Harriett placed the two knives in the cake at the base.

"Orane and Annalisa are you ready?" Selvin asked.

"Yes," we said in unison.

"On the count of three...1...2...2 ½..." We began cutting. Our faces said it all, much to the amusement of our guests.

"Okay...3." With that, we cut the cake to thunderous applause.

"Orane, cut a piece of the cake and place it in your mouth," Selvin gleefully instructed.

My eyes widened and I swallowed a couple of times before my mouth fell open.

This was not happening!

My pulse took off faster than the speed of light. Selvin and I had a conversation about this. I did not want to be fed cake in this manner, a fork would do.

Squeals of excitement went up from our guests. My eyes pleaded with Orane who was having the time of his life. He had already eaten the piece of cake in his mouth and was going for seconds, much to the delight of our guests. I steadied my heart rate as he offered me the cake, with obvious amusement. I took it, albeit unsteadily.

I must confess that I was not as embarrassed as I thought I would be and the cake tasted delicious. *Truthfully*...The mouth to mouth contact was quite electrifying.

Then, I returned the favor much to Orane's pleasure and the delight of our guests.

We had just returned to our table when Selvin struck again.

"Bring in the bubbly," he said with youthful exuberance, calling for sparkling apple cider to be poured into our glasses.

My eyebrows furrowed. I opened my mouth, closed it and then eyeballed Orane. His encouraging smile did not help.

It was a moment to behold!

Yet, not to be repeated!

Orane took it all in great strides as Selvin joyfully helped us navigate the "crazy" arms crossing wine drinking bit. On the other hand, my face was contorted as if I was drinking lemon juice. Not my best self! No. Not at all!

Selvin grinned happily, very proud of his handiwork, then called for toasts to be offered to Mama and Orane's parents. At appropriate points during each toast, the ushers presented gifts to our parents.

Melissa toasted me and said it all, from college days to my encounters with Orane. Our guests had belly laughs through the entire toast as she spoke about how smitten I was with Orane which resulted in her becoming Private Investigator M. I pursed my lips and wagged my index finger at Melissa as she grinned at me before leaving the podium.

Ridley toasted Orane with eloquence. He spoke about their childhood days and their time spent working in Jamaica's tourism industry. He cited Orane's great character traits and entrepreneurial abilities. At the mention of Orane's hobby, a joyful shout went up from his football friends. Our guest clapped heartily as Ridley took his seat.

"Thank you Ridley," Selvin said smiling. "We are moving on. Next, we have a special tribute. Let's give Cheri Delgado a round of applause as she comes to give a tribute."

The tribute was my surprise for Mama and my siblings. At first, I wanted my sisters to walk up the aisle at a point during the bridal party march but that suggestion was killed as fast as it reared its ugly head. "The wedding is all about you and Orane," they murmured. I did not even bother to pursue the conversation.

Without my sisters' knowledge, I enlisted the help of Melissa and Cheri, another wonderful friend to write the tribute. We brainstormed for a suitable title since it needed to be inconspicuous on the program. Several titles came up but none was suitable.

"Lord, what should I call the tribute for my family?" I asked, one day at home. The answer came, *"The Circle of Love"*. I looked around because the voice was so audible, then I began screaming with delight. The title resonated in my spirit. *"The Circle of Love"* captured it all; my family was my circle of love.

"Mr. Master of Ceremonies, Mr. and Mrs. Conway, members of the head table, ladies and gentlemen—Good Evening!" Cheri declared smiling as she graced the podium with finesse. "For those of you who don't know me, I am Cheri Delgado, the very proud friend of the gorgeous bride."

She smiled at me and I returned the smile.

"I will start by congratulating Annalisa and Orane, and wishing them all the best in the years to come. Today, on Annalisa and Orane's wedding day, I thank God for surrounding Annalisa with a loving and supportive family. I know that her family has been there for her, at all times and I'm thrilled today, that she has added a new brother to the family. Welcome to the family, Orane!" She smiled at Orane before continuing. "I've always admired Annalisa's relationship with her sisters and brothers. Annalisa has six sisters and four brothers." She chuckled knowledgeably. "A lot of names to remember. I am going to ask each family member to stand when I called your name."

Flawless!

I looked at the surprised yet smiling faces of my siblings. I had instructed the ushers to present a rose to each sibling as Cheri spoke about them.

With a wave of her hand, Cheri said, "There is Maydine, aka Sister Maydine—mother hen, madam principal and confidant."

Maydine eyeballed me smiling then mouthed, "I love you," before accepting her rose and taking her seat.

Cheri looked around the room. "There she is. Bella, aka Sister Bella—Bella we finally meet," she smiled at Bella before saying, "Bella is a woman with a heart of gold, always shopping for Annalisa." Cheri went into a dramatic tone. "Sister Bella, I know you don't know this, you've been shopping for Annalisa's friends too."

Bella grinned from ear to ear and accepted her rose as laughter erupted around the room.

When the laughter subsided, Cheri remarked, "Sister Bella is very humorous and according to Annalisa, she makes her laugh until tears flow…You know, those belly laughs. Bella always puts her family first. Annalisa calls her a walking example of kindness in the flesh.

Now, let's talk about Harriett, aka Sister Harri, Doc, Dr. Selby, Madam Principal—She is a very strong God fearing woman of grace with an extremely discerning spirit, a kind soul who is very proactive in all her endeavors. Word on the street—if you want the job done, give it to Sister Harri. Everything she touches turn to gold."

Cheers went up from our guests before Cheri continued in a hushed tone. "Ladies and gentlemen, Sister Harri was very instrumental in Annalisa finding Mr. Right. For almost three years, she tried to get these two together. Finally, her hard work paid off. No wonder they call her Doc. Annalisa was a hard nut to crack. Orane you are a lucky man, thanks to Sister Harri."

Harriett blushed and accepted her rose as our guests applauded enthusiastically, beating the tables.

"It's time to talk about Idalyn, aka Ida, Miss Emotional," Cheri boldly declared. "Ida cares about the family. She is very supportive of Annalisa. The secret—Annalisa and Idalyn resemble their father most. Ida, you are a wonderful and compassionate sister."

Our guests clapped as Idalyn graciously accepted her rose then blew me a kiss before taking her seat.

"Natasha," Cheri grinned, "Teaching runs in the family. Natasha is a teacher, dressmaker and baker. This gorgeous wedding cake was done by Natasha and Harriett." Cheri paused then pointed her thumb in my direction. "Ladies and gentlemen, a little birdie told me that Natasha and Harriett did not make it to the wedding rehearsal or the wedding party's get-together because they were hard at work, decorating this beautiful wedding cake."

Loud applause and laughter broke out around the room as Natasha smiled and accepted her rose. She grinned at me and I patted my heart and mouthed, "Thank you" before she took her seat.

"Last but by no means least, Verona—Annalisa's buddy who never changes." Cheri smiled while Verona briefly waved at me. "Verona, Annalisa appreciates that whether she calls you today or next year you remain the same."

Cheri's eyes widened. "Ladies and gentlemen, Annalisa also has four brothers." Pockets of snickering were heard around the room before she continued. "Yes. Let's start with the first male born in the family. Tahime, aka Tai. He looks like their father and he is very protective of Annalisa." Cheri grinned. "Yes. He seriously goes into what Annalisa calls "big brother protective overdrive mode." Cheri paused as smiles and knowing chuckles broke out. "Thanks Tai, for being a wonderful big brother to Annalisa."

Tai smiled proudly. He acknowledged us, accepted his rose then took his seat.

"Next in line is Junior, aka SJ—SJ is not at the wedding but Annalisa says talking to him is very encouraging and uplifting. Naila, Junior's wife is here. We will ask her to accept this rose on his behalf."

A smiling Naila accepted the rose while our guests applauded.

"Codel, aka Cody," Cheri beamed. "Cody you have a special place in Annalisa's heart. She loves you dearly."

Cheri paused for Cody to accept his rose. He bowed deeply towards me and I waved and smiled at him.

"And lastly, there is Wayne, aka Waynie—Unfortunately, Wayne is not at the wedding. He is Annalisa's competitor. They have been competing for the last position in the family." In melodramatic fashion, Cheri declared, "Today, Annalisa is giving that position to him. Ladies and gentlemen, Wayne is really the last member of the family. Annalisa is only the last girl."

Pockets of chuckles were heard in the room before Cheri continued. "And, the cord that holds this whole family together is the indomitable Mama." Cheri paused as our guests hooted and clapped while giving Mama a standing ovation. Orane and I stood and clapped heartily.

"Go Mama!" I yelled.

Cheri smiled broadly before saying, "Mama is a strong, gentle and gracious lady. Thanks mama from all your children. Thank you ladies and gentlemen. You may be seated."

She waited until our guests were all seated before continuing. "Ladies and gentlemen, on this wonderful day, I want to pay tribute to two very special people, the first born in the family, Sister Maydine and her husband, Gerade Mohan. Annalisa lived with Sister Maydine and Mr. Mohan from the latter part of her elementary school years through high school and college." She paused as the usher presented gifts to Maydine and Mr. Mohan who were smiling happily.

"Sister Maydine and Mr. Mohan, Annalisa is very proud of you. She feels extremely thankful for all that you have done for her."

I clapped ecstatically in acknowledgement and our guests followed suit.

"It's time to let the cat out of the bag," Cheri said in hushed tones.

A unanimous "Yes" came from our guests.

"Okay, just a few!" I hollered, grinning as Cheri eyed me.

"Speak," shouted a lone ranger in the back of the room.

Everyone laughed.

"Alrighty!" Cheri said. "The family usually teased Annalisa when she attended kindergarten school because she had to walk double steps to keep pace with Sister Maydine. Most of you know," Cheri whispered as our guests listened keenly, "that Sister Maydine is a principal. In the early years of middle school, Annalisa had to write essays almost every weekend; assignments given to her by Sister Maydine. Annalisa told me that Sister Maydine returned her essays with red lines through every sentence. The red lines went on for a while until Annalisa's creative skills kicked in."

"Ahhh!" our guests responded.

"Not to worry. Because of that, Annalisa has developed a love for reading and writing. So, thank you Sister Maydine. I know that you are a great listener and you've offered Annalisa wise counsel. If fact, you are her second mother."

I grinned at Maydine who grinned right back as loud applause broke out.

"For those of you who don't know, Mr. Mohan is a retired Agriculturalist. Mr. Mohan, Annalisa has great respect for you. Ladies and gentlemen hear this," Cheri said dramatically. "At one stage, I thought that Mr. Mohan was Annalisa's father. She would say, Mr. Mohan wants to know when I'm getting married."

Pockets of snickering echoed in the room.

Cheri grinned at Mr. Mohan. "Well Mr. Mohan, today is the day."

Our guests laughed and cheered loudly while Mr. Mohan shook his head in disbelief and mouthed, "I can't believe we are talking about this."

Cheri smiled widely before continuing, clearly enjoying the moment. "Sister Maydine and Mr. Mohan, thank you for the important role which you played in Annalisa's life. On this very special day in Annalisa and Orane's life, we honor you. God bless you both."

With that Cheri left the podium and returned to her seat amidst warm and enthusiastic applause.

"Thank you Cheri," said a smiling Selvin. "Now, ladies and gentlemen, the moment we have all been waiting for. It is that time of the evening!"

Our guests squealed and cheered loudly.

"It is that time of the evening when we will hear from the big man, Mr. Conway himself."

Our guests clapped heartily before Selvin continued. "Orane, when I asked Annalisa about you, the first thing she told me is that you are a Christian. That was the first thing, she told me. The good looks, the charm and everything thing else came later on. So everybody, you see where her priority is. Orane is a God-fearing man. I dare say this is what is sadly lacking in this country, God-fearing men with everything else." Selvin paused as everyone digested this. "Ladies and gentlemen, let's put our hands together as the groom comes to give his reply."

Orane walked to the podium amidst loud cheers and applause.

"Good evening ladies and gentlemen!" he said smiling.

"Good evening Orane!" Our guests responded in unison and pockets of laugher were heard all around the room.

"I would like to start by saying, to God be the glory."

"Amen," our guests replied.

"Amen!" Orane responded. "Can I hear another amen?"

"Amen!" they said with exuberance.

"I would like to hear you, so don't just sit there. This is a special moment; a very special night and you are here to have fun. So enjoy the goodness of God. Amen!"

"Amen!" our guests responded with zeal.

"I sound like a preacher, right!" Orane said smiling, followed by laughter from our guests. "Ladies and gentlemen, on behalf of my wife and..." Spontaneous applause and beating of the tables broke out. "Would you like me to say that again?"

"Yes!" our guests shouted.

"On behalf of my wife and myself…"

I gazed at him with pure adoration as loud cheers rang out and someone yelled, "Alright now!" before he continued.

"I would like to thank you for coming out today and celebrating our special day with us." He paused and smiled at me and I returned his smile. "My wife, you look wonderful this evening. When I saw you coming down the aisle everything was so impeccable. Babes, you look absolutely stunning." His eyes burned through me before he turned his attention to our guests.

"I'm so happy tonight. I am really happy. As I had mentioned to Annalisa during our planning stage, I am a quiet person. I did not actually want a big wedding but ladies and gentlemen, I am so happy that it went this way." Orane paused in obvious thanksgiving to God, before he continued, "It has brought back, it has helped to unite, to reunite, to reconcile and to resuscitate a lot of relationships."

Thunderous applause occurred along with the beating of tables. A smile broke out across my face as I gazed proudly at my husband…my husband.

"Today has really been spectacular. You can…" Orane paused to gather himself. He lifted his head and sheepishly declared, "Annalisa told me not to cry."

Our guests roared with laughter, before he continued, "I held it together until Reverend Fuller asked me to say my vows." He eyed me and pretended to be ashamed much to the amusement of our guests, before enthusiastically stating, "Yes! Today has been spectacular. You can feel the presence of the Lord here."

Murmurs of agreement filled the air.

He smiled at me again. "Babes, I am blessed to be your husband. I don't have to hope whether or not our future will be a happy one because God is in the center of our relationship." His appreciation was obvious and I smiled pleasantly at him, with understandable recognition, before he continued amiably.

"Of course, ladies and gentlemen, today I have not only gained a wife but a family. Thank you to all the members of our families for all of your love and support over the years. Thank you mom and dad for your love and support throughout my life. I am very proud to call you my parents. Thank you also to Annalisa's family, especially her sisters. They have been a tower of strength to us during the planning of our wedding."

I clapped my hands and nodded vigorously and our guests followed suit.

"A very special thank you to Mrs. Jones and Mr. and Mrs. Mohan for giving me their blessing to marry Annalisa. From day one, you have made me feel like a part of your family. Thank you for raising a beautiful, intelligent and strong daughter. Annalisa has a wonderful Godly character and a very caring nature. She is a true credit to you. I want to assure you that her happiness is my absolute priority."

"Absolute priority!" someone shouted.

"We are holding you to it!" another yelled.

Others cheered Orane along.

"Now, Ladies and gentlemen, it would be remiss of me if I did not say a very special thank you to Dr. Harriett Selby, Annalisa's sister, for introducing us. Dr. Selby, please stand."

A chorus of awwws echoed around the room from our guests as Harriett gracefully rose from her seat. Her medium, 5' 7" frame was decked out in a beautiful gold toned satin evening gown and accessories.

Orane laughed before saying, "I remember going to Dr. Selby's office. She is someone I can talk with, so I told her that I wanted to find a wife, someone nice, someone who loves God. And…she gave me the solution…Annalisa."

Our guests beat the tables and cheered wildly, before Orane continued. "Dr. Selby, you are very special to me."

Harriett smiled broadly and nodded demurely, moving the tresses of her long black hair behind her ears.

In great comedic fashion, Orane said, "One day, I went to Dr. Selby's office and she showed me photos of Annalisa, this nice looking girl. I didn't even know that she gave so much trouble."

My mouth fell open in mock disbelief as Orane eyeballed me, grinning from ear to ear. Our guests laughed loudly, they could not wait to hear more.

"Annalisa has all the attributes of a wonderful woman," Orane said, smiling at me. "Now back to Dr. Selby; she is such a wonderful person. She said to me, I have the number for you."

Our guests were having the time of their lives. They laughed loudly and again, began to beat the tables enthusiastically, raising the level of excitement in the room.

"So ladies and gentlemen, I took the number home and thought about it. I said to myself, Conway you must approach this thing carefully. This is not an ordinary person; you are dealing with an extraordinaire. I remember saying to myself, I am going to deal with this professionally."

Loud cheers and hooting broke out and our guests were all ears.

"So, I called Annalisa," Orane continued in a deep dramatic voice, "and I said to her, you are a wonderful person. I am blessed to have your number. You know, I went on. It's a long story and I cannot give you all my lyrics...because I went on."

Our guests howled with laughter, clapped and hammered the tables again. I grinned at Orane, quite taken and tickled by his dramatic skills.

After laughter subsided, Orane continued. "Annalisa and I spoke but our emphasis was really on the goodness of God and that was what actually brought my heart to hers. She was steadfast in her arguments about God. She was consistent about the goodness of God and all my life, I wanted to be in a relationship with somebody who loves God. It is of utmost importance that I have someone in my life who I can pray with and someone who I can talk with about God. I know that I have found such a person."

246

Loud applause followed and I smiled gently at Orane.

"Not to punish you Dr. Selby, I know that you have been standing for a while but it is important that I get this across to our wonderful guests. So, I said to Annalisa, this is what I like and she told me the things that she likes. We talked and talked..." Pockets of snickering and suppresses giggles broke out as Orane emphasized, talked and talked. "We talked on the phone for three or four hours per night."

Orane smiled at our guests. "Now, this is so amazing. I went back to Dr. Selby and told her that I was going to visit Annalisa in Tallahassee. She said, Really! Gosh! You won her heart."

Roars of laughter erupted as Orane displayed the full range of his dramatic skills.

"Another evening, I visited Dr. Selby at home and told her that Annalisa and I had spoken and we are going to get married. She said, welcome to the family!"

Raucous laughter broke out again and all eyes focused on a blushing Harriett.

Orane smiled at Harriett. "Dr. Selby, please step forward. I would like to offer you a gift. Ladies and gentlemen, this is a very special woman to me because she has given me the most wonderful woman in the world. Not for you gentlemen to feel bad about your wives, but, I have to speak it the way it is."

Spontaneous laughter erupted and loud beating of the tables continued as Orane hugged Harriett before she took her seat. He waited patiently for the laughter to subside.

"I would also like to thank our bridal party for making our wedding day a blessing. Thank you for doing such a wonderful job."

Our guests clapped enthusiastically.

"Special thanks to Melissa and Simon Bassick and their entire family for all that they did to ensure that our special day went off without a hitch. I would also like to thank Mr. Selvin Bassick who filled the role of MC effectively, leading to the enjoyment of our reception. A big thank you to our Ministers—Reverend Fuller and

Bishop Barker, our wedding coordinators—Dr. Selby, Mrs. Mohan, Sister Bella and Melissa and our ushers—Arianna, Petra, Vanessa and Allera. Thank you also to our videographer, photographer and decorator. Thank you Kevin Bassick—our director of music, Mr. Joseph Devon—our pianist, the staff of Genova All Suite Hotel and everyone who helped to make this day special. Your creativity, attention to detail and preparation made our special day outstanding."

Orane waited until the applause dwindled. "As I sat on the plane coming from Tallahassee, I thought of what I wanted our wedding day to represent." The whole room fell quiet. Orane smiled perceptively. "I am going to do this, the way the Lord has instructed me. Today is the beginning of what is inevitable. The plan of God is without a doubt exact, on time, perfectly orchestrated and always carried out by the humblest. Today is a demonstration of such an exclusive plan. This occasion without a doubt has served its purpose to unite, reunite, reconcile and resuscitate God's plans for His people. Your love, sacrifice, support and of course your presence has helped to foster the perfect plan of God. Thank you all for coming out today. God bless you all."

Orane returned to his seat amidst sustained thunderous applause and cheers. I jumped to my feet, kissed and hugged him. His reply was brilliant, bringing much laughter to an already joyful occasion.

Bustling my gown was no fun...for Melissa and Anaya.

I am indebted to them for finding white loops and buttons on a white bridal gown in dim lighting. During Orane's speech, after much effort, they bustled my gown.

I felt elegant and sophisticated as I made my way to the dance floor to do the traditional tossing of my bouquet. Ripples of laughter and cheers exploded around the room as my bouquet landed among members of our bridal party then caught by a self-conscious, Shadae.

There was no tossing of my garter!

Thank you Lord!

Actually, I felt like doing a victory dance. I was extremely thankful that Selvin remembered.

"No garter toss," Orane told me firmly. He had no desire to remove my garter publicly.

I concurred.

I was heading back to my seat when Selvin declared, "Ladies and gentlemen, let's give a round of applause as Orane and Annalisa perform their first dance."

Ugh!

I dreaded the first dance!

Imagine that! Me—dreading the idea of dancing. So unnatural!

While Orane was a great dancer, the dance instructor in me wanted to choreograph our first dance. "Babes, just follow my lead," he said confidently. My eyes widened and he laughed so hard that I had to laugh too. I even suggested that we take dance lessons. You guessed it right. He was not in for that either.

So there I was, being led to the dance floor and praying; praying that my wobbly knees wouldn't buckle beneath me. As Celine Dion's version of *"At Last"* started, Orane smiled and pulled me into his arms. "It's been dull, really dull being away from you," he whispered with an appraising glance.

My lips hovered under his. "Huh?" I giggled foolishly as butterflies flew around in my stomach begging to be released. Orane had that look in his eyes. He was ready to play with fire. I was captivated and wanted to play too. I wrapped my hands around the nape of his neck and I remembered no more.

"Did we dance the entire song?" I asked Orane as he escorted me to my seat.

He chuckled softly. "We sure did."

"Ladies and gentlemen, that was beautiful," Selvin said smiling. "We thank God for bringing this union together."

Our guests cheered loudly before Selvin continued. "We would like to acknowledge and say a special thank you to our guests who

Ann Marie Bryan

traveled from overseas, especially Annalisa's coworkers who are sitting at the table across from me."

Cheers went up as our overseas guests waved.

"Ladies and gentlemen," Selvin said. "Did you see Annalisa's face during the dance? I said when we started this evening that we would not have done our jobs if the bride and groom did not leave here smiling. Ladies and gentlemen, we have done our jobs."

Our guests cheered wildly, hammering the tables.

"We are almost at the end of a wonderful celebration," Selvin said. "Thank you for coming to celebrate this special day with Orane and Annalisa. Orane and Annalisa, we wish you all the very best as you start your new life together."

Our guests applauded wholeheartedly.

"The dance floor is now open for dancing," Selvin concluded.

Orane and I moved to the dance floor and immediately our guests converged around us. The musical selections were impressive and our guests danced the night away. Later, Orane and I waved goodbye and headed for our honeymoon suite where the real celebration would begin.

CHAPTER 36: A NEW SEASON

"Mmm!" I purred in total contentment, cherishing the last moment of blissful sleep before grudgingly opening my eyes. Sunlight streamed through the balcony door flooding our room with glowing light, announcing morning. In a daze, I watched the sunbeams and shadows danced playfully over the comforter and sheets to rest on my husband, lying next to me.

A soft smile pulled at the corners of my mouth. An indescribable night! Raging fires crossed paths igniting an inferno, rupturing explosively before submitting to the mastery of each other. My smile widened. *Totally delightful!* Far more wonderful than I ever dreamed...

Our luxurious ocean front suite at Orion Golf and Spa Resort in Montego Bay, Jamaica exceeded my expectations. The burgundy weave patterned carpet, unique octagonal ceiling and exquisite tropical plantation-style decor were absolutely impressive. Double glass doors led to an expansive balcony offering breathtaking views of the sunrise and magnificent grounds. Perfectly placed details create a unique and intimate setting to commemorate our extraordinary season.

Quietness stole over me as I gazed at Orane. Rolling slightly away from the curve of his body, I propped myself upon one elbow. Smiling, I reached out and played with his neatly trimmed beard then trailed light butterfly kisses across his shoulder. Shivers shot through me as his hand crept slowly up the small of my back. Perfect lips curved in a slow satisfied grin and he gazed at me mischievously through sleepy eyes.

"My beautiful wife, good morning."

My heart melted.

I gazed at him tenderly. "Good morning, my wonderful husband."

He kissed me and I snuggled comfortably on his chest, enveloped in the gentle scoop of his arms. He placed his lips to my ear and whispered, "I love you now and forever."

I smiled, utterly satisfied. "You are my love for eternity," I murmured.

He pulled me closer.

A good morning indeed!

This was an exhilarating start for the beginning of us, two hearts celebrating God's faithfulness. Above all, we have the faith to walk through this new door and enjoy the scenery. This was an unforgettable journey, perfectly orchestrated by a mighty God. *"This was the Lord's doing; It is marvelous in our eyes." (Psalm 118:23)*

Dear Readers,

Thank you for reading *"Unforgettable, My Love Has Come Along"*, the first of the *"Circle of Love Novels"*. This book was based in part on my personal experiences as I embarked on my remarkable journey from singleness to my amazing marriage.

I have labored over this book night after night, hoping to give you a glimpse of the faithfulness of my Lord and Savior, Jesus Christ, who understands and meets all my needs. This book is my written testimony of how God perfectly orchestrated my marriage. Albeit, I was an unwilling vessel, at first, so I thank the Lord for choosing me.

I declare and decree that salvation, deliverance, restoration, joy and gladness shall be to all who will come in contact with this book. Lord, let praise, thanksgiving, glory and honor be yours as you use this book as an instrument to change and transform lives, in the name of Jesus Christ.

Unforgettable, My Love Has Come Along, was intentionally designed for your empowerment and reading pleasure. Let me hear from you! Visit www.victoriousbydesign.com and leave me a note.

You are Victorious By Design.

With love,

Ann Marie Bryan

ngramcontent.com/pod-product-compliance
q Source LLC
burg PA
36170626
00002B/637